W9-AGP-023

about face

james calder

about face

a bill damen mystery

CHRONICLE BOOKS

SAN FRANCISCO

acknowledgments Many thanks to the following people for their help and expertise while I was writing this book: Jay Schaefer, Ted Conover, Patrice Gelband, Amy Critchett, Victoria Garzouzi, Maribeth Back, Greta Jones, Andrew Black, Bruce Hoyt, KT Wilder, Phil Cohen, Dr. Jennifer Beachy, Dr. Ann Leibold, Hansel Bauman, Nurshen Bakir, Shannon Gilligan, and Bill Reifenrath. Any errors are mine alone. —*James Calder*

Library of Congress Cataloging-in-Publication Data:
Calder, James.
  About face : a Bill Damen mystery / James Calder.
    p. cm.
  ISBN 0-8118-4179-0 (hc) — ISBN 0-8118-3680-0 (pb)
1. Private investigators—California—Santa Clara County—Fiction. 2. Santa Clara Valley (Santa Clara County, Calif.)—Fiction. 3. Biotechnology industries—Fiction. I. Title.
  PS3603.A425A64 2003
  813'.6—dc21
                              2003004529

Manufactured in the United States of America

Book and cover design by Benjamin Shaykin
Cover photo by Jean Laughton/Nonstock
Composition by Kristen Wurz
Typeset in Miller and Nillenium

Distributed in Canada by Raincoast Books
9050 Shaughnessy Street
Vancouver, British Columbia V6P 6E5

10 9 8 7 6 5 4 3 2 1

Chronicle Books LLC
85 Second Street
San Francisco, California 94105
www.chroniclebooks.com

Ye gipsy-gang that deal in glamour,
And you, deep read in hell's black grammar.

—Robert Burns

SPENCE: You worried about saving your own skin?
TERRY: Yeah, I am. It covers my body.

—Ronin

1

There are certain looks on certain faces that make you stop and think. I didn't know Alissa, but my opinion of her was not high. We had a film to shoot and she was an hour late. From the attitude of those around me, I inferred that waiting on her was customary. Anything to be done with Alissa was done at her pleasure and on her schedule. Well, I had a schedule, too.

Then Rod showed me her picture. I've been shooting for ten years and I've dealt with my share of divas. Good looks are no excuse for bad behavior. But there was something about this photograph. Alissa was curled in a bentwood rocker on a deck, feet tucked underneath herself, cobalt blue water and a careless blue sky behind her. The highlights in her almond brown hair caught the sun; a few wayward locks were feathered by a breeze. The setting was leisurely, yet her back was straight, her hands folded. Her green eyes looked down a fraction from the lens; the brows hinted at mischief. It was her smile that got me, the corners of the mouth turned up ever so slightly, the lips full, relaxed, a little amused. It was nearly a Mona Lisa, but more impish, offering much yet simultaneously retracting it. Like she knew that you knew that the smile was a mirage—but you'd fall for it, anyway.

And I did. The smile had a natural quality, free of guile. If she was a diva, she was the most dangerous type: sweet, sincere, and somewhat oblivious to her powers.

Before I knew him, I'd have thought it implausible that the man standing next to me would be the smile's recipient. Rod Glaser was older, not nearly as good-looking as Alissa, and not particularly rich—yet. We were standing on the lawn outside his company, Algoplex. He'd hired me to shoot an image piece for the company and today was the last day of the shoot. It was the day devoted to "the man behind the technology," a subject with which Rod was not comfortable. He had plenty of intelligence, wit, and even genius, but it froze in front of the camera. Alissa's name had been uttered all week like a magic potion that would unlock his personality when she joined us on Friday. Now Friday had arrived and we were still awaiting results. In the meantime, we'd shot about an hour of the company's weekly Ultimate Frisbee game. Rod had fumbled the disk and made looping throws that somehow ended up behind him in a display of full-frontal nerdity. Then he'd come over to apologize again for Alissa and show me her picture.

Rod was a Silicon Valley engineer of the old school, a man who respected technique. When I complimented him on the picture, he blushed and proceeded to apologize for its deficiencies in craft. He hadn't treated me and my two-member crew like most executives do. Rod recognized my job required technical art, too, and treated me like a fellow engineer. In his world, there was no higher token of regard.

"It's still a great picture," I said. "Alissa's photogenic."

It was meant as a compliment. But Rod frowned and looked at his shoes—cross-trainers that showed little sign of use—as if ashamed of his luck with her. He tucked the photograph back into his wallet and tucked the wallet into his satchel.

My crew—Rita on camera, Alan on sound—kept shooting while Rod and I stood watching the game. Rod paced nervously, his hands searching for nonexistent pockets in his sweatpants, small loaf of a belly pushing out his Slashdot T-shirt. He was my height, about six feet, with sloping shoulders, thinning reddish-brown hair, and a superfluous mustache. Its color made it nearly invisible, as if he might have carrot juice on his upper lip. His lips were plump and his blunt features appeared to have been rounded down by some process of erosion. His gangly arms and floppy feet did not help him in Ultimate Frisbee.

I was feeling more patient now that I knew who we were waiting for. There was no harm in letting the camera roll: It was only video. The grass was thick and aromatic, the sun warm. The faux red sandstone and glass curtain walls of the Algoplex building furnished what passed for local color. But the more Rod paced, the more agitated he became.

"I can't imagine what's keeping her," he said. "This is anomalous. She's been late before, but she's always come."

"Why don't we just go pick her up at her place?"

Rod shook his head. "I've called her twice now. No answer."

"Maybe her phone's not working. Or she left her computer online."

"We're not going." His voice took on a sudden severity, one I'd heard before only when he argued the utter wrongheadedness of a rival engineer's theory.

Now Rod was the one trying my patience. "Well, we've done all we can with this setup. I know you said Alissa likes Frisbee, but we need to move along. If you want a rough cut of this film in time for the dinner on Monday night, that is."

Monday was the night Rod was set to sign a strategic alliance with a company called Plush Biologics. Plush was developing a line of gene-regulating treatments for the skin, therapies that would renew elastin and collagen, producing not only the appearance but also the reality of youthful epidermis. Already there was a long waiting list for Eternaderm, the first in the line of ultra-lucrative products. Rod's star would rise with it.

Rod tapped his front teeth with a knuckle. It was a little habit that meant he saw your point. "This is anomalous," he repeated. "She's never failed to keep an appointment with me."

"Is there anywhere else we can check for her?" After his quick shake of the head, I said, "We'll have to move on to the next setup, then. Leave a message telling her to meet us at your house."

Rod stood paralyzed, his back slightly hunched. He never quite looked comfortable in a standing position. Only when perched in front of a screen, mouse in hand, did he forget himself: A tranquil absorption came over his face, the tension left his shoulders, and he took on the look of one transported to a more perfect realm.

Mike Riley, the company's CEO, broke away from the game to join us. "Whatcha doing on the sidelines, Rod? We need you in there." Sweat was pouring down Mike's temples in spite of a white headband. He had short, powerful legs and managed to rule the Frisbee field among employees who were younger and faster.

Rod's long face told him he would not be rejoining the action. Mike's expression turned sympathetic. "Still no Alissa, huh?"

Rod perked up with a new idea. "Maybe she emailed," he said. He bent to retrieve his hiptop from his satchel. It was a compact device about the size of a camera that had replaced the array of gadgets once holstered on Rod's belt. It could browse the Web, send and receive email messages and files, make phone calls, and take pictures. Its top flipped open to become a screen, revealing a keyboard underneath.

"Don't you love this guy?" Mike said. "Engineer to the bottom of his toes."

Following a series of beeps, Rod got a wireless connection to the Web. His lips pressed together in silent disappointment as he scrolled through his messages.

Mike touched Rod's elbow. "Don't worry, champ. She's probably just putting her makeup on for you."

"Is everything—" I hesitated but had to ask. "Is everything all right between you and Alissa?"

Rod shrugged. "I haven't heard of any revisions."

"We're always the last to know, aren't we?" Mike meant it as a buddy remark, but Rod's shoulders only drooped lower.

"Send her over to Rod's house if she shows up, would you, Mike?" I said. "We'll be there the rest of the afternoon." Mike gave me a thumbs-up, then sprinted back into the game.

"Let's pack it up," I called to Rita and Alan.

Rita gave a smile of relief. She wanted to keep things moving. Rod just nodded with resignation. He was staring out at the field, where the players swerved from one end to the other, like a flock wheeling over a meadow. "Frisbee up!" someone called, and there were whoops as players jumped for it. Spirits were high at Algoplex: The deal to be signed Monday night would guarantee its future. Yet Rod looked like the most forlorn man in the world, gripping his hiptop, grinding his jaw, as though he feared he might never see Alissa again.

» » » » »

Rod's company did data visualization and simulation. He designed software that navigated huge databases to represent in intuitive three-dimensional form veins of information sought by the client. In the case of Plush Biologics, the data represented the epidermis and the genes that produced its tissues. Rod's algorithms could then take this data and simulate what would happen when new gene-related molecules were introduced.

Algoplex's product depended entirely on the genius of its engineers. Rod was Genius in Chief. As hesitant as he was in social situations, he was authoritative in algorithmic matters. He viewed himself as supreme in his field, and his rivals saw themselves in precisely the same way. It was a marvel how this unassuming man could shout down a colleague when the debate turned to code sequence.

Unfortunately, this did not automatically ensure Algoplex's profitability. As brilliant as Rod's work was, until now he hadn't found the killer app, the monster client, to make the company fly. At 43, Rod was old enough to have a track record and young enough not to have been beaten down. He'd done stellar, underappreciated work at three previous companies—small, medium, and large—yet still had enough energy and idealism left over to believe his technology could change the world.

His fire and experience had convinced investors to entrust him with an initial infusion of cash. He'd burned through that first round laying down his code base. He then needed a second round to get his technology into play, but the capital markets had dried up in the post-dot-bomb era. Rod's pitch no longer had wings, and he hated the song and dance anyway. Four months ago he'd brought in Mike Riley as CEO. Rod relegated himself to Chief Technical Officer, though he was still the heart of the company and had the final word.

Mike was a few years younger than Rod. He'd declared that both Rod and the company required an image makeover. It was no longer enough to have great technology: Your company had to project the image that it could rule the field, dominate the market. Rod needed to make investors look at Algoplex with new eyes. Mike's campaign appeared to be paying off with the Plush deal. Not only would it bring new business, it would bring new capital from Plush's primary backer.

The film I was shooting was part of the campaign. Our last setup would show Rod at home, doing whatever it was he did in his free time. I was afraid that might mean Ping-Pong and computer games. It was another reason I wished Alissa would arrive to grace the frame.

We drove to Belmont, a leafy town north of Palo Alto. Rod had bought the house two years ago. It had cost plenty, yet was modest by neighborhood standards: a single story with a deep front lawn bordered by oak and spruce. He hadn't yet graduated to the square-foot-maximizing carbuncles that Silicon Valley millionaires liked to build, nor did he plan to. He disdained excess, and lusted after resources only to the extent that they were needed to get the job done.

Rita and Alan unloaded the gear while I toured the house with Rod. Jimmy, Algoplex's PR liaison, trailed behind. At the front stoop, Rod spoke: "Door open, please."

The lock clicked. Rod gave the door a small push and we entered.

"You didn't tell me the house was alive," I said.

He smiled to himself. "Just a few things I coded in. Let there be light!"

Lights came on in the dining room. I repeated the phrase as we entered the living room, to no effect. "It responds to the words," Rod explained, "but they're linked to my voiceprint. We'd have to code in your voice to give you the power of light. I've done it for others."

"That's all right. I'll stick to lighting the show."

The layout was typical, a dining room and living room in front, a couple of bedrooms and a small den in back. In the basement Rod kept a Web server, a library of computer games, and no Ping-Pong table. The decor was Standard Bachelor, including an overstuffed leather couch, a Barcalounger, and an elaborate media center. But there were signs of a new style overlay: a marble vase with flowers, a couple of Modigliani prints, a cashmere throw on the sofa, healthy green plants in the den.

We'd circled back to the living room. I touched the vase. "Alissa's influence?"

"We got that at an antique sale." Rod said it with the melancholy of one speaking of a lost time. Yet I figured she must be relatively new in his life, or the makeover would have spread farther.

"Here's what we'll do," I said. "Come inside like we did just now. We'll follow you in with a handheld camera as your house welcomes you home. Maybe you can say something funny to greet it." I was thinking of ways to humanize Rod. The technology had performed well in our previous days of shooting, but Rod had been rather wooden.

"Welcome, home," he suggested.

"Right. Then, after that . . ." I looked around for signs of an animal. "Any pets?"

Rod shook his head with that same melancholy. "I had a dog named Piston, but . . . he got kind of lonely."

Jimmy laughed at the name. Rod did have a sense of humor. He loved puns. But puns weren't cinema. This was going to be tough without Alissa. I sensed his life must have been solitary before her, with only his computer and voice-activated house for companions. No wonder he was so glum. Of all the days for Alissa to let him down . . .

Then it occurred to me that the film might be the very reason for her truancy: If she was planning to leave him, she might not want their relationship to go on record.

Rita and Alan had begun to unpack the gear in the living room. Alan drew the shades and plugged in the sound cables. Rita and I chose strategic spots for lights. She was an old friend and we'd worked together many times. Usually she did the directing and I did the shooting, but this job had come to me via my friend Wes, who knew Rod professionally, so I took the helm. She claimed to enjoy the reversal of roles.

The doorbell rang. I looked down the corridor, past the dining room. A young guy stood at the open door. He was back-lit; I couldn't see his face, only his outline. He wore a leather jacket and his hair swept up in a James Dean flourish. Rita, unfolding a light stand in the hallway, asked him what he wanted. Rod went striding to the door, shouldered Rita aside, and planted himself in front of the visitor.

"You can't come here," Rod said in an angry voice, leading the stranger down the steps. They went around the side of the porch. I couldn't make out what they were saying, but their voices were raised. Rod was incensed, the James Dean guy self-righteous.

Suddenly he let out a shriek. "Jesus Christ! You're insane!"

I rushed to the door. Rod was brandishing a rake with thick metal prongs. The young guy turned and ran just as I got there. Rod sensed me behind him, and gave a look that said I wasn't supposed to see that. I went back to my job in the living room.

The house shook with his slam of the door when Rod returned. "Let's go," he said irritably. "I want to get this done."

"We'll start outside," I said. "You'll approach the door, ask it to open—"

"Forget about that. I want to stay inside." Rod's face was drawn, his cheeks hollow, his lips tight. This was not going to look good on camera.

"Try to relax," I said. "Why don't you sit here on the couch. The camera will be over there so we can get the Modigliani and the vase in the background. Rita, we'll need that light about two feet to the left. Careful of the reflection on the TV screen."

Rita moved the light stand while I framed the scene. She switched on the light. There was a flash, then a startlingly loud pop as the bulb shattered. A scrim kept the pieces from spraying onto the floor.

"Oops," she said. "Must be a short."

Rod exploded from the couch. "What are you doing!" he shouted. "You numbskull! Someone could have been hurt!"

"It's just a circuit breaker," Rita replied calmly.

Rod threw his arms in the air. "You don't get it! Now I'm going to have to reset all my embedded technology. I don't have time for this!"

Rita stared at him. Rod was supposed to be the electronic genius.

"Take it easy, Rod," I said. "We can help. Right now we need you to put on your most charming personality for the camera."

Rod's mustache twitched. "Wysiwyg," he declared, spreading his arms. It was engineer-speak for What You See Is What You Get.

"All right," I announced. I slapped the lens cap back on the camera. "I'm calling it a day. We've got enough to put together the piece. If you're in a better frame of mind, we can pick up some shots tomorrow. Maybe Alissa will show."

Rod turned without a word and walked in the direction of the basement. His lips were sealed shut, like two lines of tape. His limbs moved in robotic jerks.

Jimmy waited until he was out of earshot. "He'll be better in a few minutes."

"No, something's thrown him off. He's not coming across well. You don't want to see that look he's got on his face splashed across the screen."

"Just fifteen minutes," he pleaded.

I glanced at Rita. "No," I decided. "Our schedule is too tight. Look, I meant it about coming back tomorrow, if he wants to try again. If not, we'll be fine with what we've got. Believe me, it's the best way."

I nodded to Alan to proceed with the breakdown. Rita had already begun on the lights. She'd shown admirable restraint. But I could tell by the crisp way she snapped the equipment cases shut that she appreciated my decision. Her camerawork would not have been kind to Rod after that outburst.

We hauled the gear back to my car. I waited an extra minute or two, but Rod did not reappear. I said good-bye to Jimmy. He promised to have Rod ready first thing in the morning.

>> >> >> >> >>

An eruption happened at least once on every shoot. We knew not to take it personally. Usually the anger was meant for someone else and you were a convenient target. You tried to work through it, but in this case Rod's bad mood would have taken over the screen.

By the time we finished dinner and settled into our editing chairs to review the footage in San Francisco, Rita's ire and my irritation at Rod's outburst had melted away. Rita transferred whatever leftover offense she had to Alissa, whom she referred to as the Wayward Princess.

"You didn't see the photograph," I said. "I've always wanted someone to give me the look she was giving him."

Rita gave me a look of her own, one that included her eyes rolling around like lost marbles. My cell phone rang. I flipped it open and checked the caller ID. "Rod," I said.

"His ears are burning."

Rod dispensed with greetings. "Bill," he said, "you've got to come down here right now. I can't—I can't stand it anymore."

"Stand what, Rod?"

"We have to find Alissa. I'm afraid something has happened to her."

"Like what?"

"I don't know." His voice was quivering. "I just know that she would have called me if she was all right. She's not all right."

"Have you called the police?"

"The police, the hospitals. Nothing. We've got to find her."

"Let's give it till morning. I'll be there early."

"No!" He was on the verge of tears. "Just believe me. We've got to check her apartment tonight. I'll pay you for your time. This has nothing to do with the film."

"Okay, Rod. Take it easy."

He gave me an address in Palo Alto. I told him I'd be there in fifty minutes. Rita frowned at me as I closed the phone. "Don't tell me you're going. It's ten at night. He's not your boss, you know."

"He wasn't exactly ordering me. More like begging."

"Did he say anything about this afternoon?"

"No. He's worried and he's lost in his own world. He's got no one else to call, Rita."

"What about Mike Riley?"

"I'm sure Mike would help, but you know how shy Rod is. He won't talk to Mike about it. For some reason he trusts me."

"Not that you're not worthy of it, Bill, but—couldn't it just be this week's new-best-friend syndrome?"

I knew what she meant. Film sets fostered a kind of hothouse intimacy. You spent twelve or eighteen hours a day working on a shoot and you developed intense relationships. I was in the middle of Rod's world right now. I felt a certain closeness, a protectiveness. His blind devotion to his work was endearing.

"Maybe so, Rita. I just can't leave the guy hanging."

"He went a little off his rocker today, if you ask me."

"It can't be easy, sitting alone in that house, wondering what's happened to your girlfriend. But he's rational to a fault. You saw that, too."

"There's the problem. Too much rationality can drive anyone crazy."

I shook my head. "Something else is going on. It started when that young guy visited—"

"Young James Dean?"

"Exactly. That's what set him off. Maybe the guy's related to Alissa. Maybe he's her new boyfriend."

"Oh, this sounds like a great thing to put yourself in the middle of, Bill."

I shrugged on my jacket. "He found my weak point. Curiosity."

"Nosiness," Rita corrected. But then her mouth twisted into one of her wry smiles. "I know you'd do the same for me. It's nice to have someone you can count on. As long as it doesn't get you hurt someday."

2

A man was moving in the bushes to my right. My fists tightened. I was in a dark spot on the street, between two lights, on my way down the sidewalk to Alissa's apartment. I stopped and checked around me to see if I'd walked into some kind of trap.

The man's shape loomed, then I recognized the sloped shoulders and splayfooted gait. "Rod, why are you hiding in there?" I said.

He shrugged and whispered, "I thought it would be safer."

We were in an old Palo Alto neighborhood. The trees were tall and their leaves rustled in the breeze. A black iron fence ran along the sidewalk. Rod and I followed it to the gate to Alissa's apartment building, the Granada. It was designed in a hacienda style, three stories with overhanging tile roofs. Through the wrought-iron gate we could see a fountain and a thick oak tree. Beyond it was the building itself, split into two L-shaped halves by a single story in the center.

"Pretty swank, for someone her age," I said. "Whatever she does, she must be good at it."

Rod didn't answer. His shoulders, his arms, his whole body shrank into itself. He hesitated in front of the intercom telephone, which was set in a pillar beside the gate.

"Have you tried her yet?"

He shook his head and peered at the phone as if it would bite him. I couldn't fathom why he should be so frightened. "What apartment number?" I asked, picking up the receiver.

He told me and I punched in the numbers for 304. A woman's recorded voice picked up after two rings. It had a mellow, buttery tone, but withheld her name. I handed Rod the phone. He stared at it, then slammed it into the cradle.

"Was that Alissa?" I asked.

"Yes. We have to get in. Her light's on."

A few windows twinkled through the iron bars. "You want to climb the gate?"

"Let's go around back," he said, already walking along the wall.

I followed him around the corner to an alley that led to the rear of the building. Several cars were parked in a narrow lot. A Dumpster was pushed up against the single story, probably a utility room, between the building's two halves. We stood under a large elm, which provided cover of darkness. Rod pointed to a small balcony on the third floor, above and to the right of the Dumpster. A faint light glowed through a sliding glass door.

"That one's hers," he whispered. "You can get in, can't you?"

"What, break in? Forget it. We'll ring the manager."

"No! Absolutely not!" Rod clasped his hands in my direction. "Please. Just believe me. She may be in trouble. The manager's not the person to try."

I refrained from asking how often he spied on her from this spot. But I did ask if he'd seen something happen through that window.

"I'm—I'm not sure. I wanted the police to check on her, but they said she can't be reported missing until twenty-four hours go by. It might be too late by then."

"Too late for what?"

Rod spun, looking to his left, then his right, as if an invisible fiend lurked in the dark. "*I don't know*. That's what I mean. I'm afraid she's in there, I'm afraid she's . . ." His lower lip trembled. Again his hands clasped. "I want to hire you, Bill. I have to find out what happened. Wes told me you had some experience. I'll pay you the same rate as the film, plus expenses. I'm serious about this."

That got my attention. Film work had been very, very slow lately. I wasn't turning down jobs of any kind. "You're that worried about her?"

"Worried sick," he said miserably.

The climb looked feasible. The Dumpster could get me to the single-story roof. A combination of drainpipes, wisteria vines, and balcony railings could get me to Alissa's balcony. The sliding glass door would be open, if I was lucky, or could be pried open.

"Does she live alone?" I asked.

"Yes. That's why the light concerns me."

I fixed my gaze on him as well as I could in the dark. "I might do it. But I want to know what's going on here. Who was that young guy who came to your house today?"

"He's—" Rod faltered. "He gave me reason to believe something's happened to Alissa."

"Yeah, but who *is* he? I'm not going up there until you spell this out."

"I will," Rod promised. "Afterward. Please just find out for me if she's there. If she's alive. Then I'll explain."

"Explain first. Then I'll tell you if she's alive."

A wild look leaped into Rod's face, as if the fiend was closing in. He grimaced, made a run for the Dumpster, and managed to swing his legs over the edge. But the lid was open and he promptly toppled into the bin, disappearing with a soft thump. The Dumpster wasn't empty. He emerged a moment later with a vexed whimper.

"Let me help you out, Rod."

"I'm going up there!"

"Come on out of the Dumpster."

"Go to hell, Bill." He gained a precarious knee-perch on the lip.

"Rod . . . Rod, listen to me. I'll go. Now calm down."

He came all at once, pitching forward. I caught him and lowered him to the pavement. "I'll go," I repeated, "assuming you haven't woken half the neighborhood."

Rod brushed himself off. "I'll take full responsibility. You're in my employ."

Rod had done nothing in the past week to make me think he wouldn't keep his word. And I hated to say it, but in addition to the pay I was drawn by that sense of not wanting to see what I might find, yet feeling a compulsion to look. Alissa's smile lingered in my memory.

We waited a few more minutes to make sure we hadn't attracted attention. Then Rod gave me a boost up on the Dumpster. I balanced on the lip for a moment, hands pressed to the windowless wall, trying not to inhale too deeply. A sideways jump allowed me to grip a drainpipe that ran down the wall. Climbing it hand over hand brought me to the roof of the utility room.

If I spent more of my free time rock climbing or lifting weights, I might have been able to pull myself up the drainpipe to the third floor by arm strength alone. Being a mere camera jock, I needed footholds. The Granada was a vintage forties building: The wisteria twining up the drainpipe to the balconies had been there for decades and the vines had grown thick as cords. I hoped they were strong enough to hold 175 pounds.

My arms still did most of the work. Using the wisteria cords for toeholds, I made it to the first balcony and rested, bending over the iron rail, my feet wedged between the bars. The sliding glass doors here were dark. At the second-floor balcony, a murmur of voices came from inside the apartment. I leaned forward and saw the blue flicker of a TV. The curtains were open. I couldn't rest here.

I let the vines take more of my weight as I climbed to the third floor. They twined vertically around the drainpipe, making the toeholds slippery. My right foot slid and suddenly I was dangling from the pipe. I looked down to see where I would splatter. If I could propel myself out and to the left, there was a chance I'd land in the Dumpster. I hoped my landing would be as soft as Rod's.

My arms were feeling the burn when my feet finally found a bit of leverage. I wedged my hands under the pipe to give my arms a second of rest, then ordered them to pull me the final yards to the third floor. I thrust a foot between the bars of Alissa's balcony and threw myself around the corner and over the top of the railing, gulping air. Once I was on the balcony, I stood up and gave Rod a wave.

"Are you okay?" he whisper-yelled.

I shushed him and made my way past some planters and a plastic chair to the door. The white curtains were drawn, illuminated by a weak light inside. I gave the sliding glass door a pull. Locked. I waited a minute, gathering my strength, then took the handle in both hands. Simultaneously lifting and shaking as if to rip it from its track, I popped open the door.

I stepped back and waited. No sound came from inside. By now I was focused simply on the job and not on what I might find in there. Crawling was the way to go, I decided, in case someone was waiting to take a swing at me.

The floor was cool tile. A single table lamp lit the room and its brass-riveted, Mission-style furniture. The plaster ceiling curved in the direction of a Moorish arch. A large TV sat across from the couch and a desk stood against the opposite wall beneath a leaded glass window. My hand slid under something soft and silky. I lifted it to discover that my wrist had been lassoed by a black lace bra. I decided to stand up.

The apartment had a galley kitchen, a darkened bedroom, a spacious tiled bathroom, and no dead bodies. The closets stood open. Clothes were littered in the bedroom and living room, on furniture and on the floor, as if they'd been considered and abandoned in a marathon dress-up session. The bed was unmade. The medicine cabinet was empty save for a few fallen vials. A leather purse sat by the front door. It was empty.

I went back to a small message board attached to the side of the refrigerator and turned on a light. The name Erika was scrawled on the board, as if owed a return call. Below it were letters and numbers that had been erased. I leaned in to decipher and memorize them.

The wall phone next to my ear rang, jolting me upright as if I'd been caught.

I shut off the light and made for the balcony. Then the phone machine on the desk picked up. I heard Alissa's answer message again. Another woman was on the line, her voice young and throaty, but strained.

"Alissa, it's me. Are you back? I've been worried about you, I wanted to check up." She paused and said, "Are you back? The thing is, when I was parking, I think I saw someone in your apartment, and I was afraid it could be an intruder or something." A longer silence followed. The voice turned shivery. "Oh my God . . ." she said as it dawned on her that that someone was probably listening to her.

This was bad news for two reasons. First, it meant the woman had seen me break in. Second, it meant she was close by. I considered exiting by the normal route. Then I considered witnesses in the hallway and the manager about whom Rod had warned me. I left everything as it was and went back out the sliding door.

Going down was easier than coming up. I kept a grip on the drainpipe and shimmied down. The balcony railings gave me points of balance. From the roof of the utility room I slid straight down the pipe. I grabbed Rod and told him we had to get out of there.

"And Alissa?" he asked, dreading the answer.

"She's not dead." At least not in there.

>> >> >> >> >>

I'd fulfilled my end of the deal. Now I was looking forward to Rod fulfilling his. We were in the doughy embrace of his brown leather living-room couch. Rod had commanded fire in the brick brass-plated fireplace. A glass of apple juice sat in front of him. I'd requested a stronger beverage and he'd produced a light beer. After I'd explained to him why I had to make such a quick exit from Alissa's apartment, he wanted only to talk about the interior. It was as if he heard none of my insistent questions about why he'd wanted me to go in. He was particularly interested in her clothes.

"Surely you've seen what she wears," I said.

"She dresses very nicely. But was there anything more, uh, like what she'd wear to a nightclub? Kind of racy?"

"I didn't seen any spangles. But she has nice underwear."

Rod's face went red. I saw my opportunity. "It's your turn now, Rod. Clearly you've never been inside her apartment. I don't think you've even been to the front door. You've only spied on her from the back."

Rod jumped to his feet and began to pace in front of the fire, arms folded. "It's not like that," he said. "I was just worried about her safety."

"You never even called her to ask, did you?"

"I didn't want to intrude." He'd circled around behind me, and for a moment I thought he'd left the room altogether. It was unsettling, but I'd seen him do this before when he was working on a particularly difficult problem. "I didn't want to frighten her. Did you—you didn't see blood anywhere, did you?"

"No. And the clothes didn't look like they'd been flung around violently. It was more like they'd been laid in place."

"It seems like she'd be neater."

"The apartment looked nothing like your desk. But then, neither does mine." Rod's desk was spotless every morning and it was returned to that state by the end of each day. His idea of organization was having everything put away. Mine was having everything out where I could see it. "Tell me what you know about this. An email address was written on her message board." I spelled it out: Foxldy77@telikom.crm.nu.

"It sounds like a spam address."

"What about a woman named Erika? Her name was also on the board."

He stopped behind me. "Erika. Yes, she's mentioned her. Erika works with Alissa."

"Where do they work?"

He waved the question away as if he didn't know and resumed his pacing in front of the fire. My patience was at an end. "Rod, who the hell is this woman? You've allowed me to believe she's your girlfriend, your fiancée, or at the very least someone you date. She's none of those, is she?"

"Is that what people think she is?"

"Of course they do! That's how you talk about her. Now, what's this all about?"

Rod knotted his arms tighter. His expression had become inert. His voice was barely audible. "We really were very close. I'm telling you the truth."

"All right, I believe you were close. Who is she? Where does she work?"

A little brightness came into his eyes. "She was the one who told me about Plush Biologics. She introduced me to Dr. Plush."

Plush Biologics had sprung from the work of Ronald Plush, an elite dermatologist with a cult following in the Valley. Eternaderm was their gene-based wonder therapy for skin. Rod's Algoplex had done such a good job providing molecular simulations and data visualization for Eternaderm that Plush's primary backer, Sylvain Partners, had agreed to fund the elaboration of Algoplex's technology.

"Fine," I said. "She works for Plush Biologics. What does she do there—she's a scientist?"

Rod looked at the fire, not me. "She's done other types of things. Here's the point: I really need her to be at the dinner Monday night when we sign the Plush deal. I'm at ease with her around. I feel more like *myself*." He returned to sit on the couch, facing me, the pleading back in his eyes. "That's why I need you to find her. By Monday. Forget about the film; it doesn't matter. I really need her that night. I don't want to blow it."

"You don't mean stop working on the show. You mean find Alissa and have a rough cut to screen Monday night."

"No!" Rod waved his hand as if erasing a blackboard. He started to get up again, but I held his arm. "I mean yes, if you can. But Alissa is the priority. The rest truly doesn't matter."

"All right, then," I said evenly. If I hadn't seen him pour the apple juice myself, I'd have thought he was inebriated. "If you want me to find Alissa, you have to answer my questions. What's her job at Plush Biologics?"

Rod looked away again. He didn't answer immediately, and when he did, his voice was soft. "She's had a hard life. Her mother, Wendy, was very young when she had Alissa. Alissa never even knew her father. She sort of got in the way of her mother's ambitions, and Wendy let her know it. Wendy always had some scheme going, she was always sure success was just over the horizon. Not real stuff, a glitzy kind of success. They lived in L.A. As soon as Alissa was old enough to be put in front of a camera, Wendy started pushing her, too. She was smart enough to get away from her mother eventually. But it may have been too late. Alissa learned word processing, project management, Photoshop, a few programs that got her executive-assistant jobs in high tech. She was playing it straight, working her way up from the bottom, unlike her mother. It was her way of rebelling. But she never succeeded in completely escaping Wendy."

"Where does Alissa work now?"

"She's a kind of hostess." Rod still wouldn't look at me.

"You'll have to tell me where. Tomorrow I'll interview her manager and her coworkers. I'll find Erika."

A calm seemed to settle over him. His shoulders relaxed and for the first time he looked me directly in the eye. The words came evenly spaced, as if from a computer. "She works for Silicon Glamour Associates."

"What is that, some kind of agency?"

"That's exactly what it is." Rod looked visibly lighter.

"It's an escort agency," I said. Things were falling into place. "She's assisting executives in a different way now."

An incongruous, high-pitched giggle emitted from Rod's mouth. His arms unfolded and he pressed his hands to the sofa as if trying to levitate. "An escort. How stupid of me. Yes, I suppose that's what she is. It's not what they call themselves. And it's not what you might assume."

"What do they call themselves?"

"Associates."

"And you hire them to accompany you on social occasions."

"You'd be amazed at how people look at you differently when you've got someone as smart and beautiful as Alissa on your arm. She made a difference in the Plush Biologics deal." He spoke as if letting me in on a great find. "But it was more than that with her. We had a chemistry. We genuinely liked each other."

I phrased my next question delicately. "What else is in her job description?"

Rod missed it. "Charm. Warmth. Alissa had them down." A bitter strain came into his tone. "I suppose she can just turn that on and off. Some charm algorithm is coded into her neural circuits. Here comes Rod, flip on the charm. He's such a sucker for it."

"I thought you said there was something real between you."

Rod gave a helpless shrug. "So did I. Or do I. I'm not sure which."

"What about the guy who came to your door today—is he connected to this agency?"

"Yes," Rod answered. "He works for Silicon Glamour. He was looking for Alissa."

"Does anyone else know about Alissa's real job?" I asked.

"Mike. He brought her in the first time. He's been the one pushing this whole image change, as you know."

"Well, it might be just as well to keep her out of the film. And away from Monday's dinner, too. People will ask questions. They might ask the same questions I am now. Are you sure you want me to find her?"

"Yes! Without qualification. Bill, it seems I've failed to make you understand that nothing supersedes this. For me personally, but also for the company. Forget about shooting more film tomorrow. Alissa promised to be at that dinner. I want her to be there."

"All right. Rita will do her best to have the film ready on Monday. But I take you at your word—the cut may be very rough. Meanwhile, I'll start looking for Alissa first thing in the morning."

"Thank you." Rod slumped back into the recesses of the couch. "The last thing she said to me was, 'Have faith.' That was a week ago."

"What do you think that meant?"

Rod shrugged. His body was drained. His pale eyes had turned inward.

I touched his arm. "Well, it sounds like good advice. Let's go with it."

3

Rod did not want to go to Silicon Glamour. I'd told him I'd go by myself, but Rod said I'd never get in without an introduction. Silicon Glamour was not open to walk-in business.

"In that case," I said, "you'll have to come with me."

Still he resisted. "It's Saturday," he said. "No one will be there."

"I'd think Saturday would be a busy day for an outfit like theirs," I replied. "But look, if you don't want to go, don't. My search for Alissa will end before it begins."

Only then did he admit he ought to make an appearance. The James Dean type had visited Rod yesterday to tell him the director of SG wanted to see him.

Rod sketched their methods as we drove in his Volvo down Interstate 280 to Palo Alto. It was not easy to retain the services of Silicon Glamour, but it was even harder to leave. They were unlisted and did not accept calls unless you were dialing from an approved number. You had to have an introduction from a previous client or an endorsed contact, and even then had to undertake a wooing process before you could actually hire their services. Once you were hooked, their rates began to rise.

"I'd think they'd do it in the reverse order. Does it work?" I asked.

"Consider their market. Executive-level Silicon Valley people who don't have the time, or maybe the social data set, to secure the right companion for a big event. You don't want to be one of those guys standing around with your hands in your pockets, talking shop with the other stag engineers. So you've got an exceptionally high-percentile group, and the last thing they want is some cheap escort. SG is smart. They play hard to get. It works like a real date: You have to convince them you're SG material and then you have to pay a premium price, all of which makes their services more desirable. It's all very high class and aboveboard."

I kept my opinions about its classiness to myself, but got to ask the question I'd attempted last night. "Meaning no hanky-panky?"

"Exactly. It's in your service contract. You're liable for damages. The associate can be fired. The people who work there, both men and women, sign a four-year contract. SG invests a lot in them in terms of training and appearance, and they don't want the associate to run off with the first high-tech millionaire they meet."

"They tell you all this up front?"

"No, Alissa told me. As we got to know one another."

"Did you pick her out yourself?"

Rod gave me a glance of wide-eyed dismay. "God, no. I didn't initiate this. It was Mike Riley's idea. I told you that."

"He just sprang her on you?"

"Precisely! We were going to this banquet at the close of a data visualization conference. Big event. He met me at the door. This great-looking girl was with him. I remember she was wearing a little black dress that fit her perfectly. Her hair was down and she wasn't wearing too much makeup. I thought, Jeez, Mike really knows how to score. Then he put her on my arm. He says, 'Rod, this is Alissa, she'll be your date tonight.' And she gave me this smile."

"Like the one in the picture."

"Yeah, that catlike smile, that Egyptian goddess look. We were in this flow of people. She hooked her arm into mine and I couldn't get out of it without making a scene. It made me angry, though, Mike springing her on me like I couldn't take care of myself. I wasn't very nice to her at first. I made some sarcastic remark, asked her what her specialty was in data visualization. She said she had a special power to visualize the CEO over there in his Armani suit naked. There was something about the way she said it, I had to laugh—I happened to know the guy and he's a real ass. She was young, but she had this savvy. She kept on making comments that were quite funny about the attendees. It was fascinating; we just clicked. I never understood what people meant about chemistry before that night."

"So you kept seeing her."

He jerked the car over into the right lane and frowned. "Yes, I did. I was hooked. Just like they planned."

We took the Page Mill exit and followed winding roads into Los Altos Hills, on the edge between town and country. I didn't know what to expect of Silicon Glamour headquarters, but I didn't expect to turn into a small driveway guarded by a tall oleander hedge. Behind the hedge was a two-story cube of a building, the kind that could have been built as a medical office in the sixties.

Rod parked in the small lot. We were in his car for a reason. I drove an ancient International Harvester Scout, its color faded burnt orange by the sun. It didn't go very fast or offer much in the way of comfort, but it kept me connected to the road and to the days when a machine was a machine. It was the automotive equivalent of shooting on film instead of video. Rod had said we wouldn't make it to the front door if we turned into the SG parking lot in the Scout. They had someone whose only job was to watch by remote camera the cars entering their driveway.

A screen of perforated concrete block channeled us into an enclosed space in front of the door. We could not escape the eye of the camera mounted on the wall. The door, like the building, was marked with only its address.

Rod was fidgeting madly. He pressed an intercom button and announced his arrival in a thin voice. The door buzzed. We went into a small lobby with a polished terrazzo floor. An open-tread stair lead to the second floor, but the view into the rest of the office was blocked by an interior wall with only one discreetly placed door. A pair of tall weimaraners, carved from concrete, flanked the front entrance. A small fountain bubbled. Gauzy white curtains covered the windows. Oversized pseudo-Etruscan vases marked the corners.

The receptionist was a burly man with a thick mustache and muscular sideburns to match. He gave me a quick appraisal, from my white shirt to my jeans to my boots. "Mr. Evans is waiting upstairs," he said to Rod. Rod wore a business shirt, slacks, and brown shoes for the occasion.

Rod hesitated, and I led the way. Rupert Evans stood at the double door to his office about halfway down the corridor. He frowned until he saw Rod. Once the introductions were made, he invited us in. The plate on the outer door denoted him Director. If the lobby was a curious mix of luxury and hygiene, walking into this office was like being taken into an old-style gentleman's club. Oil paintings—dogs and hunting scenes—in gilded frames decorated the walls. The windows were hidden behind heavy brocade curtains with tasseled cords. The idea flashed through my mind that behind each door in this building was a new and different world. I wondered what all went on in them.

Evans was a small-shouldered man in his fifties, neatly dressed in a double-breasted suit, hair combed back so that a few sprigs peeked from behind his ears. He told Rod how glad he was to see him and conducted us through the sitting area, a maze of stuffed furniture that included a zebra-skin couch and a leopard-pelt throw. We sat in chairs in front of his desk. He circled behind it, and I half expected him to offer a decanter of whiskey and a box of cigars. Instead, his eyes darted over me like a bird's. The inspection was quicker but more thorough than the receptionist's. "In what capacity are you here, Mr. Damen?"

"He's helping me find Alissa," Rod said. His voice was a croak.

"Very good, we need all the help we can get." His manner was at once ingratiating and paternal.

"You haven't heard anything at all from her?" I said.

"We have neither seen nor spoken to her." He folded his hands. They were smooth, the fingers tapered. "We're protective of our associates. Overly protective, perhaps. We provide them with housing. We provide them with cars. We take very good care of them."

"How long has it been since you talked to her?"

His gaze shifted to Rod. "How long has it been since *you* talked to her?"

Rod finally found his voice. "A week. Maybe more. She wasn't available last weekend. Yesterday she was scheduled to see me, as you know. She failed to appear. She's also scheduled for a dinner Monday night. It's an important event. This is a big problem."

"It certainly is. I take *personal* responsibility for our employees. Do you know what that means? Do you know how it tears me apart when I'm unsure about the well-being of a girl such as

Alissa? She's like a daughter to me, Rod. It's going to go very hard for the man who's hiding her. Unless, of course . . ."

"I'm not hiding her," Rod snapped.

A darkness clouded Rupert's face. "If some harm has come to her . . ." He shook his head, apparently at a loss for words.

I said, "I take it you've been to her apartment. You must have a key."

"We respect her privacy," he replied with a slight huff.

"What about her car? I imagine it's registered to you. Maybe some credit cards, too?"

Rupert ceased looking at me. I began to see how it was. No actual information would be forthcoming from him, only from us. His words were directed at Rod. "I'm sorry. This whole affair is extremely distressing. Naturally we look to you. We know how well you two got along. How much time you spent together."

I saw the fear building on Rod's face, and cut in. "Alissa will officially be missing, from our point of view, early this afternoon. We'll go to the police then."

"No you won't. The police stay out of it. It's in your service contract, Rod."

"That won't apply if there's been foul play," I insisted.

"All the more reason. You'd be the first suspect, Rod. I'll make sure of that. We're far more efficient than the police, in any case. We have fewer limitations. I hope you understand what I'm saying."

"I genuinely don't know where she is, Rupert." Rod's pleading tone was back. "I'll do everything I can to find her. I told you, I would really like her to be there on Monday. Give me until then."

Rupert sat with his hands folded, his head down, considering whether Rod deserved his mercy. "We know about your unauthorized visits with Alissa," he said at last. "That alone is a serious breach of contract. But we want to give you a chance, Rod. We want to think the best of you. I know you were a good man when you first began to see Alissa. I am willing to give you the benefit of the doubt, but that benefit is growing slim."

I tried to catch Rod's eye, to understand why he was knuckling under. He just stared at a pen set on the desk and nodded submissively. One of the pens pointed at Rod and one at me. I resisted, for the time being, the impulse to grab it and puncture Rupert's pretensions.

His tone turned hard. "Monday at the latest. You know the consequences."

"Just one request—please don't send people over to my house."

Rupert sat back, simulating chagrin. "I do apologize for that. But you see, we were in a state of anxiety about Alissa."

He stood to show us out. Rod's tail was fully between his legs. Until he fully explained why, I had to hold back on getting tougher with Rupert.

I did reveal a bit of information when we reached the corridor. I wanted to catch Rupert off guard. "Foxldy77@telikom.crm.nu," I said. "Do you know that email address?"

"Not our type of person," he replied. His eyes still did not meet mine. They'd avoided me since halfway through the interview.

A door at the end of the corridor opened. I glimpsed another world behind it, a severe world of clean, rectilinear lines, of chrome chairs and polished granite. A woman stood silhouetted in the door. She had come out to watch us. Her legs were jacked up on a pair of pumps sharp enough to open a letter. With her padded shoulders, she cut a figure far more formidable than Rupert. From the position of her office and the way she watched, I sensed she was the boss. And she had the power to back up every threat Rupert had made.

4

Men handle humiliation in different ways. Rod, cowed though he was by Rupert, did not appear more troubled on the way back to his house than he had been on the way down. My surmise, after a week of working with him, was that the pecking order in which Rupert operated was not one Rod recognized. The tokens of status by which most men judged one another held little inflection for Rod. He saw them as merely that, signs in a system: He himself, as a master of codes, floated above it all, decrypting the systems, not so much to manipulate them as to comprehend the nature of code itself. The algorithms he designed performed a kind of magic on obstinate databases, unlocking new and unexpected insights hidden within them.

What bothered me so much, then, about Rod's meek submission to Rupert? Was it his failure to stand up for himself, or the fact that, hamstrung from defending him, I had to submit as well?

I let my steam burn off a little before I started putting questions to him. I kept it basic. "How do you feel, Rod?"

"I'm disappointed," he said. "They really don't know where Alissa is."

"What about the way Rupert pushed you around?"

He shrugged. His voice was calm and resigned. "It's his area of expertise. What could I do? He's got the control key."

"I think we should go straight to the police."

"No. That option is closed. If we do that, everyone will know Alissa was an . . . associate."

"Rupert was bluffing," I said. "He doesn't want the publicity any more than you do."

"He wouldn't publish it in the newspaper. Just a few well-placed calls and I'm a laughingstock. You know how people are." Here was one social convention he recognized, if only in recognizing that others recognized it: It's not cool to pay to have a girlfriend. At least not through a middleman.

"Is that how Rupert forces you to keep using the service? And can keep raising his rates on you?"

"That's their method," Rod said. "But it's different for me—I wanted to see Alissa. She wanted to see me, too. So she said."

"And you did have unauthorized visits, like Rupert claimed."

"Yes. Alissa started them, but that's beside the point. Rupert's still got me for violating the contract."

"I'm sure we can get around that."

"The language is airtight. When I signed it, I thought the chances it would come into play approached zero. But it's not what Rupert can do to me I really care about. It's what he'd do to Alissa."

We reached his shady Belmont street a few minutes later. He methodically pulled the car into his driveway, made sure it was straight, put on the brake, and locked the doors after we got out. This time he said to the front door, "Open, dammit."

I expected Rod to start his habitual pacing and compulsive putting away of things. Instead, he sat down at the kitchen table. I sat across from him. He gripped his knees and looked up at the ceiling. He did this often, as if absorbed in a screen in the corner of his eye. The real action was on the screen, and you were a bit of flickering distraction that happened to be in the room. He called it "deep hack mode" when he was working.

"Alissa's unique," he said at last. "She plays a unique role in my life. I always thought she cared for me, too. Don't get me wrong, I had no illusions, but . . ."

"But you hoped anyway?"

Rod shook his head as if shaking off the idea. "No, it was absurd. But I did think she would treat me right. That she was doing her job but it was a little more pleasant with me. That she'd like to see Algoplex succeed."

I waited for him to explain. He wouldn't without a prompt. He was contemplating the corner again. "Is there some reason she *wouldn't* want your company to succeed?"

"No, I just . . . I wonder now why she got so close to me. She was bright, but no wizard. I wonder about her motives. I wonder if they have something to do with her disappearance."

"It sounds like you're talking about theft of Algoplex secrets."

Rod's face was a virtual blank, but he gave a minuscule nod.

"Did she have access to your files?"

"I was careful. I've learned that lesson. When I started out in this business, I'd share my ideas freely because I was excited about them. Then they'd show up in an executive's memo as if he'd done the work. That's why I started my own company."

"So you were careful, but then you got closer to Alissa."

"It was unexpected." His features glowed for a moment as he thought back. "We did hit it off that first night at the banquet. But also, as the night went on, I noticed the difference in how I was perceived. Before, people tended to avoid me if they didn't have some work issue to discuss. I don't do small talk. Mike pointed out this was a drawback in gaining the confidence of investors. He was right about the need to change my image. That night, with Alissa on my arm, the other guests sought me out. They wanted to know who this beautiful woman was. They wanted to know me, too. They realized there was more to me than they'd thought. Alissa turned on the charm and I found a new conviviality in myself. It was remarkable."

"It makes sense you'd call for her again."

"Yes." He gave me a bashful glance. "You saw her picture. I think you understand. It seemed a good investment, in any case. There were the public events, but she helped in other ways. She suggested clothes I should wear. Shoes—she said they were significant. She recommended a person to cut my hair."

Somehow his mustache survived, though. I nodded at a giant platter in the shape of a fish leaning on a shelf by the stove. "She started to redecorate your house, too."

"That was more recent, as she began to spend time here. She would call me—this is the honest truth, Bill—she would call me on her own on the weekends and volunteer to come over. For free. We took hikes, rode bicycles, went to the Santa Cruz boardwalk— places we weren't likely to be seen by Silicon Glamour people. She'd get in terrible trouble if we were. She did it because she wanted to see me. So she said. She never asked me for a thing."

"I assume you took the photo on one of those outings."

"Yes. In Carmel. What a glorious day that was."

"And you managed to put up with her visits."

I smiled to let him know I would have, too. But Rod wasn't in a smiling mood. He zeroed in and held me with his slate-gray eyes. They were incredibly intense when they ceased their wandering and focused on you. Suddenly I understood why he didn't do it often.

"It was amazing, Bill. New synapses started to fire. I felt doors being opened inside of me. It was so easy to talk to her. I wanted to tell her everything. Favorite books, films, foods. Stories from childhood, things I didn't know I remembered. Personal quirks—she thought they were so funny. I couldn't stop talking. I won't lie to you, Bill, I haven't had a lot of relationships. In school, I never understood why other students were so obsessed with dating. Now I know."

"Intimacy is addictive."

"I find myself thinking that. But I didn't let myself go. I didn't let myself fall in—" Rod halted at the word. "I knew the score. Yet still, she seemed as surprised by it as I was."

"Did she talk about herself?"

"Oh yes. We're not such different generations—she's thirty, older than she looks. We had very different upbringings, yet we seemed to share so much. Mine was reasonably standard: Ohio, civil engineer father, chemist mother, jock older brother who beat me at everything. Alissa's was hard. Always on the move, always new men in her mother's life, always being told she was a drag on her mother. Yet she talked about it in such a sweet way, not laying blame, not asking for pity."

"Yet she stayed in touch with this mother of hers."

"That's something I wanted to mention to you. When you asked Rupert about that email address, foxylady, it occurred to me it could be Alissa's mother. It's the kind of name Wendy would give herself."

"Does Rupert know Wendy?" I asked. "Because the way he reacted was interesting. He said he didn't associate with such people—as if he knew who it was."

"God, I hope not. I hope it wasn't Wendy who got Alissa into this business."

"I sent a query to that email address last night, asking if they knew where Alissa was."

Rod's plump lips formed a pout. "I wish you'd checked with me first. I've been telling Alissa to stay away from Wendy."

"It's worth the risk," I said. "I'm going to work on getting inside Silicon Glamour. I want to talk to Erika, that friend who works with Alissa. But it'll take some time. The email is the best lead we've got right now."

"I felt so bad for Alissa." Rod's attention strayed into the corner again, where he seemed to see the past. "I wished I could make it all better. I was thinking about helping her, Bill, sort of adopting her, like an uncle or something. Getting her out of that life, giving her a chance to acquire more advanced skills. What a fool I was."

Now we were back to the real subject. "You think Alissa set you up somehow?"

Rod tapped his teeth with a knuckle. "Maybe."

"You're afraid she got close to you in order to get access to Algoplex technology?"

"Maybe." His voice was getting miserable.

"Is there any evidence?"

"Maybe. I checked the log on my computer downstairs. Some crucial files were copied on an evening when Alissa was here. I may have done the copying myself—I just don't remember."

"Who would she have been working for?"

He kept tapping. "There are a lot of things that don't make sense. First of all, I didn't give her any IP. I talked about what we do, but not with any granularity. She's not a technologist anyway; she wouldn't know what to look for. The one possibility I can think of is that she strung me along to the point where I was comfortable having her in my house, where she could copy files. That would assume someone told her which files to copy. But who? I can't imagine SG has any use for my work."

"They could sell it. If you had this suspicion, I really don't understand why you didn't challenge Rupert."

"I keep hoping it doesn't add up. Alissa was unhappy at SG. She still had three years to go on her contract and she felt trapped. If Rupert had gotten what he wanted from her, why send Brendon over to harass me? Rupert convinced me he didn't know where she was."

"I agree that he believed you had information he didn't. Still, I think it was an act. His reasons were not what he said."

"What were his reasons, then?" Rod said.

"We need to find out. That's why we shouldn't have buckled."

"Possibly. I know there's a grammar and a syntax to social behavior, but in my world we say what we mean. We solve real problems. We scream and we argue about how our technology will get us there, but our motives and ends are shared."

"Rupert's problem is real enough. Money is to be made."

Rod glared at me. "By *real* I mean a problem whose solution will improve life in some way. Making more money just trans-fers resources."

"Rod, I know there's a difference between you and him. That's why I'm on your side. And you could be right, he may be as in the dark about Alissa as you are. Which would mean she's diddled you both."

He flinched, and I wished I hadn't put it so bluntly. "Sorry," I said. "Look, I know it's hard. I've been there. Remind me to tell you a story about a woman named Lynda someday."

His little giggle came out again. "She diddled you?"

"In every sense of the word. But then, it happened to every-one in those days." I didn't have to spell out which days I meant: The late nineties seemed like ancient history now.

Rod's face softened into relief that he wasn't the only chump in the room. He fidgeted with a napkin, tearing it into uniform strips. "It's like getting a spell cast over you. You become helpless in its power. Someone else is pulling your strings."

"Yes," I said. It was an embarrassingly old story, but everyone had to discover it for themselves.

"A glamour," Rod went on. "I remember a Dungeons & Dragons–type game where you could cast a glamour over some-one. It's like a spell but more—well, glamorous. I looked up the origin of the word. I always thought it meant the appearance of beauty where none existed. But it came from a Scottish variation on the word *grammar*. That's because in the old days, only the magician-priests knew how to write. Inscription was one of their occult powers. I used to play computer games where you had a *grimoire*, a book of spells. See, I've always thought the spelling of a word contained the spell of its meaning. For instance, the origin of *algebra* is the Arab *al-jabr*: bonesetting."

"That would explain my experiences in high school math class."

Rod laughed. He was back in his element now. His face scrunched with squinting blinks every time he made a point, as if it came at the price of a small sting. "Actually, the root mean-ing is reduction. The word *algorithm* comes from the great Persian mathematician al-Khwarizmi, who wrote a treatise called *The Calculation of Reduction and Restoration*."

"Code is a kind of magic, too," I said. "Combine a string of bits in the right order and you've got a computer that can beat the best chess player in the world. String together three billion nucleotides and you've got the instructions to build a human being. Put them in a different order and you've got a mouse."

Rod squinted, then looked up at his private screen in the corner again. "The way I see it, Alissa was a master of her particular code. I was a beginner. I'd learned a different alphabet. My principal failure was in not recognizing that we were speaking her language, which I could learn if I chose to study it. Expertise is nothing but time: Ten thousand hours equals an expert."

He gave an oddly triumphant smile. He'd succeeded in convincing himself that no inexplicable voodoo was involved in her spell. It was merely a matter of allocating resources. Any problem he could break down into its logical components was a problem he could solve.

I steered us back to the subject. "Who else could Alissa have been working for? I imagine Plush Biologics would like to have a look under the Algoplex hood."

Rod shook his head. "I was quite open with Plush about what we could do. Even if they get their hands on some base code, they need me to make it work. Our patents are secure. I'm the key man."

"What about the business side, then? You said Alissa introduced you to Plush."

"True. But they did their due diligence. Alissa and I talked about the people involved in the deal, the companies, their potential. But I gave no confidential data to her. If anything, she gave *me* inside information. She knew a lot about Eternaderm."

"I'm sure you got independent confirmation of what she said."

"Naturally. I'm scouring my memory, Bill, to think what she could have done and for whom. Nothing adds up. Of course, you could be right about Plush in some way I haven't foreseen."

"I guess we'll know for sure if they spring something on you Monday night at the signing dinner."

"You'll be there, won't you?"

"Yes. I'd like to get a few shots for our final cut. I'll also bring the rough version of the film and make sure it's screened correctly."

"Good. Speaking of which—I have a lot of preparation to do. Mike is waiting for my call. We'll be working all weekend."

"All right, Rod. I'll keep searching for Alissa. Do you have a picture I can take?"

He went to the fridge and extracted a sheet of paper from under a bitmap magnet. It was a high-res printout of the photo of Alissa I'd seen before.

"Take it," Rod said. "I can print another one. . . ."

His voice trailed off and his mouth sagged. We were silent for a moment, looking at that smile again. It did have a catlike quality of unreadable motives. And cats were not known for their loyalty.

"Maybe this will turn out okay, Rod. Maybe she's safe and she stole nothing. Maybe there's a simple explanation—Wendy got in trouble, Alissa went to help, and she was embarrassed to tell you."

Rod made an effort to compose himself. "That would certainly be preferable to the alternatives."

I waited for him to look at me. "What does your gut tell you?"

He paused, as if to get a reading. Again his mouth turned down. His voice wavered. "I miss her a great deal, Bill."

It was a simple statement, spoken without drama. I said I'd do whatever it took to find her.

5

The magic of email appeared to solve all of our problems by the next afternoon. It was a good thing, because the day—or rather, the people in it—had been getting on my nerves up to that point.

Normally I'd start a Sunday with a long cup of coffee and the newspaper at Scoby's, our neighborhood café, then get out of the city with some friends. Today had a different plan from the beginning because Rita and I had to map out our rough cut of the Algoplex film to be shown on Monday night. Wes made me late for that by showing up at Scoby's during the coffee.

Scoby's was a homey place with a well-supplied magazine rack, big windows, and very good coffee—a comforting constant as the neighborhood around me changed. Potrero Hill had been my home for eight years. Its industrial building stock made it a prime target for the loft-seeking peoples of the area. The city's determination to redevelop Mission Bay—landfill surrounding a now-buried tidal slough that cut through the Mission district to empty into the bay—succeeded with the completion of the Giants ball park in 2000. The rail and ship yards disappeared quickly after that. Glass-curtain structures sprouted like mushrooms: a UCSF research lab, Macromedia,

Sega. The old waterfront life had mostly disappeared, the long-shoremen's bars having been turned into restaurants and dance clubs for the leather-pants set.

Wes had referred me to Rod. Now Wes wanted to hear how it had turned out. I gave him a quick rundown as I finished my coffee. He wanted the juicy details, but I was not in a chatty mood. Instead, I mentioned the role I had in mind for him. I wanted him to set up a date with Erika and another Silicon Glamour associate.

His first reaction was not to say it was a ridiculous idea, nor to say he didn't need to hire his dates. Instead, he asked if the associates were good-looking.

"They couldn't charge what they do if they weren't," I said.

His sneaky smile told me he was into it. This was a side of Wes that amused me. I'd known him since college, when he was a skinny physics major with a hangdog look and a shyness about dating. We made a couple of goofy Super 8 films about existentially perplexed sci-fi insects. He'd also been the first person to show me the Internet, when it was used only by government agencies and science departments at something like 2400 kilobytes per second.

Wes was as loyal as a friend could be, but like all of us he had his fixations. I figured he felt compelled to make up for all the lost time he'd spent in the physics lab. Everyone has their own way of feeling off-beam. Wes was good-looking now, with sharp features and dark hair sweeping across his forehead. He was also CTO of a net company that had beat the startup odds. But in his own mind, he was still the nerdy boy endlessly trying to prove he could get a date.

The fact that he was a tech exec—a mind-boggling fact, to me—made him the best candidate I knew to apply to Silicon Glamour. I told him to play up his geek side and to be sure to ask for a date with Erika, the name that had been scrawled on Alissa's message board.

Wes rubbed his hands together. "No problem. We'll show them a good time."

"I believe that's *their* job. What we need to do is earn their trust so that they'll tell us about Silicon Glamour."

"Trust. Right. You did say Rod was footing the bill?"

"It'll go on my expense report."

Wes then insisted on coming with me to Rita's. I warned him it was not a social hour. We had work to do. He said he just wanted to see how Rod looked on screen.

Rita's place was in the Mission, a backyard bungalow almost a hundred years old. An editing suite was set up in her basement: an Avid system loaded on a G4, two nineteen-inch monitors on a shelf, a vector scope, and speakers spread in a semicircle in front of her chair. The hard drives were under the worktable. A Beta deck and an eight-track mixing board occupied the ends of the semicircle. Out in the garage, under a plastic cover, she kept a Steenbeck flatbed for old-style analog film editing. We didn't get to use it nearly enough for my taste.

Wes dragged a folding chair into the tiny carpeted room. Rita sat in a rolling desk chair in front of the screen. A poster of *The Third Man* hung on the wall.

I brought her up to speed on the Rod story. "Silicon Glamour," she said. "Isn't that when you don't wear your pocket protector, Wes?"

"Nobody uses pens anymore," he shot back.

Rita had to needle me, of course, about sticking her alone with the editing. It was already a big job for two of us. But she understood. The film business was all about last-minute changes. Besides, she was still raising money for her next documentary, and film work in San Francisco had gone quiet since the Internet bubble burst. All those filmmakers who'd been sucked into Web producing suddenly needed jobs. The good stuff—documentaries and features—only came around so often, and TV commercials had moved to Vancouver. I was lucky the Rod gig had come along when it did.

Rita said, "So what's your take on this Rod and Alissa business, Wes? You're the one who introduced us to him."

"Rod is the real thing when it comes to engineering genius," Wes said. "He's a good guy, too. But I never said he was Romeo Montague."

"I don't get why he's so desperate to have Alissa at this dinner tomorrow," Rita said.

"Nerves," Wes answered. "Everyone's alert for reasons to back out at a signing. Rod's the kind of guy who could get jittery and blurt out the wrong thing. It sounds like Alissa keeps him on an even keel."

"It's also for his peace of mind," I said. "He'll be upset if he finds out she stabbed him in the back. It'll be worse if he finds out she's hurt or dead. If I can at least tell him she's okay, he'll feel a lot better."

"Who are these people Rod's signing the deal with?" Wes asked.

"Plush Biologics has a genetic skin treatment called Eternaderm," I said. "It rejuvenates your elastin fibers by regulating the enzymes that break them down and promoting the synthesis of new fibers. Your skin gets looser and more brittle as you age. Healthier elastin proteins restore suppleness and resilience."

Wes's eyes widened. "That's going to *score*. If it works."

"It's being tested. They're still 'ironing out the wrinkles' before it goes commercial," Rita said, repeating Rod's favorite phrase to describe Eternaderm's progress. Wes rolled his eyes.

"Rod did some work for them that fast-forwarded Eternaderm," I said. "That led to the strategic alliance. Plush is working on genes to regulate melanin, too. You'll be able to change your skin color at will."

Wes peered at his reflection in a blank video screen. "I think I'm going to need Eternaderm. I've been out in the sun too much lately."

Rita peered with him. "Yeah, you're losing that pale engineer tone. But keep the wrinkles, Wes. They give you character." She liked to give him a hard time. Wes got nervous around her because she was so forthright in her opinions. "Anyway," Rita went on, "you can't afford Eternaderm until your company's IPO. This is a high-end market. Silicon Valley has lots of wealthy people who are terrified of getting old."

"Rod needs to retool and extend his technology," I said. "That takes money, which Algoplex doesn't have. So the third leg of the triangle is new capital coming from Plush's big backer. Sylvain Partners will fund Algoplex's next stage."

Wes ceased his self-inspection. "I hope Rod isn't giving away too much equity."

"You know how it works. Bargain your soul to the VC's. But Rod seems satisfied with the deal."

"What is Alissa going to do, hold the pen for him?" Rita said.

"You don't understand business, Rita." Wes had found a way to get a little revenge. "You've got to make all the right moves at an event like this or you'll spook your partners. Especially if Alissa's been spying."

"Wouldn't Alissa being there make him even more shaky?"

"Not if he's sure she's on his side," I said. "And if she's still missing, he's got Silicon Glamour to worry about. I need to throw Rupert off the trail for a few days. String him along with progress reports. Tell him Alissa is on her way back. As a matter of fact—can I check my email down here, Rita?"

"Sure," she said, swiveling to bring up a browser on her G4.

"I got an email back from foxylady77 late yesterday," I said. "They forwarded my message to Alissa's mother, Wendy. I'm waiting to hear from her."

"Rod's such a nervous nelly," Rita said as the throat-clearing sounds of connection came over the wire. "He's got to take charge. He owns the company, for heaven's sake."

"Where were you when the sympathy genes were handed out, Rita?" Wes said. "Rod was in love with this girl. She's vanished, and she might have double-crossed him."

Rita smiled at Wes. She was talking tougher than she really felt. Because of her Botticelli face and long, wavy hair, people expected only sweet words from her. She enjoyed surprising them.

I scooted forward and logged on to my account. "Nothing yet," I reported. "Let's get to work, Rita."

Rita brought the Avid to life. I took the camera originals from a cabinet behind me and stacked them on the table. Rita cued the first tape. There was Rod, pacing and squinting as he talked about the intricacies of code writing. I'd take notes on a yellow pad while she selected shots on the Avid.

Wes watched for a little while, then got bored with our stops, starts, and fast-forwards. He clapped me on the shoulder. "Later, Billy-boy. I'll let you know how it goes with Silicon Glamour."

"Thanks, Wes." I waited until the door closed, then explained to Rita that he was setting up a date with one of Alissa's co-workers.

Rita laughed. "He's the right man for the job."

We moved on through the raw footage from the past three days. I already had a structure for the picture in my mind. The limits on what you could do in a piece like this were always a little frustrating. Not that I hated it, but on the other hand I'd seen a documentary about the Russian army recently. It was full of very long takes, during which, through some magic, you began to feel drawn inside the subject's interior life even though you saw only silent exterior. When we kept the camera on Rod too long, he'd start fidgeting and offer to show us a card trick.

"Rod *is* kind of sweet," Rita said during one of the fidgeting shots.

"We could use this shot if we want Plush to think he's sweet, too."

"Depends," she answered, pulling the old wool sweater she was wearing over her head. The space was unheated and she always started an editing session with three layers. As the machines warmed the room, she'd peel down to a loose camisole. We'd been a couple once, and every so often I wondered whether we ought to get back together. "How sweet are the Plush people?"

"I got a glimpse of them when they came for a meeting, but no more," I said. "Dr. Plush seemed quite full of himself."

"It's his wife who runs the business side."

"No fidgeting," I decided.

We moved on. I was creating a list of shots on my pad while Rita sorted them into virtual bins. A few hours later we were down to the tape we'd shot on Friday, the scenes meant to show Rod's personal side. We watched him fumble the Frisbee in the Ultimate game. Mike trotted by, gave Rod a pat on the butt, and told him he'd get 'em next time. Rod looked at the Frisbee like it was some kind of alien saucer.

"That's not bad," I said. "We need a little humor."

"Can't leave out the full-frontal nerdity," Rita said. She skipped ahead to a shot in which several players leaped as one for a floating Frisbee. It was tipped, tipped again, and landed in the hands of a young woman who then quickly passed it to a teammate. "Here we go. Teamwork. Striving. Grabbing for the plastic disk."

"If they like this sort of thing, they will find this the sort of thing they like."

Rita chuckled. The old Abe Lincoln line was a motto we used when we created a scene that we thought was a little cheesy but knew the client would appreciate.

"Mike will love it," I said. I tipped back in my chair. "Okay, I think we've enough to build an assembly. Will this keep you busy for the rest of the evening?"

"Plenty. You can go look for Alissa."

"Thanks, Rita. Mind if I check my email again?"

She brought up her browser and we switched chairs. As soon as I logged on, the message popped out at me. "Look at this," I said. "We're on a roll."

Subj: alissa
From: sPcLdy

this is alissas mother wendy, please do not worry about her. she will be present for the dinner, she knows its important. send place and time and i will give her the information.
wendy :)

Rita lifted her eyebrows at me. "In the nick of time."

"Yeah." I frowned. "I don't know if I believe it, but . . ."

"Quit looking on the dark side, Bill. The whole Alissa thing has been blown out of proportion from the start, if you ask me. It's been a product of Rod's nervousness."

"It's interesting that Wendy doesn't know the place and time," I said. "Then again, maybe Rod hadn't told Alissa yet."

"And the message fits with your theory that Alissa had just gone to help Wendy with something and didn't want to tell anyone."

"I suppose. Well, you're in luck, Rita. You're stuck with me tonight after all."

"Joy. You'll go with Rod tomorrow night, too?"

"Oh, yes. To shoot the happy ending: Rod signs the deal and gets the girl. The company's saved and everyone's satisfied."

"Even if that doesn't come true, you've got a legitimate way to string Rupert along now."

"Yeah. I'll call Rod and tell him. Then I'll call Rupert. I just have to be careful which strings I pull. I don't know what all they're attached to."

6

"Do you think she'll really be there?"

It was only the 89th time Rod had asked. I knew he wanted me to say yes. But for the 89th time, the best I could offer was, "Wendy said she would." And for the 89th time Rod said that was what worried him. I was looking forward to the dinner if only to put an end to the questions. I was also hoping I'd at last get to meet Alissa.

He was in the bathroom when I arrived. I waited outside, feeling like a best man.

"Rod," I called, "we're supposed to be there in five minutes."

The bathroom door swung open. He was still in his boxers and a T-shirt that read LIKE YOU, ONLY SMARTER.

"How does this work, Bill?" he said. "How do you get your hair under control?"

I stood next to him facing the mirror. Rod was trying to get a strand of reddish hair to sit down over a thin spot. The strand kept popping up like a jack-in-the-box. My own hair was a study in chaos theory, a landscape of swirls and eddies the color of dirty flax.

"I keep it short," I said. "If it grows out too much, it looks like a place in the grass where a deer spent a bad night."

Rod wet his hand and smacked the offending strand down again. It would not stay.

"Do you have any hair gel?" I asked.

"You mean like Brylcreem?"

I searched through his drawers for something to improvise with. He didn't even have hand lotion. Alissa must not have spent nights with him. I found some antibiotic ointment and applied it to the strand.

Rod let out a sigh of relief. "That's better."

"Good. Now let's get going."

He dressed himself up in a charcoal suit and unobtrusive tie. I straightened his tie and gave him a little push toward the door.

We drove down 280 in the twilight. I'd already assured Rod that Silicon Glamour would leave us alone. Rupert had gotten my message about Alissa. He wanted to see her first thing tomorrow morning; I told him that would be up to Alissa. Meanwhile, I just wanted to get Rod through the dinner. I said I'd been able to spend most of yesterday and today cutting a decent rough version of the film.

Rod's nervousness only increased. "Are you sure we should show it? It seems kind of, I don't know . . . egotistical."

"You're supposed to have some ego as an executive. I know you've got it as an engineer. You can let the film do your talking for you."

"Good point. I'll just sit back and enjoy."

Sylvain Partners, the VC firm, had arranged the dinner. It was in a private room at a restaurant in Palo Alto. I brought my camera and laptop with us in through the main part of the restaurant and then through a dimly lit corridor, off of which branched the kitchen and rest rooms. A fourth door, attended by a young man in a suit, led into the windowless private room.

A fire blazed in the flagstone hearth. A small bar in the corner was stocked with martini glasses. The long, oval table was set for sixteen. A baroque painting with lots of pink cherubic flesh took up one wall. The flesh was given extra glow by rose-tinted halogen lighting and candles on wall sconces. The painting came with a pair of curtains that could be closed, but this was a dinner in which skin would be in favor.

My eyes immediately went to the focal point of the room: a woman in a short beaded dress. Her back was to us. Highlighted almond hair cascaded down her shoulders. Seven or eight guests were gathered around her. They burst into laughter at something she said. Rod picked up his pace. From the eagerness in his step, I thought he might bend her back in a big, dramatic kiss. Instead, he stopped three feet behind her.

"Alissa?" he said.

She turned. "Hello, Rod. Where have you been?"

The guests beamed. Alissa wore a smile, but not quite the one I expected: It was more coy than mysterious. Rod froze, and as I came even with him, incredulity flashed across his face. Then he forced a smile and stepped forward to meet her embrace. A chorus of oohs and aahs went up.

Rod swiveled with Alissa so that I saw his face. It showed panic. Putting his arm around her waist, he pulled her toward the door. "Alissa, honey, could we go over here—"

She squirmed. "Rod, honey, what about the guests?"

I grabbed my video camera case and stepped in. "We need a picture. If you'll just come over here where the light's better . . . "

Voices rose in mock protest, imploring Rod not to deprive them of Alissa. Mike said, "Let the lovebirds have their fun. Lucky guy!"

We hustled the complaining Alissa out through the door. The guy tending it stood there gaping at us. I told him to go inside.

Rod disengaged his arm from behind Alissa's back. They stared at each other in the passageway between the restaurant and the private room. Rod's face was flushed.

"Who are you?" he demanded.

She took a step back toward the private room. I blocked the way. She cast a resentful glance at me, whirled, and said, "Rod, what is wrong with you?"

Rod stood trembling, his gaze fixed on a small gem around her neck as if he'd become hypnotized by it. Alissa had been wearing the same necklace in the photograph.

I scrutinized the woman's face. It was a close facsimile of the one I'd seen: The hair was done as Alissa's had been, the eyebrows had the same contour, the nose the same slight upturn. . . . But this woman had too much swagger, too much insinuation in her manner. In place of the mysterious playful smile was a calculated pout.

"Where is Alissa?" I said.

She gave a miffed shrug. "I'm just trying to help. Don't look at me like I'm some kind of witch."

Rod found his voice, but it was subdued. "Who are you?" he repeated.

She sighed again, then lowered her eyes. "I'm Cindy. Alissa's sister. She couldn't come after all." The eyes grew wider. "My mother couldn't get hold of you to tell you. She thought it would be better to send me than to have no one show up."

"So Wendy's behind this," Rod said. "Alissa never mentioned a sister."

She turned her palms up in a gesture that said that was Alissa's fault, not hers. I looked more closely. Though from a distance she appeared to be Alissa's age, up close the rilled forehead and sag around the jaw were visible. The coyness clashed with the hard, worn grain of the voice.

"You're not Cindy. You're Wendy," I said.

Rod jumped back as if he'd stepped on a snake. "I don't want her here," he said to me.

"Oh, come on, Rod." She switched on a winning smile. My discovery didn't faze her; she seemed proud of having pulled off the illusion, even if just for a moment. "Don't be such a prude. You weren't with my daughter, were you?"

"Where is she?" he demanded.

"You don't know?" The smile remained glued to her face as she waited for an answer. When it didn't come, she said, "Well, if you're good, I might tell you."

I reached for her elbow. "Tell us now. Then we'll go."

The transformation was instant. Her preternaturally green eyes flashed. Her lips became thin and hard, her voice terse. "Don't you touch me. I'll scream and everyone in that room will come to see what you're doing. How you're hurting Alissa."

Rod grimaced. "She smells like cigarettes," he said to me, as if this were the final insult. "Alissa doesn't smoke."

I thought about clamping a hand over Wendy's mouth and physically removing her. But I'd have to drag her through the main part of the restaurant. I looked at the rest room door.

She saw me looking. "Don't even think about it. I'll press charges."

I wavered, then decided against it. The rest room was a dead end, anyway. "You better be careful," Wendy said. "We've got our eye on you."

I stepped up to her. "We? Are you talking about Silicon Glamour?"

The door to the private room opened and a busboy rushed out with a tray of used glasses. He gave us a curious look as he went by.

"Let's go back inside," Wendy said. "Your colleagues will start to gossip. They already know me as Alissa."

Rod's face shriveled with capitulation. "Why are you doing this?"

"It'll work out well for everyone," she answered. "You'll see."

Rod edged in the direction of her proffered hand. "Wait, Rod," I said. I was at the pay phone opposite the rest rooms. "I'm calling the police. Unless you'd prefer not to be arrested for impersonating your daughter, Wendy."

"My daughter the hustler? Sorry, I mean escort. Sorry, I mean *associate*. Won't your guests be fascinated to hear about that?"

"No," Rod said. "No police."

She slithered her hand under his elbow. "You boys just won't trust me, will you? Be patient. You saw how well I did with the guests. You'll learn in time. I know what's best."

Rod hung his head. I put down the phone. "You better live up to your word," I said.

She gave a little fling of the hair toward the banquet room. "They like me. I'm here to help. Just relax, Rod."

She took him back into the party. I followed, camera in hand. This was going to require documentation.

>>　>>　>>　>>　>>

I found Sylvain's AV guy and explained what needed to be done to play our video. I'd brought my laptop and could run it off that, if necessary, but he said he had all the equipment. I wouldn't have to do anything until the time came to cue it up after dinner.

I returned to the party and got my camera ready. Rod's teeth remained clenched through the cocktail hour. At the same time as he had to endure Wendy, he didn't know if his new business partners were going to spring some Alissa-inspired surprise on him. Wendy's charade made that scenario seem all the more likely. Yet I had to admit she stayed in character, deflecting questions that could have embarrassed Rod, keeping him from having to open his mouth too much.

For the time being, I hung back, drinking soda water, watching the guests, taking in the buzz of conversation. Appetizers were consumed and the time came for the first round of toasts. They would be followed by the signing of the contracts, then dinner and more toasts. Dr. Plush, the dermatologist who'd started the company, gravitated toward me when he saw my camera.

"Are you from the press?" he asked hopefully. Two wings of peppered hair flanked his big fleshy ears. His nostrils flared, his eyes were big. He had a reputation for charm and charisma.

I explained who I was and what I was doing.

"I see," he said. "When do we get to see the masterwork?"

"Tonight after dinner."

He raised his glass, which was full of tomato juice. His wife, Connie, came over with a martini glass in her hand. She was elegant in an Armani suit and a string of pearls. Her skin had a surprising amount of topography for the wife of a dermatologist about to introduce a new therapy to the world. She ran the business side and moved with an air of being in charge.

"Ronald," she said, "it's time for the toasts." She looked me up and down and looked at the camera. "What's that for?"

The doctor told her. "I didn't sign a release form," she said.

"It's not necessary. This won't be distributed," I replied.

My insolence brought a glare. Her eyes were cold gray marbles. "It's not myself I'm concerned for. You'll clear any footage you shoot with the principals involved."

Dr. Plush winked at me. I winked back, raised the camera, and framed him. He produced an ingratiating smile. He struck me as a fundamentally nervous man, the kind who turns his nervousness into egotism.

A high, narrow table sat against one wall. Above it were gator-board posters representing each of the deal's three partners. The contracts were on the table. I kept the camera on Dr. Plush as he made his way toward them. He had a smile and a pat on the back for everyone. Rod was also making his way to the table. Wendy had his arm securely in her grip. As Rod finally extricated himself, Plush gave Wendy a knowing wink.

I clenched the camera a little tighter and kept him in the frame. What had that been about? He'd winked at me, too, but not like that. Was he in on the game? Connie Plush entered the frame a moment later, a scowl of disdain on her face. Her eyes were on Wendy. My viewfinder stayed with Wendy as she worked her way back toward the bar. She had a talent for small talk, but I also noticed she asked a lot of questions about the deal, questions the men in the room were glad to answer.

Glasses were tapped and attention called to the table where Rod, Plush, and a handful of others had gathered. Mike Riley, Algoplex's CEO, was there, along with the men from Sylvain Partners—and they all were men—in their respectably somber suits. A Sylvain lawyer led off the toasts with some words about the great venture Plush, Algoplex, and his company were embarking upon, one that soon would be unveiled. Epidermal gene regulation would make headlines.

Dr. Plush stepped up next. "This really is a proud day for me. I started my clinic as a small practice in Palo Alto, taking cases of every kind: eczema, bullous diseases, melanoma, you name it.

I never envisioned the growth it has enjoyed, nor the fruits my research would bring. But, as my wife likes to say, I've always had a special *feel* for dermatology."

He paused for the chuckles. "The market for cosmetic treatments hardly existed when I was in medical school. It's been a tremendous boon to the field. But I don't want to forget that, as significant as that market is, our business is more than cosmetic. Eternaderm may also be able to treat a number of other conditions involving connective tissue. Sylvain has given us the resources, and now Algoplex will give us the computing power to develop those treatments. Here's to you, Rod and Mike, and to our old friends from Sylvain: May we all enjoy an enduring and profitable relationship."

After a round of clinks and "Hear, hears," Mike gave Rod a little push. His glass trembled as he set it on the table. Rod was not a drinker, but he'd downed two vodka martinis in preparation for this moment. He fumbled for a piece of paper in his pocket, unfolded it, and squinted at the crowd.

"Until I met all of you, I never knew how deep skin was." Rod got a laugh or two. "Seriously, this opportunity is very, very exciting for us. We think Eternaderm and its offshoots will be a perfect application for our technology."

He looked up from the paper. "To speak personally for a moment, I've put in a number of years at my work, always with the same faith it would find the right outlet, just as Dr. . . . Dr. . . . ." His face reddened as the name eluded him.

"Plush," Wendy said. "Like the carpet." Everyone laughed.

"Thanks," Rod mumbled. "Just as Dr. Plush did . . . have faith, I mean . . ." He couldn't recover from the gaffe. My own face reddened in sympathy. He finished his toast by going back to the piece of paper and reading quickly. He talked about how Algoplex's software would enhance Eternaderm and how Sylvain's capital would make it all possible. It was a little more detail than the crowd needed, and the claps and clinks and gulps at the end may have been as much for the fact that Rod was done as for what he'd said.

I kept shooting as the contracts were signed and a check was handed to Rod. After it was over, Wendy rushed up to Rod and planted a kiss on his cheek. "That was very nice, Rod. Don't worry about your mistake."

Rod flinched and shook his head.

"No, really," she said, taking his hand. "You were fine. I'll get you another cocktail."

I kept the camera rolling. If nothing else, it was fascinating theater. I wondered what the real Alissa would have done.

"You're finished now," a woman said, speaking into my ear. "We're going to start dinner."

I lowered the camera and turned. It was Connie Plush.

I said, "Rod will let me know when I'm done."

Rod saw what was happening. "I want Bill to be here," he said.

"Why?" Connie demanded. "The other AV guy doesn't have dinner with us."

The room lights were being adjusted. A gobo projection appeared on the floor, the Plush logo revolving in a ghostly dance. The other AV guy at work.

"Nonetheless, I would like Bill to be here," Rod said. It occurred to me he was trying to compensate for his toast performance by asserting himself.

Dr. Plush joined us. Wendy was with him. She stuck a new martini glass in Rod's hand. "Is there a problem, dear?" the doctor said.

Connie Plush gave a jerk of the head to her husband. "This gentleman—*Bill*—seems to think he's invited for dinner."

Wendy said, "You don't need any more pictures do you, Bill?" She smoothed the pocket of my linen jacket as if, having staked a claim to Rod, I was also her property.

"Ladies," Dr. Plush responded, "I don't think it would hurt for him to stay." He didn't want to miss his chance for screen time.

"Confidential information will be discussed," Connie said. "And we don't have a place set for him."

I looked straight at her. "I don't need a seat. I don't care about eating." The truth was, I'd be happy to go out to the bar, except that I wanted to keep an eye on Wendy.

"Bill's been NDA'd," Rod said. "Please, Mrs. Plush, I've hired him to do a film." He took another gulp of his martini. He was already beyond his limit. I'd need to keep an eye on him, too.

"The film's done, though, isn't it, dear?" Wendy said. Connie seemed surprised that Wendy was on her side. I wondered again what was going on with those two and Dr. Plush.

By now a Sylvain man was listening in. "If it's all the same to you, Rod—"

"It's not," Rod cut in.

This stunned the Sylvain man into temporary silence. He looked at Mrs. Plush. "Well, if there's no real danger . . ."

She glared at him. "You're on the hook for this. I don't want to hear about some insider-trading case down the line." The glare turned on me. "No cameras during dinner."

Our little group disbanded. Connie had lost out, and I could see by the way she marched the doctor to his seat that she wasn't used to it.

"I'll bring you a doggie bag," Wendy said, putting her hand out to give me a pat.

I stepped out of her reach and said, without smiling, "My bite's worse than my bark." She withdrew her hand quickly.

In the end, I was squeezed in next to Mike. Rod's face had a numb look by the time the first course was served; it had been anesthetized by alcohol. His lips remained parted in a blubbery kind of way. I was the recipient of a certain amount of sympathetic small talk from people nearby, who had seen my encounter with Connie Plush. It gave me the sense that I was not the first to get the treatment from her. I responded politely, wishing the courses would move along.

Just before dessert, Wendy excused herself to use what she called "the little girls' room." I was pretending to listen to a discussion between Mike and an Eternaderm scientist. I'd draw too much attention if I bolted after Wendy, so I waited fifteen seconds before excusing myself as well.

As I got to the door, the waiters came marching in with dessert. I stepped aside to let them pass, then went into the corridor. A closed ladies' room door stared at me. I knocked and called Wendy's name. Somehow I knew I wouldn't get an answer. I knocked again to make sure no one else was in there, pushed open the door, and called, "Hello?"

A quick inspection of the stalls confirmed that she'd given me the slip. I burst down the corridor and into the main restaurant. Scanning for Wendy, I froze when I saw a form I knew. It was the receptionist from Silicon Glamour, the beefy man with the thick mustache. He wore a polo shirt. His arms were huge.

"Did you see her?" I said.

He didn't look up from his beer. "See who?"

"Alissa. Wendy."

"I don't know what you're talking about, man," he said, then turned away.

I ran out to the parking lot just in time to see a pair of exiting taillights. My keys were back in the dining room, in my camera case. I went back inside and stood behind the SG guy. "Tell Rupert he can get off of Rod's back about Alissa."

His head didn't move an inch. "You better get off *my* back."

His voice was a soft, deep rumble. Speaking low as he did, he left me with the sense that he could blow my eardrums out if he chose to. His argument was convincing, and in any case I couldn't leave Rod alone with those vodka martinis. I was left to return to the private room, cue up Rod's film, and ponder why Wendy would go to such lengths to pass herself off as her daughter.

7

Algoplex was in motion the next day. Now that the deal was sealed, teams were being assigned, milestones scheduled, supply chains activated. The halls were abuzz with the task of tailoring Rod's software to Plush's program.

The only person looking less than energized was Rod himself. It was eleven o'clock and his desk was an uncharacteristic mess. He tended to fill coffee cups and then abandon them in various locations. Today no fewer than six cups were sprinkled around the office.

I'd covered for him at the end of the dinner last night by saying to the others at the table that I'd seen "Alissa" on my way out of the rest room. She wasn't feeling well, had to leave, and had asked me to give Rod her apologies. Now I was in his office to talk to him about what I'd really seen.

Rod had been in no shape to discuss it last night. He'd taken it upon himself to drink to every round of the after-dinner toasts. He dozed most of the drive home and his hangover was under way by the time I left his house. His face was the color of chewed paper this morning.

Mike Riley strode in whistling a tune, as he was inclined to do. A look from Rod caused him to shut his lips. He reported that the first check from Sylvain had been deposited. This would take care of Algoplex's immediate needs. The rest of the money was due seventy-two hours after the signing.

"Good," Rod grumbled, "we can actually pay our employees this month."

Mike smiled. He was a stocky guy with square shoulders and a square face, quick to smile or joke. His dark hair was cut short and parted on the side. "Fun night, huh? You kept up with the big boys on the martinis. That impressed them."

"Then they're idiots," Rod said. I could hear how dry his mouth was.

Mike couldn't be stopped. "Alissa was looking good."

"That wasn't Alissa," Rod replied.

"Okay, take it easy, Rod. I had a feeling something was up. I figured you made some other arrangement. It was a gutsy move."

"I need to talk to Bill, Mike. Thanks."

After absorbing Rod's stare for a few seconds, Mike left. I felt bad for him. He revered Rod's genius. Though he treated him at times like an awkward little brother, he was Rod's biggest cheer-leader. Today he'd cheered the wrong team.

"I hate those events," Rod said. "Nothing but head-patting and bogon flux. It's business, not a love affair."

"Connie Plush wasn't in a petting mood. You stood up to her, though. She was right, you know, I shouldn't have stayed for dinner."

"Yeah. It wasn't like her to back down."

"That's what was interesting. Nobody else would say no to you, especially not the Sylvain guys. They must want this deal pretty bad."

"Connie's all right in my book—tough but fair. Ronald leaves all the business to her."

"Maybe they don't like a tough woman."

"The only thing I know for sure is that Plush needs my technology. It's the future of biotech. It's the reason Stanford started their Bio-X program and Berkeley started QB3."

I was glad to see Rod's confidence bouncing back. I moved on to the primary business at hand. "I sent Wendy an email this morning. I took the diplomatic route so as not to scare her off. Thanked her for her performance. Suggested we get together to talk about Alissa."

"I don't believe in hell, but I hope she fries in it," Rod said.

"I'd say she's pretty well-done already. We can put some heat on her ourselves, but first we have to make her believe it's safe to be alone with us. Did you notice how she pretended like you knew where Alissa was?"

"She asked me if I knew."

"She was testing to see if you had any idea. I wonder if she knows herself."

Rod lowered his head to the desk, resting his forehead on his arms. The bravado spurred by the grain of irritation with Mike left him. "It's the only explanation that makes sense. Unless Alissa's been the victim of some random . . ." His muffled voice trailed off. "What the hell was Wendy doing there, Bill? And what the hell was she doing wearing the necklace I gave Alissa?"

"She needs something from you. I don't know what it is yet, and she chose a strange way to get it. But she knows how much you dislike her. She might have thought it was the only safe way to see you."

"All she would have had to do is tell me Alissa was with her. I can't believe Alissa would lend that necklace to her."

"Wendy could be up to any number of things. Do you remember I told you on the way home that the muscleman receptionist from SG was lurking in the bar?"

Rod looked up again. "Really? What's his name—Gary, I think. You saw Gary?"

"If Gary's the guy with the billboard mustache and arms like tree trunks, I saw Gary. He pretended he didn't know me and that he didn't see Wendy leave. Now, he might have just been there to watch for Alissa. But he and Wendy could also have cooked up something. And we can't count out the possibility that Wendy and Alissa are working together."

Rod's face turned a paler shade than it already was. "That's an unbearable idea."

"Tell me more about Wendy. What her motives might be. Contacts, places I might be able to track her down."

Rod shook his head. "I preferred not to know. Alissa was born in Phoenix. They moved to L.A. when she was young. That's where Wendy did most of her scheming. She'd leave Alissa at a friend's house while she went out on a casting call or whatever bogosity she was up to, then neglect to pick her up until the next morning. Sometimes Alissa would make her way home herself and find Wendy in the house with a man. Or two men. There was always a new one around: the one who was going to transform their lives. Every week Wendy promised Alissa they were on the verge of moving to some grand life with swimming pools and manicured gardens. Alissa believed it for a long time. She was crushed when it dawned on her it might never happen."

"The illusion that real life is just around the corner can keep a person treading water for years."

"I don't know where to look for Wendy now," Rod said. "Last I heard she lived in Reno."

"Dr. Plush winked at her last night. It was the kind of wink you give someone who's in on a secret. Would he know her?"

"Oh, God. Yes, I forgot about that. That was Alissa's original link to Plush. Wendy knows half the plastic surgeons in L.A., of course, and she heard about Plush. She wanted in on his treatments a few years back, before Eternaderm. I don't know what happened with that, but she ended up in some of their promotional materials. Before and after photos, that kind of thing."

"Which was she, before or after?"

Rod came fully upright, stricken. "I don't know—but shit, Bill, if the Plushes recognized her, they know she was a phony date. They could spread the word."

"I wouldn't count on it, unless Connie has some reason to undermine the deal. The doctor doesn't talk about anyone but himself."

"Connie was cooler to the deal than Sylvain. Sylvain were the ones who grokked the fit between Algoplex and biotech. Connie kept warning me not to give up too much of the company to them. Maybe it was her way of trying to sabotage the deal."

"If Connie really wanted to stop it, she'd have done her damage before the contracts were signed. Was Wendy still in touch with Plush?"

Rod shook his head. "I hope not. She came back into the picture when Eternaderm was being developed. She was desperate for it. I advised them to bar the door."

"Connie Plush is no fan of Wendy's, either, judging from a look she gave her."

"That's good." Rod cocked his head. "Bill, I just remembered something. You'd better know about it. I said some things to Wendy last night during dinner. I leaned over to whisper into her ear. What I whispered was that she'd been a poisonous mother to Alissa. And that if she ever bothered me again, I'd perpetrate some fairly egregious acts on her. I'd rather not say what they were."

I nodded slowly. "Those things happen."

The color had flushed back into Rod's face. "As you know, I'd been drinking, and, well, I just let out my real feelings. I don't usually lose it like that. I believe in rationality. I've always been able to sublimate my most dangerous emotions. But right now I feel out of control. I'm embarrassed."

"That may be why Wendy left when she did," I said. "I kept waiting for her to deliver the punch line, tell us what it was she wanted."

"It was such a relief when she left. I finally felt relaxed. I'm afraid I may have embarrassed myself again while our film was being shown."

I chuckled. Rod had become garrulous during the show, probably because he was self-conscious about seeing himself on the screen. He'd tossed out a number of remarks making fun of himself. "Oh my God," he'd said during the Frisbee scene, "getting in touch with my inner dork."

"Don't worry," I said, "your commentary won them back."

Rod massaged his temples. "Never again."

The intercom buzzed. Rod glared at it as if it were deliberately adding to his pain. He pressed the button and said, "What?"

"A Wendy is calling for you. She said it's urgent."

Rod looked at me. I nodded. "All right," he said, and switched the phone to speaker.

Wendy pitched her voice high. "Hello, Rod. I'm sorry I had to leave early last night. I hope the rest of the dinner went well."

Rod's jaw set. He showed me two pairs of crossed fingers and said, "I'm the one who should apologize. I had a little too much to drink. I'm sorry if I said—"

"Don't be silly, Rod, it was your big night. You should celebrate however you like. Honestly, I was just trying to help because Alissa couldn't be there."

"Yes. Well . . . why don't we put our heads together on this, Wendy? We both want to find her."

"Oh, I thought I told you, Rod. I'm in touch with Alissa. You don't need to worry, she's fine."

Rod gulped. It pained him horribly for Wendy to have this apparent knowledge while he didn't. "I'd like to see her."

"Of course, honey. She'll meet you tomorrow night. Go to the Cheshire Cat nightclub on Currey Drive at ten-thirty."

Rod's relief overcame his aversion. "Thank you very much, Wendy. Please tell her I look forward very much to seeing her."

"She says the same. I know you'll dress up nice. And you'll come alone. She'll only see you if you come alone."

I was waving madly at Rod. Finally he looked up. "Uh, Wendy, could we . . ." He paused a moment to read my lips. "Could we meet later today? I feel I've been unfair to you."

"Oh, that's nice. But I'm really busy. Don't forget about tomorrow night."

I leaped for the phone myself. By the time I had the receiver, only the static of a dead line could be heard. I replaced it in the cradle.

"Sorry," Rod said. "I tried." He gave me the same entreating look as when he heard Wendy say Alissa would meet him. "Do you think it's true that she'll be there?"

"I think we should assume Wendy is setting you up. I could be wrong—it's possible you really did give her a jolt last night. Either way, I'll be there to keep an eye out."

"But she said to come alone. I don't want to scare Alissa away."

I smiled at him. "You won't recognize me."

Rod's forehead crinkled. "O-o-o-kay . . . Bill, none of this makes any sense to me. I don't know why Alissa doesn't just call me herself."

"That's the question, isn't it? I don't buy anything Wendy says, including the fact that she's in touch with Alissa. She's trying to smoke you out—but why, I don't know. Can you think of anything else you have on her, anything you have that she wants?"

Rod took a moment. "I can't, Bill. I told you about the Plushes—that I said they should keep her away from Eternaderm. And, of course, I was trying to convince Alissa to cut off contact with Wendy. Making progress, too."

"So she might think you're the one who's got Alissa and you're hiding it from her."

"But it's so obvious I don't. Can't she tell that?"

"You heard her just now. You saw her at the dinner. She can put on any voice, act any role. She probably assumes other people are doing the same. I could tell that you're genuinely hoping to see Alissa Wednesday night, but she might assume it's an act."

"I don't understand these kinds of people, Bill. I was right to try to get Alissa away from her." Rod stood up, began pacing, then stopped. "I thought you also said Alissa and she could be working together."

"That's the other theory."

Rod paced again. My cell phone rang. "I better get that," I said, digging it out of my camera bag.

It was Rupert Evans. He said he wanted me to come to SG immediately. The greatest importance and so on. "How did you get my number?" I said.

"Just come," Rupert replied. "If you're with Rod, don't mention my name. This concerns him. You'll see him in a new light."

"Right, Rupert." I clicked off.

Rod looked up when I said the name.

"I'm going over to SG. Rupert has some big secret to share with me. What else have you done that I should know about?"

He raised his eyebrows and laughed. "You know more about me than any living person ought to, Bill."

"You'd make a great subject for a film."

Rod snorted. "I didn't get the chance to tell you—your work was first-rate. I wasn't too drunk to see that last night."

"Thanks, Rod. I'll let you know what Rupert has to say."

He waved to me as I closed the door, an expression of utter trust in his eyes. It did not occur to me it could be unwarranted.

8

Rupert Evans had an awfully smug look on his face. I would have felt better if there was more guile in it. His expression told me he felt confident he had the goods on Rod.

He gave me the red-carpet treatment: hung my jacket with care, sat me down on the zebra-skin sofa in his office, and offered me tea, coffee, soda—every time I shook my head he thought of another beverage.

"I don't want anything, Rupert," I said. "Except to know what your man Gary was doing at our restaurant last night and why he pretended he didn't know me. He wasn't at the desk when I came in just now, or I would've asked him myself."

Rupert was clinking bottles at the bar. He looked over his shoulder and gave me a sebaceous smile. "Please forgive us. Gary is rather shy. You know how I want Alissa safe and sound. We were hoping to see her."

"She was there. He missed her."

Now I was indulged with a laugh. "You like to test me, don't you, Bill? I understand. But surely you also understand our position. Your presence was a surprise at our first meeting. I did not know what kind of man I was dealing with. However, from what I've learned, you're a reasonable man. Especially in the face of hard evidence."

"Who did Gary see, then?"

"The same person you did." Rupert smiled again and joined me on the sofa. "Let me ask you a question. Your assignment is to find Alissa. Now, are you more true to the assignment or to your employer?"

I stared at Rupert, waiting for him to get to the point.

"I'm about to show you evidence that convinces me Rod is behind her disappearance," he went on. "If your loyalty is strictly to Rod, you may leave. I'll hand the materials over to the police. If you want to know what happened to Alissa, I suggest you look and learn."

I'd been paying attention to the way his thin lips moved like clockwork. A hunting idyll played above his head, hounds baying after a frightened fox. "If you're going to show me, show me," I said.

He unzipped a document pouch. The first document he handed me was a photograph. It did cause an intake of breath. Rod's arms were wrapped around Alissa, and not in a tentative way. He was squeezing her, pressing her against a stucco wall, pressing his mouth forcefully to hers. The compressed look of the picture told me it had been taken with a telephoto lens.

Rupert chuckled. "Not the meek engineer he seems, is he? We have more explicit fare. But you may prefer to respect your client's privacy."

"So they kissed. Maybe more. Maybe there's more to SG's services than advertised."

"We are not an *escort* service." He said the word as if it were in quarantine. "We do not provide *massages, suntans,* or *photo sessions*. We provide legitimate—"

"Where'd you get your tan, by the way?"

The question threw him off. He touched his cheek before recovering. "I enjoy the fresh air, Bill. I'm an outdoorsman."

The poolside kind, I thought, then glanced at the painting above him. "Big hunter?"

"I'm more the protector type. It's stated explicitly in Rod's contract that there's to be no sexual contact with our associates. He's clearly violated the contract."

"Maybe they liked each other. It's against your rules, but rules can be trumped by the laws of human nature."

The rigidity in Rupert's spine slowly relaxed. He leaned forward and, with a tic of a smile, handed me a letter from the document pouch. Alissa had written it on salmon-pink stationery with a filigree border. The script was swooping and girlish. It began "Dear Mom" and went on to talk about how she planned to decorate her apartment, clothes she'd buy courtesy of Silicon Glamour—all the new vistas her job was opening up for her. I paid closer attention when she came to the subject of Rod.

> *He's very possessive and hates it when I talk about the loved ones in my life. He wants the full-on Girlfriend Experience. Somehow he knows when I talk to you, so I have to go "underground" for a little while and you may not hear from me. He's my best client and I'm afraid to tell him to get lost. Let him live out his fantasy. I am hoping he is harmless. Don't worry about me. I'll send letters whenever I can.*

It was signed with a giant loop—either an A or a C—a dot, and a heart.

Rupert spoke before I could. "You may say we invented this letter. But we had a graphologist analyze it. The police labs will confirm Alissa wrote it."

I hid my dismay and said, "Wendy must be on your payroll, too—or did you steal the letter?"

"This letter is evidence of Rod's intention to have Alissa for himself," Rupert said, ignoring my question. "She says in a hopeful manner that he's harmless, but we can hear her fear underneath. She was terrified even to call her own mother."

I had to admit—though only to myself—that the letter put a new spin on Rod's insistence that Alissa break with her mother. For the first time it occurred to me that Wendy may have had reason for her charade. She may have been on a rescue mission.

Rupert handed me another photograph with a grunt of satisfaction. It showed Alissa trying to get out of a red Cabriolet whose top was down. The man behind the windshield had hold of her wrist and was pulling her back in. Though the reflection of the glass partially blocked his face, I could tell it was Rod.

"That's Alissa's car," Rupert said. "Look at the date stamp. Ten days ago. It's the last time we saw her or the car. He pulled her back inside and we lost them. No one—her mother, her friends, our office—has seen or heard from her since."

I sat back and stared at the documents spread on the table. I needed more time to think. "I'll check out this information and get back to you," I said.

Rupert tucked his chin under and gave me a disappointed-father look. "Bill, we have the information. What we want to know is if you're going to join the right side and cooperate with us in getting Rod to come clean. A trip to the police station would be messy for everyone, but especially for Rod. We'd like to spare him. Return Alissa and all is forgiven. Of course, he can never see her again."

I shook my head. "I've kept you informed, Rupert. We honestly expected Alissa to show up last night. You had your own man there; he saw the reality. You know Rod. How can you think he would contrive something like that?"

Rupert stroked the corner of his lip. "Perhaps he didn't, Bill. Perhaps you did. It doesn't matter. You may not have known the truth about Rod. Now you do. Now you have a chance to put everything right."

"Give me the photos and Alissa's letter. I'll get to the bottom of it." I wondered if he knew about the Cheshire Cat rendezvous scheduled for tomorrow night.

"That's your offer?"

I rolled my eyes. "It's not an offer."

Rupert sank back into the couch. "If we must go to the police, we must."

"I can't stop you." I stood up. "Thanks for having me over. After we find out where Alissa's really been, we'll deal with the fact that you've been spying on Rod."

"Bill?"

I turned at the door. Rupert hurried after me. He thrust the photos and a copy of the letter into my hand. His voice was as earnest as it could be. "When you find out I'm right, you'll let me know, won't you?"

I couldn't give him the satisfaction of a nod. The truth was, he'd sown plenty of doubts about Rod in my mind. I said, "I'll be in touch."

>> >> >> >> >>

Rod was in meetings the rest of the day at Algoplex. A workstation had been improvised for me near his office. I tried to do my job, which at the moment meant searching for Wendy. But I couldn't concentrate. I kept wondering if Rod really had forced himself on Alissa. It didn't fit with what I knew of him.

The pictures told a different story, though. The only times I'd seen the same unbridled emotion were the day he yelled at Rita for blowing the lights and the moment on Monday night when he found out Wendy's true identity. Both incidents involved Alissa.

Five o'clock came and I asked Rod's assistant to let me into Rod's office. Rod kept a recliner in the corner where, he said, his best ideas came to him. I told the assistant I wanted to take a nap while I waited for Rod to return. Naps were an approved part of Silicon Valley culture. The assistant let me in.

There were plenty of reasons Silicon Glamour would want to frame Rod: To cover up their own crimes in relation to Alissa and to get back at him for "cheating" with her were two that came to mind. I tilted the chair back and looked carefully at the photographs. They hadn't been doctored. The letter had the scent of authenticity, too.

The kiss was forceful, passionate. It was hard to read Alissa's response—most of her body was hidden by Rod's. Tentative fingers touched his shoulder blade. I thought about Rod's secret urges and how he might be overcome by a wave of longing for Alissa. Touching her hair, smelling her skin, after so many years in his wilderness of code: Silicon Valley was a cauldron of pent-up desire, the lid clamped tight by disciplines of command language and deliverables. If Alissa gave Rod a glimmer of hope, he may have seized on it and seized on her.

His laptop sat mute near his desk. A fractal screensaver displayed ever-new self-recursive patterns. I considered getting up to snoop into what dreams lurked on his hard drive. Most likely I'd find the same kind of thing as on ninety-five percent of single engineers' drives in the Valley. It would tell me nothing. He was careful about exposing his desires; unauthorized access would leave me feeling dirty.

I was dozing when he came back. He said his head was pounding and he wanted to get out of the office. I suggested we go for a beer: I wanted him to be relaxed when I showed him Rupert's pictures.

"Isn't that what they call the hair of the dog?" he said. "It's like curing anemia with arsenic."

We ended up at a Chinese restaurant with semiprivate booths for an early dinner. Rod ordered a Coke and sweet-and-sour pork. I told him sugar worked as a temporary treatment for his hangover. He asked me what Rupert had wanted.

I slid the photographs across the mint-green Formica to him. The look on his face was not quite guilt; regret pulled down the corners of his mouth and eyes, and there was a small twitch of longing at the sight of Alissa. He threw them back at me and said, "Those *bastards*."

"Rupert's got a story that goes with them. Did you have sex with Alissa, Rod?"

"God damn Rupert and Trisha. I swear to you, Bill, if I knew anything about how to get someone killed, I'd do it. They're worse than pimps."

"Who's Trisha—the woman we saw at the end of the hall when we visited Rupert?"

"Yes. She's Rupert's sister. She's the boss at SG."

I tapped the kiss photo. "Did Alissa enjoy this?"

Rod stared at me, his jaw slack, before he exploded. "What kind of question is that, Bill?"

The waiter, arriving with a steaming plate of pork, jumped back to avoid Rod's waving arms. I said, "Just tell me straight, Rod, what you and Alissa have done together."

Rod momentarily lost his ability to speak. The food was slipped under our noses. I had Szechuan beef. Rod stared at his sweet-and-sour. His mouth quivered.

"We did make love. She—I couldn't stop myself. She said she was in love with me. That kiss—I don't know, it was a moment when I let myself go. We both did."

It was my turn to be speechless. A chili pepper stung my mouth. Rod dabbed the moisture from his eyes and said, "I know it seems implausible that she was in love with me. That's why I didn't mention it before. It was too . . . ridiculous."

"She said it in a way that wasn't convincing?"

He speared a pineapple. "No, it was very convincing. She said she'd finally found a man she could trust. She herself was surprised, but it was true. I can show you little notes and drawings, if you don't believe me. It still seemed improbable. She's a woman who could have any man in the world. Why me?"

"Women aren't as shallow as men. They're better at seeing beneath the surface."

"I don't know, Bill. Maybe I made the biggest mistake of my life."

"You have absolutely no idea where she is?"

Rod's eyes opened like saucers. "Are you some kind of idiot? What did I hire you for?"

"A program for which you never revealed all the initial conditions. Garbage in, garbage out."

Rod's head sunk. "This is not easy for me. I thought you'd laugh if I told you what she said. She claimed she wanted a life with me but SG wouldn't allow it."

I showed him the picture in which he was pulling her back into her car. "Did you two have some kind of fight?"

He inspected the picture, then played with his food. "I don't know what got into her. We were on a drive in the country. She picked a fight with me and demanded I pull over. She tried to get out and walk home. It was ridiculous. We were all the way up on Skyline Drive."

I showed him the letter last. As he read it, his features curdled and the blood drained from his face. It was as if a plug had been pulled. His shoulders shook, and after a long pause, he said in a small voice, "I guess that seals it. She was—what was the word?—diddling me. That's what it divides down to. I *paid* her to *use* me to steal my technology."

"We have no direct evidence she pilfered files."

"Deduce it, Bill. Why else would she go beyond the requirements of her job? Why add the 'Girlfriend Experience'? I've thought about how accommodating they were to us at the signing dinner, letting you stay. They wanted to lock me into the deal. Now they'll lower the boom, using whatever they got from Alissa."

I couldn't say he was wrong; his theory was too plausible. He halfheartedly ate a few bites of food, then put down the fork. "I'm not going to the club tomorrow night," Rod said. "Even if Alissa herself is there—especially if she is. I don't want to be humiliated again."

"I can't make you go, Rod. But it'd help us nail her—or whomever."

He conjured up a twisted grin. "I make good bait, don't I?" The grin disappeared. "Let's just drop it, Bill. Let's admit that I'm a sucker. Focus on controlling the damage instead."

I let him sit with his emotions. It was not a time to talk him into anything. He pushed his plate aside and jammed his chin down into his palms. The faraway look that so often glazed his features returned. When he looked back at me, his face was vacant. It was the look of a man who'd lost hope.

"Beauty," he said. "What a trick. I presumed it impossible that someone as beautiful as Alissa—not just her exterior features, but the intelligence behind her eyes, the glow inside—could not be good all the way through. She spoke of children and pets. What she wanted more than anything, she said, was to get off the treadmill and have a quiet life in a snug house with a few trees and a hammock in the back yard. She spoke of me as being the one with her in that house."

He shook his head. This man who'd been such a believer in the power of the mind now trusted nothing and no one. "All of it was conjured from her grimoire. An algorithm coded to produce an utterly predictable effect in simple-minded organisms like me. I'd presumed there was a law of physics that made her incapable of double-speaking. Even with the 'Girlfriend Experience,' I thought she was doing it as a favor, to make me feel good. All right, so she's no different than the other operators and schemers in the Valley. And I guess beauty's like any other code: It can be put to whatever application the owner chooses. It's as opaque to me as any nonlinear system."

We sat in silence. There was no point in confirming his naïveté by asking if he'd never seen Barbara Stanwyck in a noir role. The fluorescent lights buzzed. A busboy took our plates. The waiter hovered, then left. I thought back to my conversation with Rupert, to my own suspicions about Rod and how I'd put them to him, how hurt he'd looked. It seemed he was speaking truly to me now.

And yet I thought back to the times I'd felt equally certain of someone and had been ambushed all over again. A shred of skepticism remained; it refused to dissolve now and perhaps it never would. How sad, I thought, I couldn't give my whole trust to this devastated man. Melancholy as it was, I could not shake the notion that no one in this mess was innocent. It would not be the first time in Silicon Valley.

9

The Cheshire Cat club was not what I had pictured. If it was Alissa's choice, to match her enigmatic smile I figured she'd summon Rod to a mod place done in minimalist black and white, or else to a cozy English-style pub. Instead we got burgundy velvet curtains, Tiffany lamps, Naugahyde banquettes, and corseted cocktail waitresses.

"Yeah, this joint sure has class," Wes said as we tucked ourselves into a corner at the end of the bar. It did seem more like Wendy's style than Alissa's—unless Alissa was the predator Rod feared she might be.

Rod had not arrived yet, but he had changed his mind about coming. He admitted he couldn't stay away. A part of him still wanted to believe in Alissa: to believe she would come and that there'd be a good reason for everything that had happened. "I know it's a long shot," he'd said to me this afternoon. "But hope plays its tricks on everyone. If there's one thing I've learned, Bill, it's that I'm not immune to human emotions. It was an illusion that I could *think* my way around them."

I'd spent most of the day trying to get more on Wendy, and failed. I couldn't get past the front desk at Plush Biologics. Connie must have posted my mug shot or something. Rupert continued to claim ignorance. That left me to snoop on the net for Wendy Bevins, of whom there are plenty in the United States. None of them was our woman. She and Alissa might not share the same last name, anyhow.

Wes ordered a Manhattan and faced outward on his stool, blocking me from view. I doubt I would have been recognized, anyway. I wore long, black curly hair, a goatee, shades, and a studded jean jacket. The original intention had been a latter-day D'Artagnan, but Wes said I looked more like Frank Zappa. A mirror in back of the bar allowed me to keep an eye on the room and the entrance. A full-length curtain divided the bar from the dining room. Every few minutes Wes got up to check inside, in case Alissa or Wendy had slipped in the back way.

The stage was empty now, but we were told when we came in that a go-go show would commence at eleven. That apparently justified the three-drink minimum.

"We can bring our Silicon Glamour dates here," Wes said. "I think I'm in, Billy. They're setting me up with Erika and a friend on Friday."

"Oh yeah, this'll impress them." Friday was two days away and a lot could happen between now and then. "Did you ever talk about dating or girlfriends with Rod?"

"Sure. He had a wicked crush on someone at every conference we went to, but he was always too shy to do anything about it. It got a little tedious. I wouldn't think he'd go so far as to pay for it, but maybe he was lonelier than I realized. The girlfriend interface can be a tough one."

"Alissa told her mother she was giving him the full Girlfriend Experience."

"Hey, experience is the latest commodity. The Explorer experience—as if you become one by getting into an SUV. You can make a lot of money selling simulations."

"Well, reality has its ways of biting back. All I need to know right now is whether Alissa's safe. And then I want to find out if she diddled Rod."

Wes drained his glass and ate the cherry. "Ready for another?"

"Sure. But I'm sticking to two parts H and one part O, with bubbles." I checked my watch. "Damn, Wes, it's ten-thirty. Where's Rod?"

"Maybe he wants to make sure Alissa shows first, so he's not stood up."

"Like she's going to sit around waiting for him."

Wes swatted my arm. "Here we go. At two o'clock, headed for the dining room."

"Don't be so obvious," I said. I took off the shades to track her in the mirror. The hair was piled high. The cashmere minidress, the knowing walk: It was Wendy, dressed to be noticed. She made no secret of inspecting the bar patrons.

I told Wes to follow her around the curtain. She came back into my mirror view sixty seconds later. I turned in time to see her exit the front door. Wes sat down next to me.

"No Alissa?" I asked. He shook his head. "Follow Wendy," I said.

Wes went out the door. He returned, breathless, two minutes later. "She took off in a Toyota. Do we go?"

"It's too late. Shit. Rod's still not here. He may have blown it." I got out my cell phone and dialed him. His voicemail answered. I warned him that Wendy had come and gone and he'd better get over here. Then I turned back to Wes. "You'll have to give him the bad news when he comes in. Tell him to stay put and eat dinner or something."

We went back to our drinks. Wes finished his second and I drank my six-dollar soda water. At eleven, a few bass thumps from the drummer announced the start of the show. The band members took their places and the house lights went down. I decided it was safe to turn around. The dancers wore suede out-fits tiny enough to have come from the same small patch of steer.

Strobes flashed and the band cranked up the volume. The minutes stretched on. Still no Alissa. Still no Rod. Still no answer on his phone.

After his third Manhattan, Wes plucked the cherry and showed me the stem. "Ever had a girlfriend who could tie one of these in knots with her tongue?"

"You've got to chew on it first. Softens it."

Wes leaned away from me in mock amazement. "You've got skills."

I checked my watch. Eleven-thirty. "Let's take one more look around, then go," I said.

We had to dodge beer-slopping patrons to make our search and get out of the place. I held out my hand for the car keys. We'd come in Wes's Jeep in case Wendy knew my Scout. "I'm all right," he said.

"You still working on that cherry stem?"

His tongue did a quick inventory of his mouth and came up empty. He gave me the keys.

» » » » »

Rod's Volvo was in the driveway. The front porch light was on, and a dim glow slanted from the rear of the house. I rang the bell. There was no answer. I rang several more times, then tried the door. It was open.

Wes started to say something. I signalled for him to keep quiet and stay at the door. The only sound in the house was the lonely tick of a clock in the dining room. I took a few careful steps inside. The smell of coffee came down the hallway.

I motioned Wes to close the door. "Stay here," I whispered. "He might have freaked out or something."

The living room was empty, the hearth dark. In the dimness I could see that items on the shelves had been knocked over and the sofa cushions were disarranged. Lights came from the bathroom and kitchen down the hall, along with a sound of faint static. I had a sensation again of peering into recesses of Rod's psyche he wanted no one to see.

"Rod, are you all right?" I said before turning left into the bathroom.

No answer. The sink tap was running. It was the source of the static. I turned it off.

The bathroom was a mess. Dirt was spread across the floor. An amaranth plant and its pot—an Alissa item, I was sure—lay broken on the floor by the toilet. The idea came to me that Rod had learned the truth about Alissa and had smashed the plant. A crumpled towel lay next to the shower. I found a nail file next to it. It had made small tears in the towel. The cabinet drawers had been pulled out. Antibiotic ointment lay on the sink counter.

If Rod did this, he was in bad shape. If he didn't, he was in worse.

I looked into the bedroom. His best shirt, jacket, and tie were laid out on the bed. He'd been getting ready to go to the Cheshire Cat and for some reason had stopped. The chest drawers were open, as if he'd been searching for something. A pair of dress slacks hung on a closet doorknob. The bed was made neatly. I glanced at a pair of books on the bedside table: *How to Romance a Woman* and *Why Sex Is Fun*. A bottle of massage oil sat next to them.

I called Rod's name again as I came into the hallway. He might be in the basement, taking refuge with his computer, if something had made him decide not to come tonight.

But he wasn't, and the laptop he usually brought home with him wasn't there, either.

I found him in the other room with a light on, the kitchen. Coffee was splattered over the floor and on the wall. The phone had been ripped from the jack and the line was tangled in his socked feet. The handle of the coffee pot, with some Pyrex still attached to it, was near the back door. Other shards were close by. So was a dented toaster.

Rod was in the middle of the floor, on his stomach. He was wearing only a pair of boxer shorts. His back was a mottle of pink scalds and brown stains, like temperature zones on a weather map. His left arm was crooked so that it touched his waist. A series of cuts marked the arm like a broken alphabet, along with a dark ruby port-colored streak.

In his right hand was a cutting knife. The seven-inch blade was stained crimson. His carotid artery had been severed. Blood had spurted on the floor to form a glistening maroon lake. I could only bear a quick glance at his face. Smears of shaving cream ran down the jaw. The eyes bulged with surprise and the lips were stretched in a scream. The skin was drained a worm-white that told me it was too late to call an ambulance.

A piece of paper torn from a notebook rested near his head. I didn't see a pen. Scrawled on the paper was the word "Sorry."

» » » » »

I drank coffee because I didn't know what else to drink. I didn't figure on sleeping tonight, anyway.

Wes and I sat in an all-night diner on El Camino Real. I couldn't say where it was or how we got there. I'd been going through the motions for the past three hours. After I'd found Rod, the room had begun to spin. I went out to the living room and sat with my head between my knees until Wes's inquiring voice forced me to stand up. We called the police and then picked through the house for some hint of what had happened and why. The towel, the nail file, the toaster and coffee pot, the note—we couldn't make sense of it.

The police came and I told them what I knew. Evidence was collected and photos shot. The corpse was wrapped and taken away like a piece of discarded furniture. I'd gazed at the yellow tape marking off the scene and thought: My job had been to prevent the arrival of the yellow tape.

But I was not fixated on my failure just now. I was only trying to grasp the fact that Rod was dead. My brain was numb, like a useless limb, my stomach still queasy. Everything in the diner— the chipped porcelain, the scorched coffee, the hideous fluorescent lights—was a nightmare simulation in which I was trapped. Real life was stuck in the moment that knife went into Rod's neck. My mind was frozen there, picturing the gash. The fountain of blood. Picturing myself preventing it, somehow. Picturing Rod alive and, like as not, still agonizing over Alissa. Pacing in front of the hearth. Tapping his front teeth. Berating himself for his naïveté yet clinging to a thread of hope.

I wondered if Alissa, wherever she was, had gotten what she wanted. If she would care when the news reached her. Or if she herself . . .

There were too many variables to solve for. Wes had barraged me with questions when we sat down. I'd told him to shut up. The same questions were swirling in my mind: Did Rod kill himself? If so, that could mean he was implicated in Alissa's disappearance, as Rupert accused, and guilt had overwhelmed him. But then why all the signs of struggle? He could have done it himself if his lid had finally blown, the volcano erupted. Denial drove him berserk and he self-destructed. *Sorry,* the note said.

But I couldn't believe Rod would do it that way. He'd have found an elegant poison or put a neat bullet through his brain. Stabbing oneself in the neck was not a typical method of suicide. Someone must have done it to him. Wendy could have set him up. But she wasn't strong enough to do the killing herself. So she had help. Who? And why at Rod's house, when they'd tried to lure him to the Cheshire Cat? We'd seen Wendy there ourselves. Okay, so maybe it was Rupert and Gary from SG. Their motive was fuzzy, but Rupert did seem to believe that Rod was holding Alissa against her will. Or maybe it was just a plain, stupid, random burglary gone wrong. A couple of cranksters who didn't count on Rod being there, didn't count on a struggle, didn't know how to finish the job, and then fled once they realized what they'd done.

Then there was Alissa. Victim? Perpetrator? Both? Maybe she was victimized by Rod in some way and had brought some muscle, a boyfriend, back for revenge. Or the hypothetical boyfriend did it on his own.

I couldn't say any of this aloud. Words were betrayals, hypotheses were lies. Until I knew what really happened to Rod, I didn't feel like speaking at all.

"I can't accept it, Wes."

He sat up, startled after my long silence. He'd been slumped back against the wall, his feet up on the booth.

"I can't get it through my head. It's so wrong."

"It'll take some time, Bill."

"Thanks for the wisdom."

He touched my arm. He knew I had to vent some anger. The room was starting to spin again. I let my head drop to my arm on the table. The coffee squirmed in my stomach. The sick feeling would not leave me any time soon.

10

Mike Riley woke me with a phone call. Somewhere around dawn I'd crumpled into sleep on my sofa. My first thought when the phone rang was that it was Rod, calling with the latest news. I ran to pick it up, disoriented about what day it was and what time it was, thinking I must be late for an appointment. Mike's voice jerked me back into the ghastly present.

I had no patience for Mike Riley and his hearty-fellowness. But, of course, he was now my primary contact at Algoplex. He was the man I'd have to work with. He was devastated by Rod's death, too, but his method was to chew the same phrases over and over: "This blows me away. Unbelievable it could happen to Rod. He was such a good guy. He never hurt anyone. Unbelievable. He was top shelf. . . ."

Mike wanted to see me right away and hear everything. I told him I'd come down later. He kept pushing. I repeated that I'd come down later and hung up.

I grabbed a blanket and collapsed back into the couch, which fit into the cove of a bay window. My flat was an Edwardian, with high ceilings and tall windows, expensive to heat. November sunlight angled in. I closed the blinds and curled back up. The living room was a wreck: camera gear, bags, newspapers, tapes everywhere. I hadn't had time to clean up since the shoot. Rita was still working on a final cut of the film. I'd have to call her. Mike would probably want us to complete it, if only as a kind of memorial to Rod. I couldn't bear to work on it myself right now.

My eyes closed, defying orders from my head. There were so many things I should do. Look for Wendy. Find out if Alissa really was back. Confront Rupert. Speak again to the police. Go to Algoplex. Yet I wanted nothing more than to escape back into sleep. It would not return Rod to life, but at least I wouldn't have to be present, either.

By midafternoon, I was ready to get back into the fray. My little cove had been warmed by the sun, even with the blinds closed, and I stayed on the couch to make my calls. Wes was the first. I told him to book the SG date with Erika for Friday night. He wanted to know how I was doing. "Busy," I said.

Then I gave Rita the news. She offered her help, of course, anything; I said that, assuming Mike wanted it, I'd ask her to finish editing the Algoplex film. I started to dial Silicon Glamour's number, then thought better of it. Rupert should have no chance for evasion. I wanted to watch his face in person when he responded.

I pushed the Scout as hard as it would go—it got up to 68 on the downhill stretches of 280 on the way to the SG offices, engine rasping. It occurred to me I should have come down earlier. Rupert wouldn't have heard about Rod's death first thing in the morning. Now he'd had time to prepare.

Rod had warned me that SG monitored their parking lot, and he was right. No sooner had I bounced over a speed bump than a young blond guy came out of nowhere. I rolled down my window. He said this was a private lot. I told him I had business with Rupert. He squared his shoulders and demanded my name.

Clearly I was not the first person to barge in with the idea of settling business with Rupert. As the blond spoke into a two-way radio, I stepped on the gas. I wheeled around a line of cars, used mine to block the walkway to the front door, jerked on the parking brake, and took the keys. I pounded on the door and looked up at the video camera. "Let me in, Gary. Rupert needs to see me."

The blond guy yelled into his radio as he scrambled over the hood of my car. I thought, foolishly, how much I'd enjoy hitting him. But then the radio squawked back and he halted. The door buzzed. I went inside.

"Where's Rupert?" I said.

Gary was guarding the open-tread staircase, his arms folded. He really was a lot bigger than me. His biceps thoroughly filled the sleeves of his black polo shirt. He said, "Sit down."

I went around the reception counter and grabbed his phone. He didn't hurry. While I searched for Rupert's extension, he took hold of my wrist and twisted it. And kept twisting it. The phone fell from my hand. He dragged me around the other side of the counter and, before releasing me, said, "Stay the hell out from behind *my* desk."

I sat in a chair by a carved weimaraner. "I need to see Rupert."

"Mr. Evans is not here. What's your name again?"

"You know my goddamned name. If Rupert's not here, I'll see Trisha. It concerns Rod and it's an emergency."

Gary shook his head. His voice never lost its deep, easy, diesel rumble. "Man, you are some piece of work. Look, buddy, this thing is over. There's no connection between us and Mr. Glaser."

"It's that easy, huh? Just erase him from the books."

"There are no books."

"Let me talk to Rupert. Or Trisha. It'll save them some trouble. Might save them a visit from the police."

"We're shocked and saddened." He said it with a straight face, as if at a news conference. "We'll do whatever we can to help."

"Where was Rupert last night? Where were you?"

"At a hospital charity dinner. A few dozen people will confirm that." The heavy lips curved into a smile.

I stood up. He moved, catlike, in the direction of the stairs. I wasn't going there. I was going to the door. "I hope you know what you're doing, Gary. I hope Rupert's happy with your work here."

"Next time, I don't buzz the door for you."

I didn't mind. While he was twisting my wrist, I'd had a glimpse of the weekly planner open on his desk. A dinner was scheduled for Friday night. The dinner was with Sylvain Partners.

>> >> >> >> >>

I don't know why I put off Mike Riley until the end of the day. I wanted to get my hands on whoever killed Rod, not deal with the formalities, I suppose. Mike grasped me in a bear hug the moment I walked into his office. He expressed more concern for my well-being than I needed, asking if I was all right, repeating again how the whole thing just blew him away. Rod was a good friend, a great man, this was a terrible, terrible thing. I felt the same way, of course, but his way of putting it made it seem less than it was.

I asked about the arrangements. Mike said Rod's lawyer would handle the estate. Rod's mother was on her way from Columbus. Mike hadn't heard when or where a service would be held, though he assured me Algoplex would find a way to honor him. The remains would be cremated and Rod's mother would take them back to Ohio.

"After the autopsy, I assume," I said.

"Yes. That will be done tomorrow. A Detective Coharie was here."

"Coharie? That wasn't the one I talked to last night."

"Coharie's the one in charge of the case."

"Okay. Give me his number. I want to make sure he's got all the information."

Mike jotted it down for me. Then he took a little walk around his desk and glanced at his computer screen. "I see that Rod had you on a retainer," he said.

"Yes. He wanted me to find Alissa."

"How would you feel about staying on, Bill? To find out what happened last night. The company will continue to pay you and your expenses."

"You got it." I would have done it for free, but the money was welcome.

Mike held up a disclaiming hand. "Not that I doubt the competence of the police. But I want to use every resource we have. They said it looked like a break-and-enter job. The lights were off in the front of the house. The burglars may have thought no one was home. After the deed they freaked out and split."

"There are a lot of possibilities. That's one."

"They also have another theory. Because of the note, I guess, they think Rod could have committed suicide. They wanted to know if he had a history of mental illness. I said no way."

"Yeah." I didn't want to admit the theory wasn't completely farfetched. "The scene looked more like a struggle to me than one guy going berserk."

"Right!" Mike jabbed a stubby finger at me. "Exactly right. The detective said you'd be amazed at what people do to themselves when they flip out. But I don't see Rod flipping out. Not that way."

"How much did you know about this Alissa business?"

Mike shook his head. "Rod wouldn't talk to me about it. Even though I'm the one who first set him up with her, after they started seeing, uh, more of each other, he clammed up. What was going on at the dinner Monday night, anyway?"

"I'm working on that. It wasn't an easy subject for him to talk about. Did he mention Alissa might have fallen for him?"

"Lord, no. Her for him?"

"Maybe. Or she might have been using him to gain access to Algoplex secrets."

Mike leaned toward me, fingers pressing the desk. "Is there anything to that, Bill?"

"These are all things I'll be checking out."

"You know that I'll help in every conceivable way. Would you mind writing up a memo for me about how you see the situation so far?"

Sure, Mike, I thought, I'll have all 500,000 words on your desk tomorrow morning. I gave what he might have mistaken for a nod and said, "I wanted to ask you about this deal with Plush Biologics. Do you have any reservations, see anything odd about it?"

"No, I don't think so, Bill." He stuck his hands in his pockets and jingled some change. He must not have heard the news until he got in this morning, because his tie was garishly floral. "Quite the contrary, this is an enormous opportunity. Eternaderm looks like a winner to me. We'll be on the inside. We had to give up a chunk of the company, of course, and they drove a hard bargain. But that's business. I see nothing but upside."

He stopped jingling and added, "Assuming, of course, Sylvain wants to go ahead with it. Most VC's would jump ship after this. They have every right to: A key-man clause was written into the deal, and Rod was the key man. But when I talked to Sylvain this morning, they said they'd stick with us. We'll see if that holds. They might just be waiting for the body to cool off."

"Can you come through on your end without Rod?"

He took a deep breath. "It'll be tough. But we'll come back. We'll fight for Rod. He gave us the blueprint. We've got enough good minds to meet the specs."

"Can you think of anyone who would benefit from Rod being out of the picture?"

Mike's eyes went wide. "Someone wouldn't *kill* Rod because of this contract—to steal it from us in some way?"

"You never know. Can you think of any advantage Plush or Sylvain would gain by having intellectual property Alissa might have stolen?"

"Jeez . . ." He scratched his chin. "I don't know what they'd do with it. Rod was the man with the plan. Why hand it off to some other engineer when they just inked with us?"

"What about Silicon Glamour?"

"They seemed all right. Prudent, discreet. Rod took charge of his account with Alissa. I guess you know more than me by now."

"So how is Sylvain connected to SG?"

"Sylvain and Silicon Glamour? That's a bizarre idea. I don't like the sound of it."

"I don't, either. They're meeting tomorrow night. Don't let on that you know."

"These are very weird ideas, Bill. Where are they leading us to?"

I stood to leave. "Like I said, there are a lot of possibilities. Just think about these questions and let me know."

"Will do. And you'll go ahead and work up that memo for me?"

"Sure, Mike," I said as I left. I'd changed my mind. It would be a short memo after all. Four words, five at most: *I have no fucking idea.*

» » » » »

I found myself back where it started. In the alley behind Alissa's apartment, watching the faint light behind her sliding glass doors. I'd been here since dark, waiting for something to happen. The police still had Rod's house off limits. I was secretly relieved. But I wasn't ready to go home yet, either. I'd come here, parked the Scout down the street, and now was loitering. When a car went by, or a tenant left the building, I stuffed my hands into my jacket pockets and walked down the alley as if I had somewhere to go. As if I belonged here. I didn't belong anywhere at the moment. Not back in my flat, with the camera cases all over the floor and the clothes unhung up and the takeout food cartons on the table and the century-old lintels sagging. Not out with friends: There was no one I wanted to talk to. Not in some café or bar, with its conversations like flies buzzing. I wanted to be only what I was here: a man in passing.

The night was chilly. A November wind whistled down the bay. People walked quickly, heels clopping. I was supposed to have only passed through Rod's life, too. Passed through, improved it, shown him to himself in an uplifting way, or at least in a way that provided fifteen minutes of cinematic amusement. Pass through and get paid. The life of the cinematographer. We were notoriously hard to maintain relationships with because we were away from home so much. Rita and I had been together a few years ago, and it had worked because we understood the demands of the business. Often we shot films together. That was before the dot-com whirlwind lifted and rearranged everything, then dropped us like trailer siding in a tornado. Rod had kept a steady course through the whirlwind. It seemed unbearably wrong that he'd been taken at the brink of his own liftoff.

I stared at the sliding glass door, wondering what role Alissa had played in all this. She'd swept him off his feet, given him visions, sent his blood racing. I willed myself some kind of X-ray sight into the apartment and its past. I pictured the cool tile, the heavy wood of the Mission sofa, the unmade bed, the scattered camisoles and skirts and lingerie and shoes—had they been discarded carelessly, or in some hasty escape? Had the garments been plundered by an intruder—Gary, Rupert, a boyfriend, a kidnapper? Or had Alissa now returned and made the bed and put the clothes back in their closets?

The night got later, colder, darker. Nothing changed. The light behind the glass door seemed to flicker, but it was only a trick of my eyes from staring too long.

I couldn't stand any more. I ran at the Dumpster behind the utility room, levered myself atop it, and leaped for the drainpipe on the wall. I flashed back on Rod's sad attempt to climb this wall, when he managed only to deposit himself in the Dumpster. After gaining the utility room roof, I climbed heedlessly. My senses were blurred now, my nerves numb. I scrambled to the third floor, hardly noticing the effort or the height, then stood gasping on the balcony. The door stared back at me, unforthcoming as a judge.

I grabbed the handle and pulled. It should have opened; I'd left it unlocked after my last visit. It did not move. With both hands I shook and lifted it. The door was blocked. Its base was ramming into some obstacle. I bent and peered in the dimness. Someone else had been inside. They'd placed a metal rod in the track. No amount of shaking would open this door. Whatever answers were inside were sealed off from me now.

11

Dr. Ellen Quong was perfectly willing to help. I'd gotten her mobile number from Mike this morning, Friday, and had proposed lunch. Maybe the Chief Science Officer at Plush Biologics also wanted to get the inside gossip on Rod: She was a large, loquacious woman with a big laugh and quick eyes, and she liked to talk about people. Her black hair was cut in a page boy, which made her look younger than her fifty years. She also smiled a lot, producing big dimples in her cheeks.

We met at a Mexican restaurant a few miles from her office in Redwood City. My previous attempt at getting into Plush, on Wednesday, had been thwarted by Connie, so I wanted a neutral spot. After we ordered food, I gave Ellen an accurate but not detailed account of what had happened to Rod. Her face clouded and she told me how stunned she'd been by the news. But she wasn't the kind of person to linger in melancholy: Before long she was reminiscing about amusing moments with Rod, like his Nerd-in-Chief remarks during the film at the dinner signing. She'd done a fair amount of preliminary work with him before the signing. Ellen had been impressed by how quickly Rod got up to speed on the biology and how well adapted his tools were to the biocomputing tasks at hand. She'd also been impressed by his integrity: He didn't try to sell her on Algoplex, but interrogated her as thoroughly about the molecular targets she had in mind as she had him about his software's capabilities.

"I'd like to hear more about that," I said, "and the mechanics of this deal. I know that Eternaderm takes up the slack, so to speak, in a patient's skin by renovating elastin. It sounds like a form of gene therapy."

"It's similar," she said, "but safer." Our food had arrived and Ellen dug into a chili relleno. "In gene therapy, you insert new genetic material to modify the patient's DNA. Eternaderm won't alter your skin's genetic code; the consequences of that sort of thing are hard to control. Instead, it remodels elastin by promoting the turnover process. Normally, your skin's elastin production drops off after puberty and eventually stops altogether. We found a regulator protein that modifies the expression of elastase, which breaks down old fibers, and at the same time upregulates fibroblast synthesis of new elastin fibers. The process is reversible by withdrawing the drug."

"And elastin is a connective tissue?"

"Right. Both collagen and elastin are connective tissues made up of proteins. You find elastin in various parts of the body, including arteries. Once Eternaderm is launched, I want to look into whether it can be used for wound healing and to prevent atherosclerosis."

"Healthier elastin means skin that's more supple and relilient. I gather this is essentially a cosmetic therapy."

Ellen made a face. "A *cosmetic* is a compound that is supposed to have no biologic action. Skin is porous, but it's also our armor: Its job is to keep the outside world out. Cosmetics, in general, don't do a lot more than polish the armor and make it look and feel better for a while. You want to know what the number-one wrinkle-prevention treatment is? Using sunblock or staying out of the sun altogether. Sun does more damage than aging. Most cosmetics are remixtures of a palette of known ingredients, with new textures and smells and marketing campaigns. Don't get me wrong, it's a real art. The companies like to call their products 'bioactive,' which sidesteps the issue. Something like tretinoin, on the other hand, is an actual therapeutic, although they're still trying to understand how it works. It has a similar effect on collagen as Eternaderm does on elastin, though it's not as powerful. One problem it has is that it might cause skin to burn more easily by flattening the stratum corneum. Alpha hydroxy acids seem to improve the skin, too, but they haven't been studied rigorously. The thing is, arriving at a scientific understanding of what a particular molecule does is a long and expensive process. From a business angle, it's unclear whether clinical trials are worth the trouble. If you know how to play around with the language, you can market a cream that makes more grandiose claims and costs far less to develop."

"But that's not an option with Eternaderm."

"Eternaderm goes to the genetic level without altering genes. We've developed artificial transcription factors that target the binding domains on chromosome 7 and set the turnover process in motion. This has distinct biologic action on the skin."

"So it's definitely a medicine, not a cosmetic," I said. "But the company is still aiming for—what would you call it—an *elective* market."

"That's right." She looked down her nose. "These patients will receive treatment primarily for their vanity. I thought we were going in a more therapeutic direction, treating real problems. Ronald promises that once we build up the company with these elective treatments, we can get the big money we'll need to find out what Eternaderm can do for arteries and wound healing. We'll see what it can do for other skin diseases, too, but a lot of them are so rare, there's little money to be made in them. You do it to help people."

"I remember hearing you're also developing other treatments that work on collagen and on melanin."

Ellen nodded. "Right. I'm hoping Rod's technology will help us tweak Eternaderm so it works just as well to remodel collagen. That'll put us in the wrinkle-prevention business, which needless to say is huge. And if we can regulate melanin, we can regulate pigmentation. We're identifying control sequences and binding domains, and developing transcription factors. Every gene complex has a set of control sequences that initiate or inhibit the transcription of the genes. This is where Rod's tools come in. His software will run simulations and scenarios and tell us which ones to pursue."

"It sounds pretty magical."

"Oh, it is. He was an algorithmic wizard. Rod gave me confidence they'll work, and your video helped the suits get the picture. I heard them talking afterward about how it had branded Rod for them."

Branding was a word people used when I was making films for them. The branding mania had extended to groups within a company finding ways to get themselves noticed. "What are the chances of the deal holding together, now that Rod is gone?"

"I certainly hope it does," Ellen said, sitting back. I sat back, too, having polished off a couple of enchiladas. "I suppose you couldn't blame Sylvain for getting shaky in the knees, but the truth is we need Algoplex's technology. In fact, I'm glad you mentioned it. I'm going to talk to Sylvain about this."

"Did anyone have doubts about the deal?"

"I can't think of anyone who wasn't enthusiastic."

I remembered how the Sylvain guys had acceded so quickly to Rod's demand to have me at dinner. "What about Connie?" I said. She'd been the only exception. "What do you think of her?"

"Well," Ellen answered slowly, "I think Connie is on board. And Ronald is a dear, in his self-absorbed way. As for Connie, personally—well, I wouldn't want to be indiscreet."

A little twinkle in her eye told me she was dying to be. "Oh, go ahead."

"It's nothing really. Sometimes she just seems like a character out of a fairy tale. The evil stepmother." Ellen burst out with a little laugh. "I'm sorry, I just had to say it. But the truth is, she knows what she's doing. She keeps everyone, especially Ronald, in line. So to be honest, although we're not best friends, I do admire her." Ellen stopped and finished off her soda. "You've probably already asked yourself if Plush made up his name. No, it's real, and so is Connie's epidermis. She doesn't waste time on vanity treatments."

"I figured from the minute the doctor was born he knew he was either going into dermatology or carpets. These other programs will be equally big in the cosmetic market, if they pan out, won't they?"

"Oh, yes. I didn't exactly sign up for the cosmetic business, but the work is too exciting to drop now. I hope Ronald is serious about therapeutics, because personally I am not itching to tend exclusively to the wrinkle anxieties of the overfed or underfed rich of Silicon Valley."

"Who are the only ones who'll be able to afford Eternaderm."

"It'll be exceedingly expensive until we ramp up production and perfect the delivery system. These people will expect creamy perfection. We'll need to analyze their skin chemistry before devising the individual treatment regimen. It's a tricky balancing act."

She looked at her watch. I thought about what else I needed to ask her. "Did you happen to know Wendy Bevins?" I said.

Ellen squinted. "No, the name's not familiar."

"Dr. Plush knows her, and so does Connie. I sure would like to talk to them."

"You want to meet with Connie? I don't see why not."

"Connie doesn't like me."

"Connie has strange taste in men. You might have noticed that."

I smiled. "Well, last time I tried to get in, I couldn't get past the front desk."

"No problem. I'll take you back to her office right now."

>> >> >> >> >>

Ellen was one of the few people at Plush Biologics who was not intimidated by Connie Plush. She was a very good scientist and the company would still be groping for ways to make Eternaderm work without her, and she knew it. She breezed me past the lines of administrative deterrence that protected the suite in which Mrs. Plush, as they called her, held court. Worried glances followed us.

Connie, on the phone, gave Ellen a sharp glance as we entered. Ellen said, "Please take a minute to talk to this gentleman."

The long, rectangular suite had two glass walls, one of which faced outdoors. Most of the panels were shuttered except for one looking back into the office and one facing out to a small patio attended by Japanese maples. Ellen proceeded to a sitting area at the far end of the suite. Connie's gaze followed. I seated myself in a wingback chair before she could kick me out.

We waited while Mrs. Plush finished her business on the phone. Ellen's leg began to wag; she was not a person who liked sitting still. After a few minutes she abandoned me to Connie.

When her call was done, Connie sat opposite me. She was wearing a long black skirt and a pink shirt with a button collar. A pair of reading glasses dangled from a sterling silver necklace.

I glanced at the chaise lounges on the patio and attempted a joke about skin and sun damage. Connie looked at the patio and said, "I don't use it."

So much for small talk. I waited. She folded her legs, folded her hands on top of them, and said, "We were terribly sorry to hear about Rod." Her tone was earnest, even respectful. "It's a terrible loss for all of us. Is there any word on what exactly happened?"

I limited my answer to the police's burglar theory. She tutted about the condition of society and the unfairness of such a talented man being taken. It was boilerplate, but she acted like she meant it.

"Will this make completion of work on Eternaderm difficult?" I asked.

She focused her hard gray eyes on me. They matched her hair and its sensible cut. A trace of elegance showed in the way her hands moved, but she suppressed it in favor of efficiency. "Let's not speak of business. The man is dead, we ought to honor him properly. Are you so concerned that you went to all this trouble to barge in and ask me that?"

I drew back a little. Nothing in her appearance was specifically censorious, it was more the iron spirit animating the face. Still, I appreciated the invitation to get to the point. "I'd be very grateful if you could tell me what you know about Wendy Bevins and where to find her."

"Wendy?" She drew herself up.

"The woman with Rod at dinner Monday night. I'm sure you met her."

"Alissa? What about her?"

"You know that's not her name. Your husband winked at her."

"Ronald's liable to wink at anyone," she said.

"So you're completely clueless about what was going on?"

She looked away with a mild cluck of the tongue, as if pausing to deliver a lesson. "There's something known as discretion, Bill."

"You don't know who it was, do you?" I goaded.

"Of course I do. I know them both."

"They did some promotional work for you, right? Showing off their excellent skin. What exactly was the job?"

"That's confidential."

"Well, I need to be in touch with Wendy. There are matters of the estate concerning both her and her daughter."

Connie sighed as if I'd badgered her into doing me a favor. "Don't push that angle, Bill. Her benefit is no concern of mine. And don't get the mother and daughter mixed up like you did the other night."

"All the more reason I should speak to Wendy. Can you tell me how to reach her?"

"I'm sorry. Her address changes frequently."

"Perhaps I could talk to Dr. Plush, then."

"Ronald's not in today. He's a busy man."

"Yes, but he seemed to have a special connection with Wendy."

She smothered her anger under an indulgent smile. "He can't help you, Bill. Leave him be. He lives in his own world." Her tone made me picture Connie picking up after him as the doctor went distractedly about the house dropping skin samples behind him like socks. It also managed to put me in the position of a youngster bothering Daddy, who was busy. I had to hand it to Connie. She was good.

I had one more card to play, and I marked higher than it was. "Wendy lured Rod to a club the night of his death. The police are hunting for her. They'll also be looking for anyone who knows anything about her."

"I'm right here. Take one of my cards on your way out. Give it to them."

So far I was 0 for 2 on the threats of police investigation. I was sure Gary had been bluffing on Rupert's behalf, but less sure about Connie. Yes, she was good. I should have just accepted it. Instead, I took a moment to inspect her face. A looseness was visible in the skin. As Ellen had told me, she'd made no effort to hide the channels on her forehead or the rills inscribed near her eyes and mouth.

"Do your husband's treatments actually work?" I asked.

I should never have stooped to the implication. When she caught me at it, her victory was complete.

"I know exactly who and what I am, Bill," she said, then stood and walked me to the door.

12

Wes had left a message with news that was both good and bad while I was in Connie Plush's office. The bad news was the date with the SG associates was postponed until tomorrow night. The good part was that meant I was free to spy on Rupert's dinner tonight with Sylvain Partners.

I punched my speed-dial button for Wes as I drove from Plush down to Algoplex. "Can you believe this?" Wes complained. "They're playing a game on us, Bill."

"At least it's mutual. Erika probably got a last-minute call from a more important client. We're at the bottom of her list."

"Let's see if she still feels that way *after* the date."

I had to laugh. "Impossible as it seems, she may be immune to your charms."

"Want to put some money on that?"

"Let me remind you of the purpose of this date, Wes. First we need to gain their confidence. Then we need to get Erika and the other associate to talk about Alissa."

"There's the wager. You use your methods, I'll use mine."

I sighed and clicked off. Wes never stopped trying.

At Algoplex, I spent some time talking to people who knew Rod, including his assistants and Jimmy the PR guy. Nothing

much new came out of the conversations, except for how trau-
matized everyone was and how clearly they respected Rod.

It was late in the afternoon by the time I went into Mike
Riley's office. He looked properly haggard. He'd been up until
three last night with his senior engineers, verifying that they had
the expertise to come through on the Eternaderm deal. I noticed
he'd added a picture of Rod to his wall, right next to the photo of
Mike's old rugby team. I mentioned that I'd talked to Ellen
Quong and Connie Plush, but didn't give him details.

"Any word from Sylvain about sticking with the deal?" I asked.

"They're still talking nice, but they said they're revisiting the
key-man clause. I have a feeling they're letting me down slowly."

"How considerate of them."

"Rod's death is a shock to them, too. It came just as they were
calling in the big cash for us from a backer. Their concern has
got to be they'd be throwing good money after bad."

"Which backer exactly?"

"They prefer anonymity. That's not unusual."

"Tell me more about Sylvain. Where'd they come from?"

"We did our own reverse due diligence on them, of course,"
Mike replied. "They're relatively new, and small, but they've got
a solid record of backing winners and then plowing the return
into new ventures. No take-the-money-and-run tactics I could
uncover. One thing I found odd, though, is how diverse their
portfolio is: routers, set top boxes, Internet auctions. . . . Plush
is their first biotech company, and we're the first in data visualization and simulation. But each play's scored a touchdown, so I
guess they've got a good eye."

"What kind of equity are they getting?"

Mike made a you-don't-want-to-know wave. "Too much. I
went to the mat with Rod over this. They got major Series A

equity, three seats on the board, their own CFO, a boatload of warrants, big-time attachments—and that's in *addition* to what we gave up to Plush. Rod's argument was that Algoplex could go nowhere without him, so there was no danger of losing control. Meanwhile the upside was robust for both companies. He was right, of course, about himself being the indispensable man."

Mike stopped, cracked his knuckles, and went on. "Some execs suffer from an inflated sense of their own value. Did I say some? *Most.* I'm not like that, Bill, I'm a team player. I've got some skills and some experience, but there are twenty other guys who could do my job. Except for one thing: Rod trusts me. Trusted. He was right to, and he was right about his value to our company. He really was The Man, which meant that he was right even when he was wrong. We gave up too much, but then again, it's probably true Sylvain would have walked. Rod felt this was our main chance."

"How exactly does the key-man clause work in this case?"

"It was meant to protect both sides. It insures Rod's stake in the company, but it also says that if we lose Rod for any reason, Sylvain has the option of getting out *or* of buying 30 percent of his stock for next to nothing. Losing Rod was as big a risk for them as it was for us. People sometimes call it the hit-by-the-bus clause. No one foresaw losing him this way."

"So they could gain by Rod's loss."

"They don't see it that way. Their nightmare, of course, is that they pour money into a company that can no longer deliver without Rod. After spending half the night with my engineers, I'm convinced we *can* deliver. Rod laid down a solid blueprint. We just have to carry it through. I said this to Sylvain today. If they want to bail, it's on them. I'm sure not giving up more of the company."

Mike had switched into competitive mode. I'd noticed this at the Frisbee game: He was everyone's best friend until play started. Then he didn't care who he knocked over to get into the end zone. "Was Rod insured?" I asked.

"You bet. He was a good man. Algoplex was his child. He didn't want to leave it orphaned if the unthinkable happened. If the insurance comes through, it'll keep us going until we find another deal, in case Sylvain does back out."

"The insurance must have some conditions."

"Yes. Which means we need to clear up this ridiculous idea that Rod killed himself. I'm counting on you for that, Bill."

"What do the police say? The autopsy was scheduled for today."

"The police put time of death between ten and eleven Wednesday night. The cause was exsanguish—well, he bled to death from the stab to his carotid artery. The main theory is that a burglary was in progress and Rod surprised them. Detective Coharie figures there were two guys. No fingerprints, which supports the idea they had some experience. But at the same time he keeps harping on the fact that the lack of prints could also mean there was no one else in the house. There was no sign of forced entry, either, so he won't rule out Rod doing it to himself. It's unlikely, he admits, but he's heard Rod was psychologically unstable. Who would have said that?"

The possibilities came to mind quickly. "Rupert Evans. Maybe even Connie Plush. Rupert's the one with the biggest motive to blame it on the victim. But I have to admit, Mike, Rod was bent out of shape about Alissa."

Mike looked down. His lip quivered and his voice grew soft. "There's no way you can convince me he'd do such a thing to himself. Yet the police say they can't find clear evidence that anything was stolen."

"What about his laptop? He took it home with him every night."

"Right! But they said there's no proof he did that night. Well, it's not in Rod's office, so where else would he have left it? Anyway, it doesn't discount the robbery theory. If the robbers were interrupted, they'd just grab what they could and get out."

"You still have to wonder—why only the laptop, all the way downstairs? Why not the high-end stereo stuff in the living room?"

"Portability," Mike answered. "Look, don't lend credence to the suicide idea."

"Did they do a toxic screening?"

"Yes. No drugs, nothing." Mike gripped the back of his chair. "I find it infuriating that a couple of sleazeballs ended Rod's life like this and we're talking about whether he might have done it himself. I want to wring their necks, Bill. Personally."

"I know the feeling. Listen, I don't think Rod killed himself, either. He supposedly wrote this note, but there was no pen near him. What did he do, put it away before he bled to death? Even Rod wasn't that neat. No, I think the note was a fake and we should look closer to home. It's more than a coincidence this happened at the very moment Rod was supposed to be reunited with Alissa. Did you remind the cops to get after Wendy?"

"I did. Coharie wrote it down and all, but . . . he seemed skeptical of that avenue, to tell you the truth."

"Well then I need to talk to him. I don't understand why he hasn't called me himself." I glanced at my watch. It was after five. "Is he still in?"

Mike shrugged and handed me Coharie's card. I found out he'd left for the day. I left my number, and also told Mike to have him call me. "What about Rod's estate?" I said. "Who's benefiting there?"

"Primarily his mother. She'll keep the assets right here at Algoplex. She instructed me to do what Rod would want. He's got some money going to Caltech, his alma mater, and to a couple of friends for their startups. He also"—Mike gave a little laugh—"left some money to be passed out as bonuses to the employees. That shows what a good guy he was. I haven't decided yet whether to ask people if they want to reinvest it."

"There'll be some kind of service for him, I assume."

"Yes, a memorial service on Wednesday afternoon," Mike said. "The funeral itself will be back in Columbus next weekend. I think I mentioned his mother will take his ashes back with her. She's at a hotel. I'll give you the number."

"Thanks. Then I'll get going."

Mike came forward to give me the number and shake my hand. It was a warm, firm shake, as his always were. He looked me in the eye. "Bill, you don't need to tell Rod's mother about the Alissa stuff and—and all that, right?" I shook my head and he pulled me closer. "I feel like it was my fault for bringing Alissa into his life. I just wish Rod had been able to confide in me. He was like a brother. I feel I could have prevented it."

"Yeah. I thought I was in the right place Wednesday night. Obviously I wasn't."

Tears suddenly burst from Mike's eyes. His mouth turned down and he sobbed on my shoulder. I patted him on the arm, then on the back. He put a hand to his face and pulled away. "Sorry, Bill. I'm tired. I should call it a day and hit the showers."

were sharp and her features angular and well-preserved. She gave the waiter a glittering smile to match the stones on her neck. "There's no need for security. I'll have a cosmopolitan."

Rupert opened his mouth, but Trisha put the words into it. "Bring him a cosmo, too."

He was speechless for a change. Only a big sister could do that. "You must be the oldest in the family," I said to her.

"Old? Is that what you *meant* to say, Bill?" Her voice was a rich purr, slightly curdled.

"Wise. That's what I meant." I turned to the guys next to me and said, "How's the financing for SG going, Kevin?"

He looked to his colleagues, who glanced back at Trisha. That in itself was valuable information. "This is purely social," Trisha said. "No business of any kind."

I looked at the square faces of the bankers, then at Trisha's jewelry, a carat or two beyond gaudy, and Rupert's Gene Meyer tie. Trisha's dress was a luscious chiffon, with ruffles on the shoulders that gave an impression of big red wings. I asked Kevin how he met her. He stammered out something about his wife and social circles that was clearly invented on the spot.

"Bill, it's not polite to embarrass guests," Trisha interrupted. "Now, you know our business perfectly well. Why don't we talk about something else before our drinks arrive and you leave?"

These guys were clients, she was implying. So why was their date with the big cheeses instead of Silicon Glamour "associates"? There was one thing I knew for sure we all had in common. "I don't know if you've heard the details about Rod's murder," I said. "It was incredibly brutal."

Everyone nodded as if they did know the details. Rupert folded his hands and put a look of concern on his face. "The poor fellow. Shocking a man could do that to himself."

I acted surprised. "Oh no, they've ruled out suicide. Someone went in there and murdered him."

Trisha pursed her lips. "It's a shame. That used to be such a safe area. It's terrible how standards are falling."

"You know, Connie Plush said exactly the same thing," I replied.

The only way I knew Trisha's smile was fake was that it was too big. "Connie's a *lovely* woman."

"So we've heard," Rupert added hastily.

"You provide Plush with models for their marketing, right?" The guess was based on what Rod had told me about Alissa.

Trish gave a noncommittal smile and sipped her drink. Rupert looked away. The faces of the Sylvain guys showed no puzzlement, only hesitation; they were still waiting for cues.

"We know a lot of people in common," I went on, shooting in the dark. "I saw Connie today and she said nice things about all of you. She particularly admires your style, Trisha."

"I'd imagine so. She married that funny man—what was his name?"

No one spoke up. It was as if they were afraid to say the wrong thing.

"Donald, isn't it?" I suggested.

Still the table was silent. No one corrected me. The waiter appeared with a tray of drinks.

"Good-bye, Bill." Trisha tapped the underside of Rupert's elbow. He stood, and she gave a lift of the eyes to the Sylvain men. They stood and crowded me out of the booth.

The waiter retreated. "Do you have another table, sir?"

"I'll take it myself," I said, picking up the beer from the tray.

I raised the glass. "A toast," I said, and paused for the waiter to hand out the other drinks. When Trisha lifted her pink cone, the rest followed suit. "To those who deserve justice. Here's to Rod Glaser."

Everyone drank tentatively. It was hard to tell whether this was due to guilt or to fear of Trisha. They acted as one, like puppies watching Mom. I turned as if to depart, then swung back to Rupert. "I can save you some trouble with the police. They're awfully interested in your relationship with Rod. There's no reason for me to keep quiet about his connection to you anymore. I'll come by to talk to you about it."

The threat had nowhere near the effect I wanted. "Don't worry, Bill, the police are taken care of," he said serenely. He was back in charge. He looked away from me and made a witty remark to his guests as they sat down again.

The busboy arrived and I had to move so he could distribute water. I took my beer back to the bar. A few sips later, a man emerged from behind the bar and informed me that it was time to leave. He was big enough that I had no choice but to agree.

But I had gotten one answer for my trouble tonight. Rupert's comments about the cops confirmed my suspicion that he'd been the one whispering about Rod's instability. Still, I left with a lot more new questions. I hoped Alissa's friend Erika would begin to answer them tomorrow night.

13

You can't control when people are going to call you. It's one of the reasons email seems so agreeable, even if it only adds up to written voicemail. Email suggests an ongoing correspondence; delay is built in and therefore acceptable. Voicemail continually makes you feel as if you're missing out on things.

What I missed out on was the chance to speak person-to-person to Wendy. She left the message Saturday morning while I was on the phone with Jenny. Jenny was my ex-girlfriend. We were together for seven months. It had verged on getting serious, but we parted ways two months ago. We were in post-relationship limbo now, talking infrequently, wondering who'd be the first to announce they'd met someone new. I knew I hadn't, so when she'd called last week to set up dinner tonight, I wondered if I was about to receive some news. It would be painful to hear, but I didn't regret the breakup: As bright and sparkling and enterprising as she was, our approaches to life were too divergent.

My hope had been for the dinner to be the first step in becoming friends. Now I hoped that when I explained that my client of the moment had turned up dead, she'd understand why I had to break tonight's date. I thought she might even be a little amused by the fact that Wes and I were going out with two "associates."

She wasn't. There was a long silence after I broke the news. "Hello?" I said.

An intake of breath came over the line. "Well, that's just pathetic, Bill, if you have to go to these lengths to avoid seeing me."

"Rod was murdered, Jenny. This woman Erika was close to Alissa."

She took another breath, then let it out. "Well, I have to hand it to you, you were right about Sheila and what killed her at my dinner party. But that doesn't automatically turn you into Sherlock Holmes. Don't tell me you're too dumb to realize what these girls really are."

"There won't be any sex. That's spelled out in the contract. SG is about creating an image, casting a glamour."

"Glamour is not your area of expertise, Bill."

"I'm a babe in the woods," I admitted. "But it's interesting to watch how it works. I have a feeling I have to decipher the code to get to the bottom of Rod's murder."

"Get to the bottom of it," she said with a trace of sarcasm. "You never trust what's on the surface, do you? There's always something deeper, and by God you've got to dig it out. But then you find out there's a new layer, a deeper cause, and you get obsessed with that. And then another, and another, until you go all the way to the bone. And it's hollow at the center. Remember how you used to complain when I put on makeup, as if I was some fashion victim? Well, I *like* putting on my face; it's fun, it's creative, it puts me in control. You never understood that. You can keep going deeper and deeper and deeper, to whatever layer you want,

Bill. It's still surface. You're always right back at the top layer, and all the digging in the world won't bring back your friend."

A sudden abyss yawned in my mind. She'd put our differences in a nutshell. It was clear to me that neither of us had absolute truth on our side. The truly frightening thing was that she might be right in this case. There might be no deeper truth and no rhyme or reason to Rod's bloody death.

"Bill?" she said into the silence. "Aren't you going to tell me how wrong and superficial I am? You always have an answer for everything."

"I don't have an answer, Jenny. I don't know what else I can do but keep on driving with my eyes closed."

It was a phrase I'd used when we first met, at a point when my life had been tossed like a salad. Her voice grew softer, concerned. "I know you're doing what seems right, Bill, and that's a good thing. I've always liked that about you. Just please don't crash."

"Thanks, Jenny. I'll call to reschedule the dinner as soon as there's some kind of conclusion to this Rod business."

"I wish you all the luck in the world," she said, and hung up.

The message from Wendy had been waiting on my voicemail afterward. She sugared her voice and apologized for being mistaken about Alissa again; she could have sworn her daughter was back in town.

"I've got a line on her in Arizona," Wendy's message continued. "Honestly, I don't know what's wrong with that girl. She's acting very strangely. I was so shocked by the news about Rod. I'm really, really sorry, I know you were fast friends. People have strange inner demons, don't they? Well, I've got to go. I had really hoped to speak to you in person. I'll be on the road, but I guess you know how to reach me. Of course, I'll do anything I can to help. Ta-ta for now."

I banged the phone down, then called in for my voicemail again, noted the time of the message, and made sure it was saved. Then I phoned Mike. He wasn't in his office, but I got him on his mobile. He'd received a message from Wendy, too, the same kind of thing. I asked if he had any way to trace it. He said his caller ID indicated it came from a pay phone. I had him give me the number.

"She was just covering herself, don't you think?" I said. "It would look bad if she split town without calling. She made sure neither of us picked up. She figured you wouldn't be in the office on Saturday, and with me she just got lucky. My outgoing voice-mail message gives my mobile number, yet she didn't use it."

"I guess so, Bill. Hey, I'm sorry but I can't talk. I'm with the Sylvain lawyers."

"I'm going to the police station. I'll talk to you later."

I thought about Wendy's call on my way down the Peninsula. The entire reason I had a new cell phone, with film work getting so sparse in the Bay Area, was not to miss calls. I'd thrown away my previous one after my short, unhappy foray into the tech business. The phone broke due to a collision with a wall. Wendy knew that people around here didn't answer their land lines any-more, and took a calculated risk. She would have hung up if she'd gotten me real-time.

The day's string of unsuccesses continued at the police sta-tion. I showed the card Mike had given me for Detective Coharie at the front. They said he wasn't working today. Wasn't he supposed to be solving the Rod Glaser murder? I asked. This brought a glare and eventually, after a long wait, an interview with an on-duty detective. He nodded as I spoke, jotted the number of Wendy's pay phone, stared at his pad, and offered a perfunctory thank you. I said I wasn't finished yet. When I tried to outline the connections between Silicon Glamour, Rod, Sylvain, and Plush, he interrupted to thank me again and tell me the detectives knew how to do their job. I had the feeling he'd been warned not to listen to me—more of Rupert's handiwork.

The next place I swung and missed was the hotel where Rod's mother was staying. She didn't answer her phone and I could do no more than leave a message at the front desk. Strike three. I headed back up to the city to see if I had any clean clothes to wear for our date tonight, wondering how many outs I had left.

>> >> >> >> >>

Most of my expectations about our dates proved wrong. They did not call me and Wes "gentlemen." They did not maintain that either we or they were "high class." They gave no come-hither looks and let no lace peek out from under seams. They treated us like we were just a couple of guys they knew and we were all out for a pleasant and proper night on the town. I kept reminding myself that this was the result of training, and the training had been good.

Erika had a natural look. Her face was broad, open, and wholesome, her hair the color of freshly cut hay. She came across as the kind of hearty, athletic woman you might get to go skinny-dipping with if you were really lucky. She wore a sheer outer layer over a simple designer T-shirt, with a print skirt. Her friend Noela's pencil-lined eyes glinted with a more impish disposition. She wore a dark silk blouse, silver jewelry, and hip-hugging black pants.

We met them at a dinner club in San Jose, a retro place that had lost some of its charm because it knew retro was hip. The lounge was festive, with white lights strung across the ceiling and a parquet dance floor. We ate in the dining room, where the food was overpriced and the tablecloths too thick.

Wes and I bumped into each other doing things like pulling out chairs for our dates. I sat across from Erika. When she introduced herself, I'd swallowed a comment about having met before. I knew her voice; it had been the one speaking to Alissa's answering machine when I was inside the apartment.

Wes sat opposite Noela. He ordered a Manhattan and the table was inspired to follow suit. Noela had a healthy gulp of hers, but the level in Erika's glass decreased little in spite of her frequent sips, which she took with a smile.

I'd prepared a few opening lines, but Erika beat me to it with the first rule of dating: Let your date talk about himself. "So," she said, "tell us about your work!"

The effect on Wes was immediate. He talked about his company, which round of financing they were in, the excellence of their software, and their plans for expansion, as if offering a prospectus for investing in it—or in him as a mate. I was slightly embarrassed, but I knew it came from a nervousness about himself. He was a nerd at heart who felt he had to go out of his way to prove his bona fides in the "real" world.

Erika and Noela offered a picture of perfect fascination. They were also courteous enough not to leave me out. When Wes finally paused for air, Erika asked me what I did.

"I make films," I said suavely.

"What kind of films?" Noela said with nothing more than polite interest.

"Action-packed Silicon Valley stuff. You know, scheming CEO's, top-secret tech—in fact, you probably could tell me a lot about it. I'll bet you've met some crafty execs in your time."

Erika gave a giggle that went on a fraction of a second too long. "I really don't know very many CEO's. What happens in your story?"

"Well, maybe you can help me with it. We could use some consultants."

This brought laughs from both Erika and Noela. "Oh, the movie business is too slick for us," Noela said.

"Actually, my films are nonfiction. Well, as nonfictional as a corporate show can be. I do industrials and image pieces for companies in the Valley. The last one I did was for a guy named Rod Glaser."

I saw a brief contraction in Erika's eyes. She covered it quickly. This would be a delicate operation. I pulled back and said, "So, what movies have you seen lately? Anything good?" The question would take a good half hour to answer and would tell me something about the two.

"You know what's cool?" Noela said. "Those old James Bond movies, with Sean Connery. I've been watching them on DVD. He's so sexy."

Wes got excited. "I *loved* James Bond. I had a 007 lunchbox and—" He stopped short as it dawned on him he was dating himself. "You know what else, Austin Powers is really funny."

"Yeah!" Noela agreed. "That's why I started watching the old Bonds. Austin cracks me up. He's such a barney."

"We could shoot a groovy episode in this place." Wes gestured to the other room. "It's the right era, right?"

"It'd be perfect!" Noela said.

"I thought that updated *Romeo and Juliet* movie was good," Erika said. "You know, the one by the guy who did *Moulin Rouge*?"

"It was pretty interesting—the camera angles, the editing," I agreed, then realized I sounded like a film geek. "How about actors—who's your favorite?"

"I had the hugest crush on Leonardo when I was a teenager," she went on. "Now I think Vin Diesel is pretty hot."

"Right on," Noela agreed. "And Wesley Snipes."

The half hour passed and then some. Our dinner came, surf and turf, and I heard about the relative merits of young movie stars: which one was too seedy and which one too pretty, which too full of himself and which just right. There was a brief detour into music. Noela and Erika had their differences on hip-hop; Erika was more into the new loud bands. Again Wes and I dated ourselves by recalling their forebears, who themselves had been inspired by an earlier generation. We were in the era of third-degree retro.

On the whole I considered the diversion a success, since our dates seemed to have forgotten their job for a little while. Erika caught my quietness, though, and asked me, "What's your favorite movie, Bill? And why?"

I thought about what she'd relate to, or what would impress her, and then decided the hell with it. She'd proven herself good at seeing through bullshit. "There's an old Hitchcock film that always gets me. I've lost track of how many times I've seen it. *Shadow of a Doubt*." I tried to explain how what got me was the way this teenage girl named Charlie has a big, though innocent, crush on her uncle, played by Joseph Cotten. She's unwilling, right up until the last moment, to believe he's a murderer who would betray her.

"I'd like to see it," Erika said.

"I've never heard of those people," Noela said. "It sounds creepy."

The table was quiet for a moment. Dinner was done and the band in the lounge was tuning up. Wes extended a hand to Noela. "Let's dance."

I waited to catch Erika's eyes again. They were clear as a Sierra lake. I said, "I'm sorry if I startled you earlier when I mentioned Rod."

"Isn't Rod dead?" Her voice was neutral.

"Yes. Someone put a knife into his neck. I want to find Alissa. I'm concerned about her."

"She told me not to worry. That was two or three weeks ago. I didn't know what she meant at the time." Erika watched me, wary. "What's going on?"

"This date isn't purely social," I admitted.

"Don't worry about it. Guys schedule dates for all kinds of reasons. We don't get many filmmakers. I figured you had an agenda."

"I need your help, Erika. I need to know about Alissa."

She sat back, then smiled unexpectedly, her lips forming a sensuous curl. "Let's dance," she said. "I can tell a lot about a man by how he dances."

"Great," I said, getting to my feet. "That helps me feel real loose and relaxed."

The dance floor was not large. A Latin jazz combo was playing and the room was alive with sinuous motion. It was a nicely mixed crowd, old and young, chic and traditional. The young men were in form-fitting black T-shirts, the women in tight jeans, while the men with white hair wore suits and the women flared dresses. The older couples were slower but more elegant in their moves, a look of serene contemplation on their faces.

Erika and I plunged into the writhing crowd. Noela was teaching Wes how to samba. I laughed at his attempts to make his hips move like hers. Then I tried it myself and found out how hard it was. Erika didn't seem to mind. Her skirt swung in a nice counterpoint to her waist. We were carried along by the music, caught up in the motion. With each number we got a little closer, touched a little more often, until together we were making up our own version of the rhumba or whichever style was being played. The longer I danced, the less it seemed to matter whether I was following the rules.

When the band went into a slower number, I put my arm behind her back and we fell into an easy two-step. "It's fun to dance with you," she said.

"The only problem is the messages between my brain and my hips go astray. What does that tell you about me?"

"You dance from the heart. You don't pretend like you know it all. It's not your fault your hips are tight. That's how you were raised."

I moved in a little closer. "So there's hope for me?"

She threw in a little twist, and our thighs brushed. "It's never too late. You just need a few lessons."

We came closer yet. I felt the heat of her body through her clothes, the dampness of her back, her shape undulating with mine. Her head rested on my shoulder and I drifted with the music until I realized that might be just what she intended, leaving the question of Alissa to go unanswered. I started to speak but then took in a whiff of her hair and put it off a little longer.

When the number was over, she pulled back and checked her wrist. She must have an internal clock, I thought, because it was five minutes to twelve. The date was scheduled to end at midnight.

"You're about to turn into a pumpkin," I said. She gave a nod. I pulled her closer as the music began again. "What about Alissa?"

"Not here." Erika nodded at Noela, who was still dancing with Wes. "She wouldn't rat on me, but I have to be careful about this. *Really* careful." She moved a little closer. "I *am* worried about Alissa, though."

"Can we meet tomorrow?"

Erika made some mental calculations and said, "I'll be shopping in Union Square in San Francisco. Meet me at the Rotunda Restaurant at the top of Neiman Marcus. You know it?"

"I've heard of it."

"Come at noon. I'll get a table. But we have to have some signal I can give you in case it's not okay."

I thought for a second. "How about a scarf? Put it on if it's not okay."

"All right. All right, that's good. It'll be a red scarf." She put her eyes in front of mine and added, "I'm taking a big chance, Bill. If I'm wearing the scarf, leave."

The song ended. We clapped, then I bowed and kissed Erika's hand. She laughed and clicked back into associate mode. She found Noela, hooked arms with her, and thanked Wes for a wonderful evening.

"Can't we buy you a nightcap?" he said, scrambling to keep the date going. Midnight had snuck up on him. "How about a ride home?"

"We have our own car," Noela said. "Good night. Thank you."

We stood at the edge of the dance floor, waving good-bye. The only thing left was to repair to the bar for one last drink.

"Damn, Billy," Wes complained. "I was making progress."

"You mean with the dancing or the dating?"

"Both, I'd say. Noela was warming up."

"She timed it that way. I hope you didn't ask her about Alissa."

"No, I just tried to find out about the agency. She said she likes her job."

"They're both good at it. I wonder if Erika's really going to meet me for lunch tomorrow or if she's just setting me up."

Wes narrowed his eyes at the news, then broke out into a grin. "You *dog*. Did she say whether you have to pay for it?"

I looked into my glass. "I'm sure I'll pay for it. One way or another, I'll pay for it."

14

The elevator took its time rising to the fourth floor of Neiman Marcus on Union Square. I half expected to find Gary at the top, ready to teach me a lesson. The more I thought about it, the less likely it seemed that Rupert and Trisha hadn't known about the date last night. They'd been ahead of me every step so far, especially in putting their spin on Rod to the police. My jaw clamped as the elevator opened. If Erika showed up, it was probably only to lure me on.

The restaurant was near the top of the store's grand multitiered rotunda, with fluted columns rising to a lavishly decorated glass dome. Great windows looked out over the city. A small circular bar, set a few steps higher than the restaurant, was the first stop. The bar was jammed with people waiting for tables. I heard some Texas drawls and noticed a number of well-coiffed older men trolling for new catches.

I didn't catch sight of Erika's straw-blond hair until I turned the corner of the bar. She stood stiff and straight, letting the trollers know she wasn't available. Her neck was bare except for a small locket. She was fingering the scarf near her waist. I moved in quickly before she decided to put it on.

"Thank you for coming," I said.

"Whatever you do, don't act like we're on a date."

"You got it. This is a business meeting."

"Could you tell the hostess we're ready for our table? It's under my name."

We were taken to a small table hidden behind a column. The hostess smiled at Erika and said, "Is this is the one you wanted?"

She nodded. The table was hidden from the entrance and from most of the restaurant. A bowl of consommé was placed before us. After a few discreet glances, Erika settled a little more at ease into her chair. She opened the menu and said, "I always start with a champagne cocktail."

Her voice was different than last night. It was faster, sharper, carrying a hint of disdain. She wore a close-fitting sleeveless top that stopped just above her belly button, and low-riding, hip-hugging pants. Her eyes seemed oddly luminous, and then I realized they were a different color than last night. She was wearing blue-tinted contacts. Her lipstick today was strawberry; last night it had been clear. The nature-girl image had been replaced by an air of glamorous caprice.

A waitress came to take our order. Erika got the lobster club on brioche. On her recommendation, I started with the lobster bisque. My plan was to continue ordering as needed to keep her at the table.

"This room is amazing," I said. "I've never been to Needless Markup before."

She pressed her lips together: She took the place seriously and didn't appreciate the nickname. I myself had never presumed to shop here. I corrected my error by raving a little more about the rotunda, then got down to business. I described my relationship with Rod, our first discovery that Alissa was missing, and Rod's eventual revelation that she worked for Silicon Glamour. Erika said she'd never met Rod.

The waitress came with my bisque and a basket of popovers. "Would you like to try some?" I asked.

"Oh, I have," she said. "Keep going. I want to hear more before I say anything."

I mentioned that Rod liked Alissa, but didn't mention his suspicions about her. I described Wendy's stunt at the dinner. Finally I told Erika how I found Rod in his house that night. She stopped sipping her champagne. "That's horrible," she whispered.

I let the silence stretch. One by one the bubbles broke from the side of her glass and rose to the surface. "I come here once a month," Erika said at last. "I do my shopping. SG gives us a generous allowance. I buy a few things for myself. The rest are for the persona, that crunchy girl you dated last night. Alissa had lunch with me here once. She liked the food, but it's not her kind of place. She's no droop, she does have her own style, but . . . I don't think she fits in very well at SG."

"How does she not fit in?"

Erika shook her hair, then fluffed it with her fingers. Her strawberry lips, her small nose, her pencil-lined eyes were defined perfectly on her face. "I don't think she fully realized what the work was about . . . dates. She talked about how she wanted to move to the business side, but she'd just started. She had a long way to go to earn out her contract."

"It's a four-year contract, right? And she has three left?"

"At least. She hasn't even been working for a year yet. It takes that long to learn the ropes and groom your identity. Rupert's a genius. He can look at you and draw out a character you didn't even know you had inside. It's not you, but it's like your cousin or something, it totally makes sense that you could have been that person. He shows you what to wear, how to move your hands, how to lift your head, how to walk. He gives you certain words to use."

Erika's hands were inscribing arabesques. The direct, economical motions of last night were gone. I imagined each gesture, item of clothing, posture, and word selection as an element in a cipher. Each SG persona came with a grammar and syntax of its own.

"It allows you to keep your personal life personal. It's like being an actress," I said.

"Kind of, only better paying. It's a sort of disguise, but at the same time it comes so natural that it doesn't feel like work after a while. When you come home you can take it off and put it away in your closet."

"I do something similar in my job. Take an ordinary scene and put the right lenses, lighting, angles, filters in front of it and you've got magic."

"I like the magic." She smiled.

I smiled back. "Anyway, you said Alissa was unhappy at SG. The dating part bugged her."

"She could do it, she just didn't like it. She kept going on about moving over to the business side. I finally told her to shut up and enjoy the perks. I mean, my life is so much more comfortable than it was before. They give you an apartment, a car, good pay, special bonuses."

"But the bonuses don't involve sex?" I was double-checking.

Her nose wrinkled. "No. Most of the guys are *old*."

"So how do you feel about Rupert and Trisha? Are you treated well?"

"Mostly. They're totally super when you play by their rules. Rupert's very sweet. He's the manager. Trisha started the business. She's in charge."

"Do you know what her connection is to Sylvain Partners? Or Plush Biologics?"

"Well, I know about Plush," Erika said. "Some of us have tried Eternaderm. We get it for free."

"Nice deal. Does it work?"

She drew a finger down her cheek. The skin was smooth as butter. "It was fun to try. I think I might save it for when I'm older, though."

"Are Trisha and Connie Plush buddies?"

"I don't know about that. Some associates do modeling for Plush and work at trade shows. I think Alissa did something like that."

"She did. How do *you* get along with Trisha?"

Erika looked down. "She's fine—you just don't want to get on her bad side."

"What gets you on her bad side?"

"Whining. Not doing your job. Not earning your bonuses."

"And what do you have to do for the bonuses?"

A look of alarm crossed her face and then I realized it was just the waitress behind us. Erika didn't want to be overheard by anyone. The waitress placed Erika's club on the table and asked me if I'd be having anything else. I said I'd have the luau pork sandwich.

Erika picked a bit of lobster from her plate. Then she looked up at me with the kind of look that happens when you're about to sleep with someone for the first time and you suddenly wonder if it's a good idea. "Who *are* you, Bill?"

I wanted to hear about these bonuses, so I gave her the biography. I grew up in Davis, in the Sacramento Valley. My parents were anthropologists. They split up when I was thirteen. I had a camera in my hands from a young age. My siblings went along with the elaborate science-fiction scenarios I created and recorded on home movies. Film was my real love, but somehow I'd gotten drawn into the dot-com madness. Now, spit out the other end, I was regaining my bearings, remembering what it was I really wanted to do with my life. I shot industrials to make money. I played in a pickup basketball game every Thursday night, surfed at Linda Mar when I got the chance, and went to movies. I'd never been married. I had a small flat in Potrero Hill and still drove the old four-wheel-drive Scout my family had bought when I was a kid. That made Erika smile.

She fingered the locket around her neck. "This is one of the few things I have from my family. A picture of my grandmother is inside. She lived in L.A., she was very glamorous."

Erika showed me a tiny photograph of a woman wrapped in a fur coat. "She was beautiful." I waited another moment, then said, "So do you want to tell me about the bonuses?"

Erika exhaled. "We don't have to do that much, really. On any date, you want to draw the guy out, let him talk about himself, right? Most of them don't take much prodding. Others, the shy ones, are hard to get started, but once they do, you can't stop them. Anyway, we get them to talk about their work and then report whatever is interesting to Rupert."

"So what does Rupert do with these tips? Invest?"

Her right shoulder twitched in a delicate shrug. "All I know is that if it turns out to be good, a bonus appears in our checks. The whole thing is a pain, but it's worth the extra money. Alissa felt weird about it, especially with Rod. She said she couldn't do it anymore. I said, You can't quit. I mean, I don't know that it's so wrong. It's what everyone does in the Valley. It's the kind of stuff you'd hear at a cocktail party. Why shouldn't SG be invited to those cocktail parties, too?"

I nodded. Erika had just helped me clarify why Rupert and Trisha would be dining with the men from Sylvain. "That's helpful information. I won't tell anyone it came from you." I smiled at her, and paused while the waitress put my food in front of me. "I have to admit, I wasn't sure what to expect at our lunch today."

"You mean which one's the real me?"

"Well, I thought someone from SG might come with you."

Her lips pursed in a smile she was trying to hold back. "So you believe me now?"

I could see only shining honesty in her eyes. I wondered why she wanted to play this game all of a sudden. Maybe it was a test. "Yes," I said. "But I've been fooled before."

She laughed. "You should meet Rupert. He always knows when I'm lying."

"I've met him. Maybe he's not as accurate with men."

"He wouldn't have let on. Every word you said to him, he knew which one was true and which wasn't."

"Doesn't that scare you, then, that he might find us out?"

The playfulness dropped from her face. "Oh my God, that would be a disaster."

"What would they actually do? Fire you?"

"I've never heard of them hurting an associate, but . . ." She thought for a moment. "Well, there was someone who committed suicide a couple of years ago. And sometimes people just disappear—we're told that they were dismissed, but who knows?"

"Then I'm even more grateful to you for taking the risk. You must care about Alissa."

Her eyes went liquid. "I do. She's so sweet and she's trying so hard. She brings out something in me, like I want to take care of her—like she's my little sister, even though she's older than me."

"Do you know what was going on between her and Rod?" I asked. "Was she in love with him?"

Erika pushed her empty plate away. "Good question. At first she talked about how geeky he was but also how she looked forward to seeing him. He was her most reliable client. I think he scheduled dates just to give her business, or maybe to keep her away from other clients. Then as it went along, Alissa got more careful about how much she told me. It kind of hurt that she didn't confide in me anymore. I don't know—I think she felt she could trust me, but maybe she didn't want to put me in an awkward position." Erika looked down and pulled at a finger. Her hurt was real. "How did Rod feel about Alissa?"

"Also a good question. I think he did love her. But he didn't want to admit it. He had a hard time believing she felt the same way. He told me most engineers have had the experience, in college or grad school, of having a love interest blink her eyes and say, 'Can you do a little code for me?' For free, of course. After the guy's been burned, he's suspicious of women until he knows what they're after. Rod's fear was that Alissa was taking him for a ride."

Erika shook her head. "I doubt it. She explained what turned her on about him to me once. She said it was his gaze. He's really intensely involved in his work. When he fixes that intense concentration on *you,* it's incredibly sexy. Her feelings were real, I think—unless she was a way better actress than I give her credit for." Erika finished her drink, then added, "I *would* like to know where the fuck she went."

The anger surprised me. "Aren't you afraid something happened to her?"

"Yeah. But I'd rather believe she left on her own. There have been people in her apartment. I don't know what they were doing. I live in the same building, but I'm scared to go by and check anymore."

I feigned innocence. "Do you have any idea who it was? I imagine Rupert could get in."

"I'm sure he could. He probably did, to try to find out where she went."

"What about her boyfriend?"

Erika's eyes narrowed. "What boyfriend?"

"I thought she had one. A younger guy. Maybe I'm wrong. What about Wendy, Alissa's mother?"

"I met her once. She's a wild thing." A grin snuck across her face. "She and Alissa and I got drunk one night, did some blow, talked about guys. . . . I was amazed, my mother would cut her wrists before she'd do something like that. Alissa did complain that Wendy always wanted more and more from her. I doubt she had a key to the apartment, though. SG only gives out one, and it's not supposed to be copied."

"Do you have any idea how to contact Wendy?"

"None at all. Sorry."

"How about getting inside Alissa's apartment?"

She cocked her head and looked away. Maybe I'd pushed my luck too far.

"Let me think about it," she replied. "Like I said, Alissa has the only key."

Our plates were taken away and the waitress asked if we wanted dessert. Erika said no. I asked for some coffee and the check. Erika excused herself to use the bathroom.

My coffee came, but no check. When she returned, her face was fresh with makeup. "It's time to shop," she said. "Nice having brunch with you."

"How about if I join you for a few more minutes?"

She glanced around, then smiled. "I guess it would be okay. I haven't noticed any fishy eyeballs on me. It's fun talking to you."

That made me smile back. "Great. I'm just waiting for the check."

She waved a receipt at me. "That's sweet of you. But it's on me." Then she whirled and led the way to the escalator.

» » » » »

All I saw of the black leather jacket was the zipper. The jacket must have been open. The zipper was peeking from behind a column as we left the Rotunda Restaurant. I didn't think much of it, or the fact that the wearer of the jacket had stepped behind the column, until I noticed the jacket again in the lingerie department.

I had to wonder why Erika chose that particular department. Either she was flirting with me or she wanted to have a little fun at my expense. We'd wandered through the store for a few minutes and she'd tossed off comments about the various designer labels: which one was meant to display good breeding and which one meant you were trying too hard, why this label was worn by the new rich but not that one. As we'd passed a corner showing some heavy denim, she'd said, "Now we're in your territory. Except you're, like, the original. You don't even know you've got the look."

"What look is that?"

"The scruffy artist-craftsman look. You were just itching to get out of your suit last night. You look nice today, but you need some new pants. And new shoes."

"Wait a minute, these are not only the most comfortable boots I've ever owned, they can handle having a C-stand dropped on them. I do need some pants, though."

"You can't afford them here. We'll go down the street and find you a good pair of black pants. No pleats."

Then, with an innocent glance, she led me into lingerie. She asked me what I thought of a particularly vivid hue of green panties. "I need a new pair of lucky underwear," she said, dimples folding her cheeks.

I told her the truth, which was I thought she'd look great in them. She laughed at how my hands were stuffed into my pockets.

You don't see many men in lingerie. A black leather jacket stands out. I caught sight of it again and the frame of the young man wearing it. It resembled the silhouette of the James Dean type who'd come to Rod's door nine days ago. He stepped back among the hooks and straps, but they didn't provide much cover. I started toward him. He disappeared in a hurry.

"Ready to go?" I said to Erika.

"Oh, I've just begun to shop."

"But if we're going to get me some pants, we should go now."

She laughed again, and I let her think my discomfort came from hanging out in the underwear. She made her purchase and we left the vaulted halls of Neiman Marcus. I had to admit it had taken longer for me to get a headache there than in most department stores. We went down the street to the kind of store that would have the kind of pants for the kind of person I was. Erika took me to the second floor. She knew just the pair for me. They were a fine weave, midnight black, soft but with some structure. I scanned the store before going inside the dressing room to try them on. There was no sign of the leather jacket man.

"Well, come on," Erika called into the dressing room. "Let's see them. You could be hot if you tried."

Once again her honesty gave me pause. Not that I thought I was so hot, just that people didn't usually say to your face that you fell short.

She was right about the pants. The cut was perfect. I was zipping them when I heard her say, "Stop it, Brendon. I don't know where she is." Her voice became frantic. "*Stop it!*"

I charged out the door and saw the guy in the leather jacket twisting Erika's arm. They were on the other side of a clothes rack. When he saw me coming, he used his free hand to push the rack at me. I had to do a quick shuffle to keep it from landing on my stocking feet. Erika bent and squirmed out of his grip, but he caught her by the hair. I climbed over the rack and hit him with a tackle to the hip. We tumbled to the floor. Erika screamed in pain as he pulled her hair before letting go. She got to her feet and yelled for help. Brendon aimed blows at my head as he tried to extricate himself from my tackle. I had to loosen my grip on him to fend them off. He scrambled to his feet. I scrambled to mine and took off after him.

A young guy, not very big, hurried down the aisle in our direction, speaking urgently into a headset. He tried to block Brendon's way. "Sir! Please—" was all he got out before Brendon shoved him to the floor.

"Call security!" I said as I went by.

"I'm *trying*," he said from his prone position.

I was losing ground. The unsewn legs of my pants flapped under my feet. The tags rattled on the waistband. More people with headsets converged on us. None of them carried much heft. Brendon pushed clothing racks into their paths.

Brendon burst through a door marked STAFF ONLY. I thought this was a mistake on his part: They'd subdue him in there. I was wrong. There weren't a lot of people among the wheeled racks, sorting benches, and sewing machines. The few who were cowered from him. Brendon grabbed a pair of shears.

"How do I get out!" he demanded of a seamstress.

She pointed to an indistinct place behind some stacked wardrobe boxes. He raced in that direction. I grabbed a couple of shirts on my way after him and wound them around my forearm. When I got to the wardrobe boxes, I threw myself into them, toppling the stack, hoping they'd bring him down.

As I picked my way through the fallen boxes, I saw a metal door with an alarmed exit handle. There was movement near the door. Brendon's head emerged from under a pile of dresses that had dumped from a box. He had a stubborn jutting jaw and wide, piercing eyes. His blond hair had fallen across his forehead.

"Stay out of this!" he yelled, brandishing the shears.

He was struggling to get to his feet. I kept coming at him. He whipped his arms free and flung the shears at me like a knife. I raised my forearm. The shears rotated once and struck, point first, into the material wrapped around my arm.

I jumped for him as he got up and brought him back down among the dresses. His black boots kicked at me. I got hold of one, then the other, and raised them high in the air.

"Why are you here?" I demanded.

"Stay out of it!"

He writhed to escape my grip, his hands grasping for my ankles. I kicked him as hard as I could in the ribs, twice. The pain rocketed up through my foot, but the effect on him was greater. He coughed, gasped for breath, and stopped his struggle.

"Tell me what you want," I said, gasping myself. "You're Alissa's boyfriend, aren't you?"

He glared at me, then a mocking smile crossed his face. "Yeah." The words came out staccato, punctuated by hard breaths. "That's it. I'm in love with her. That's right."

"Tell me!" I said, shaking his legs. "I know who you are. You came to Rod's house a few days before he was killed."

Voices sounded behind me. Hands grabbed me by the shoulders and forced me to let go of Brendon. His feet hit the floor. "Watch out you're not next," he said.

"Grab him," I said to the security staff. "He attacked a customer."

But I was in their way and so were the boxes. They must have assumed he wouldn't go out the alarmed door. Brendon got casually to his feet, appearing to have given up the chase. His smile still mocked me as he turned and, in one quick motion, pushed open the door. The alarm shrieked. He disappeared down the fire escape.

15

I had a strange moment when I woke up the next morning, Monday. Images of the garments from the store—the cuts and colors, the racks and hangers—and Erika, her golden hair, the way her mouth playfully formed words, the light streaming through the Rotunda's glass dome, came back to me. And I thought to myself: Wait until Rod hears about this. He'll have some amusing observation to offer.

And then the memory of his death slammed back into me. So did the image of Brendon's sneer and the scissors catapulting toward me. He'd escaped, leaving Erika and me to make explanations to the store security people. They'd apologized, then awarded me the black pants I was still wearing as a consolation prize. Erika left quickly after that, promising to tell more about Brendon by phone today.

So I would have to relate the story instead to Mike Riley, my new boss. Algoplex had a brisk air this morning, the air of work to be done. I sensed a desperation under the briskness. When I found Mike in his office, I asked him how the sessions with Sylvain had gone over the weekend.

"We're in trouble, Bill," he said. "It's just as I thought. They were nice about the key-man at first, but now they're lowering the boom."

I sat myself down in a leather chair. "They want to pull out?"

"That's not how they put it. They claim Algoplex still has promise, but it lost 30 percent of its value when Rod died. Not only do they want that 30 percent, they want to push our peformance targets forward. They could end up with outright control. Plus, in addition to installing their own CFO, they're telling me we have to bring on a hotshot engineer they've found as CTO because we've got no one qualified to promote from within."

"And the key-man clause gives them the power to do all of this."

"The only surprise is they haven't walked already. This hotshot claims he's looked at our software and it's not powerful enough to do the simulations we promised. I don't see how he could have figured that out so fast."

"Unless Sylvain had it for longer than we think," I said. "If Alissa stole files from Rod, then Rupert could have passed them to Sylvain weeks ago."

"Jesus. This is getting worse and worse. I'm not going to give in, Bill."

"You're counting on Rod's insurance money to pull you through if Sylvain dissolves the deal?"

"I was." Mike was marching back and forth in front of me. I wondered if he'd picked up the habit from Rod. But his pacing was springy and aggressive, while Rod's had been nervous and preoccupied. "Sylvain tried to shoot that down, too. They said the insurance company will take a good long look at the circumstances of Rod's death. Yeah, they've got me bent over, all right."

"What are your choices now?"

Mike sat back down at his desk and bounced a pencil on its eraser. "I can accept their terms, which I won't. I can hope for the insurance money, which may take too long. I can try to raise more from Rod's private investors, but one of them is already making noises about cashing out—to Sylvain, of course." He stopped and stared at me. "So I don't know, Bill. My other option is to punt. The company goes bankrupt and Sylvain ends up with the lion's share of the assets, anyway. I need you to find out what happened to Rod. Soon."

"They're taking full advantage of Rod's death. Almost like they knew it was coming."

Mike stopped and gave me a curious look. "You're kidding, right?"

I didn't reply. I'd wanted to see how it sounded.

"I can't picture it. I know these guys, Bill, I know how they play. They're tough, they'll bite and kick in the scrum, but actual murder? No way."

"What about Trisha Evans? She's in bed with Sylvain. In fact, it looked to me like she was the one holding the whip."

"Maybe Trisha's got something on them. Something they'd rather their families not know about."

"Maybe. But exactly how wide are they going to open their checkbooks to her? Never mind—that's for me to find out. Next time you meet with the Sylvain guys, I want you to bug them about SG. Tell me how they respond."

Mike nodded. "Will do. Did you get a chance to talk to Detective Coharie?"

"No," I said, and told him about my fruitless visit to the station on Saturday.

"I guess they don't want to have to answer every question and pursue every speculation from friends and relatives," Mike said. "But hey, the detective told me something very strange this morning. He said that knife in Rod's hand might not be the one that killed him. The blade didn't match with the wound."

"That ought to take care of their suicide theory. Did you say that to Coharie?"

"Yes, but not exactly in that tone. Don't take this the wrong way, Bill, but it might not help for you to barge into places like you do. That Sylvain dinner Friday night, for instance. It may have contributed to their putting the screws to us. Keep your investigation low-key."

"Sure, Mike. I'd hate to offend Rod's killers."

Mike rearranged the objects on his desk, as if trying to solve some kind of Rubik's cube. "Come on, play fair. You know I want them as much as you do. Let's kick their butts if Trisha or Sylvain are the ones. That reminds me, I forgot to mention something else. Sylvain wants Algoplex's name changed. They want a more bio-oriented name. That kills me. Why not just spit on Rod's grave?"

"No need," I answered. "They're the ones who dug it."

»   »   »   »   »

Upon further reflection, Mike had a point. As much as I wanted to throw an accusation in someone's face, I didn't know whose face to aim at. Nor did I have details to back up my conclusions. I'd have to go the polite route. It was usually a better way to get information if you lacked the leverage of search warrants and subpoenas.

I assumed I'd get nothing from Trisha and Rupert Evans, so I went to Plush Biologics. It was close to noon. The receptionist was a little nicer to me this time, but said Ellen Quong wasn't at her desk. I asked the receptionist to page her. Ellen was in the lab. I said it was urgent. A technician came to escort me inside.

The one-story building was a maze of partitions and corridors. The labs were in the back, on the opposite side from Connie's executive office. Ellen was in her lab coat and goggles. I was required to put on the same outfit before I could go in to the lab. She showed me some tissue in a shallow plastic container with wells. "It's looking fresh, don't you think?" she said.

"Is that skin?" It looked like a thin sheet of pinkish-beige Swiss cheese.

"Yes, we use it to test compounds we're developing."

I wanted to ask her a lot of things, but right now the first question that came to mind was, "Where do you get skin like that?"

"A lot of it's harvested from cadavers. Nice thigh and back pieces, undamaged by sun or cosmetics." She pointed at a gray device that looked like an oversize razor with a thick electric cord and a single large blade. "You use a dermatome to peel it off."

I hefted it. It was heavy. "You get all your skin this way?"

"We use a lot of pig skin, of course. And new sources for dermal cells are popping up. Researchers in Wisconsin came upon an immortal cell line, a population of keratinocytes in a petri dish that just keeps stratifying and multiplying into normal skin. It's become quite a business for them. The line originated with a discarded foreskin. An especially happy one, I guess."

A crawly feeling came over my own skin. "Before or after it was cut off?"

"I believe the mutation happened in the dish, so—after."

"Sorry, Ellen, but that's weird."

She let out one of her booming laughs. "Lots of things like this are going on in the dermal-replacement field. Skin is being grown for burn and wound victims, as I'm sure you know. One company is using cadaver skin, another is growing artificial skin from bovine collagen. Growth factors are being engineered. Nipples are being made in the lab, too. They're constructed from pig ear ligaments. Whole breasts are next, using the woman's own fat cells. They can be grown right on site in the body."

"For women who've had mastectomies?"

"Right. But of course, there's also the cosmetic market. The company thinks they can sell two hundred fifty thousand a year. Don't worry, you guys aren't being left behind: Scientists at Harvard are growing rabbit penises in the lab. The skin's the easy part, it's the corpus cavernosum that's hard. But they succeeded by growing the cells in a collagen matrix. Apparently the reconstructed thing's fairly functional."

I watched her wrap the skin and put it back in the refrigerator. "It's easy to forget that skin is an organ like any other," I said. "You identify with it so much."

"We'd look kind of creepy without it. I suppose muscle tone would become even more important than it is now. You know, people are working on enhancements for IGF-1, the gene that regulates muscle growth. I don't know how the Olympics are going to test for that." She put her hands on her hips and looked around the lab. It was similar to other biotech labs I'd seen, with spectrophotometers, a gas chromatograph, and a clutter of beakers, tubes, autoclaves, balances, mixers, viscometers, and Rotovapors spread across the benches. "I'd love to sit around and chat with you, Bill, but I suppose I should ask what you're here for."

"I have some questions. Can we go to your office?"

We left our lab coats and goggles by the door and went into Ellen's office. It was a practical place, taken up mostly with books, journals, and a few family photographs. I closed the door, then sat across from her at her desk. "It's confidential."

She looked at the door in mock alarm and said, "Don't tell me. You've got a crush on Mrs. Plush. Sorry, she's taken."

I laughed. "Did she say anything about me to you?" When Ellen shook her head, I said, "I want to ask you about Sylvain Partners. What can you tell me?"

She spread her hands. "They've got the bags of money and they give some of them to us. That's the extent of my knowledge. Too much else on my plate."

"Have you heard of an outfit called Silicon Glamour? Trisha and Rupert Evans run it. They provide dates for executives. Alissa worked for them."

"Nope. I've got all the dates I need with my husband and daughter and dog."

"They're connected to Sylvain somehow. You probably know that Rod had a key-man clause in the deal with Sylvain and Plush. With Rod gone, Sylvain is threatening to take the money-bags away."

"I apologize, I shouldn't be joking around. I suppose you can't blame them for worrying about the future without Rod. But it would be a mistake for us to pull out of the deal. I need that technology right now to develop the next Eternaderm, the one that will work on collagen. It could blow tretinoin away."

"Well, the whole deal with Sylvain may fall apart. They're trying to use Rod's death to take control of the company."

"I'm going to speak to Ronald and Connie," Ellen said. "If we lose the deal, we'll lose months in our development cycle. You know, it seems to me we had a similar battle with Sylvain here at Plush. During our last round of funding, come to think of it— a fight about equity ownership. I wish I could tell you the details. Like I said, I'm busy with my skin."

"Who did they battle with, Dr. Plush?"

"Yes, Ronald was quite steamed, as I recall. His pate turned a brilliant red. Connie was the one on the front lines, though."

"Has there been any internal conflict here over the deal with Algoplex?"

"Not that I recall. Connie was skeptical at first, but I think we won her over. There's also been some grumbling about personnel lately: people let go, new people put in. My staff is intact, but Sylvain could be directing the changes."

"Anything else? Especially in the last five days?"

Ellen touched her finger to her nose. "There was a big fuss about a woman who came in today. She had some kind of injury, she was pleading for help. Connie booted her out."

"Who was this woman?"

"She was young, pretty, blond. Something happened to her face. I heard the name Erika."

Ellen was startled by the speed at which I was on my feet. "Is Connie in?"

"I believe so. Unless she's gone to—"

"Thanks," I called on my way out the door.

>> >> >> >> >>

After a few minutes of backtracking through the Plush maze, asking for directions more than once, I found the array of desks in front of Connie's office. She was giving instructions to an assistant. An expensive-looking couple, wearing their coats, waited nearby. They could have been social friends, stockholders, or potential clients, and probably were all three. They looked to be on their way to lunch.

I stepped in and asked Connie why an injured woman asking for treatment had been sent away. Fury flared in her eyes, then she ordered, "In my office."

I waited by the door to make sure she didn't attempt an escape. She excused herself to her friends and we went inside. "Don't *ever* interrupt me like that again."

"Why did you send Erika away?" I watched her closely. There was no widening of the eyes at the name. "You knew her, didn't you?"

"I have tried to tell you, Bill. Get out of this business. Just get out and don't look back."

"What happened to her?"

"*You* happened to her. When are you going to learn? Everyone you touch gets hurt. You have no regard for their safety."

"So you're part of it. You, Rupert, and Trisha did whatever was done to Erika."

"That is such an ignorant statement I can't even respond to it."

She appeared truly offended, but I wasn't buying it. "You all are too cowardly to come after me, is that it? Someone sent Brendon after Erika yesterday. Today they finished the job."

Connie folded her arms and looked away, as though fed up with an especially slow pupil. "What's it going to take, Bill? Another death because you insist on intruding? Well, keep pushing. You'll get it."

"You're only convincing me there's a lot more to find out. You've had your own battles with Sylvain. Tell me what they're up to with Algoplex."

A small pool of moisture had gathered in the corners of Connie's eyes. She turned abruptly so I couldn't see her dab them. The emotion was so out of place, I regretted for a moment having discarded my politeness strategy. But as she opened the door for me to exit, the chill returned to her voice. "Don't ruin my luncheon, Bill. Just leave quietly."

>> >> >> >> >>

Erika did not answer her cell phone, so I drove straight to the apartment building. She'd indicated she lived in the same one as Alissa, but I didn't know which unit and I'd never heard her last name. The directory listed three tenants with E first names. I memorized their apartment numbers and waited for someone to approach the gate. That could have taken some time on a Monday afternoon, but only a minute later I heard the metal gate being unlocked from inside. I pretended I was just on my way to open it myself. I smiled at a middle-aged man in a hat and overcoat on my way into the courtyard. He turned to watch me. I hurried up the walk before he could object.

The apartments were split into two wings. Two of the E's were in the wing on the left, so I started there. The door to the building hadn't closed all the way. The foyer was rather grand, with vaulted ceilings and a painting of a Casbah scene. I ran up the stairs to the second floor, then to the fourth floor. No one answered at either door, in spite of my banging and calls for Erika. No neighbors whom I could ask opened their doors or came down the hallway. The manager likely had ties to SG, so I avoided him.

I was on my way down when I encountered the man I'd passed on the way in. He was waiting at the bottom of the stairs. I nodded to him, and as I squeezed by, he said, "Bill."

I turned. Before I had noticed only the short white hair and the crow's feet around his eyes. Now I saw that his face lacked expression of any sort. So did his voice. I made for the door. It opened in front of me. Blocking it was a young man in a heavy jacket. They had me trapped.

I allowed the older man to herd me outside and around the corner of the building. I'd stick around long enough to hear what he had to say. We stood on a patch of grass, the younger man blocking my route to the gate.

"You must be a friend of Gary's," I said.

The older man looked at the other one. "He's Bill, all right."

The younger man didn't react. His age and build were similar to Brendon's, but he had a more fatalistic slouch. Brendon's James Dean aura had been manufactured with a haircut, a leather jacket, and a sneer. This guy's eyes were as flat as his partner's voice.

"You're smart all right," I said. "Why isn't Gary here? Too easily identified with the company, I guess."

"Jesus, you are full of stupid questions." The older man did all the talking.

"What do you want with me?"

"No problems for you, Bill." His mouth stayed open. The smile was purely mechanical. "It's your friends who are in danger. It's selfish of you."

"You should have told me earlier."

"Now you know."

"This is kind of vague. Which friends?"

"Can't tell you, Bill."

His manner was so assured, I was dumb enough to believe he'd leave me with only the threat. The young guy's fist came out of nowhere. I was on the grass before I knew it. I felt the blow but not yet the pain. A tooth rinsed around with blood in my mouth.

The older man's patent-leather toe was poised in front of my eyes. "Mind your own business," he said, not raising his voice. I shut my eyes in anticipation of the next blow. It didn't come. By the time I looked again, the men were at the gate. I deposited the tooth in my shirt pocket, got shakily to my feet, and staggered to the gate in time to see a brown Mercedes pulling away.

16

I was not well. Wes was feeding me whiskey and the room was getting cloudy. The hospital had given me Vicodin. Wes insisted that the drink would finish the job and, as I lay flat on my back on my living room sofa, my judgment was impaired enough to listen to him.

Wes had brought steaks, which was thoughtful except for the fact that I couldn't chew. He looked crestfallen when I reminded him of that, then he topped off my glass. The whiskey did a nice job of secondary cauterizing on the hole in my mouth where gauze had been, and before that my tooth. Silver nitrate sticks in the ER had done the primary job. The doctor's initial concern had been that my jaw had been fractured or dislocated. The X-rays came out negative. After she satisfied herself that I could swallow and was reasonably clear in the mind, she let me leave.

It was when my head hit the sofa pillow that the pain really came on. I called Wes first, then Mike, to warn them to be on the lookout for the two guys. Wes, when he arrived, launched into his own story about a collision between his nose and a surfboard. There was a lot of blood and a realignment of cartilage and bone. For some reason his story did not cheer me up.

"You keep resting, Billy," he said. "I'll char these steaks and figure out a way for you to get one down."

The blood thumped in my face like a big bass drum. But after a while, Dr. Wes's medicine had its effect. I had the illusion of feeling good enough to sit up and move my jaw. I tried Erika again.

A woman answered her cell phone. She wanted a complete biography from me before admitting Erika was there. I had to repeat my name several times. In the background I heard her say, "Do you know someone named *Bihhh*?"

"Hi, Bill." It was Erika's voice, small and timid.

When I said hello back, she understood immediately that I'd been attacked, too. I went first with my story, if only to explain why I was talking so funny. Then I asked about her.

It had happened this morning. She was leaving her building when someone threw a pint of liquid in her face. She had only a glimpse of a shape. It tallied with the young guy who'd sucker-punched me.

At first Erika thought she'd been blinded. She rolled on the grass, screaming and clutching her eyes, until she realized there was no pain; the liquid had not been acid. Her vision began to clear. But she could tell by the reactions of people who'd come to help that something terrible had happened. She ran back upstairs.

"You can see the pattern of how the liquid splattered across my face. I don't know what the stuff was. Everywhere it touched my skin, it turned it bone white. My face looks like a drop cloth. It's horrible. The first thing I did was cover every mirror in the apartment."

I said how sorry I was and how responsible I felt.

"I guess I should feel lucky to still be *in* my skin. But this is awful, Bill. I went to the Plush clinic because I thought Dr. Plush would remember me. Mrs. Plush sent me away, no sympathy, no concern, nothing. I couldn't believe my ears. I was crying, I made such a scene—it was embarrassing. The hospital didn't know what to tell me. The damage to the skin is mainly in the discoloration. They're analyzing the liquid. I was afraid to go home, so I'm at a friend's house."

"I am really sorry, Erika," I repeated. "I hate to say this, but I think Silicon Glamour is behind the attacks on both of us. They've proven they've got guys violent enough to have killed Rod. What can you tell me about Brendon?"

"He was a favorite of Trisha's. It seemed like he could get away with anything. I don't know why—" Her voice cracked and she sobbed. "I don't know what he had against me. He wanted me to get away from you when we were in the store. I wouldn't go. Then he started saying I knew where Alissa was. He tried to drag me off. I couldn't believe how he was acting. It was like he was possessed."

"Was it Alissa he was upset about, or me?"

"Both. I think more Alissa. He . . . well, he did have a big crush on her. She was out of bounds: We weren't allowed to date other associates. But Brendon had it really bad for Alissa. He wanted me to be, like, his advocate or something. I knew Alissa wasn't interested."

"He told me he was in love with her, but he said it in a weird way, like actually he hated her. Where can I find him, other than at the SG office?"

"I don't know. I don't know what to do, Bill." Her voice cracked again. "I mean, I don't think I can go back to Silicon Glamour, ever. They were teaching me a lesson."

"I'm afraid you're right. What about Alissa's apartment? You said you might be able to get me inside."

There was a long silence. "I just don't know if I feel like it, Bill. I *do* want you to get these guys, I want them to *pay*. But I also want you to keep me out of it. I've done my bit."

"I know, and I'm sorry to have to ask. But if we can nail Rupert and Trisha, we can probably find out what substance they had those guys throw on you."

She let out a long sigh. "When you put it like that . . . Call me again tomorrow."

"Thanks, Erika, I will."

I thought back to the elevator ride up to the Rotunda and how I wondered if Erika was about to betray me. She'd trusted me; she'd taken a risk for me and she'd paid for it. The damage to her face could be permanent. I began to feel more depressed than I already was.

"That's a good boy," Wes said as I took another sip of whiskey. He bore two sizzling steaks fresh off the grill. I made a comment about needing a blender to eat. Wes held up a finger for patience, then painstakingly cut the steak into tiny bits. His cooking skills did not extend beyond the grill, so our side dishes consisted of potato chips and salad from a bag.

A pleasant fuzziness oozed from my head down through my body after dinner. Wes, inspired by our date with Noela and Erika, loaded a copy of *Dr. No* into the DVD. Wes asked me what was happening with Algoplex. I filled him in. I also told him about the SG-Sylvain connection and the associates' mission to gather insider information from their dates. A slightly sick look came over Wes's face.

"And you thought Noela was curious about your company for its own sake," I said. "I assume Trisha turns around and makes investment decisions based on what she hears, like people in the Hamptons do."

"I'm going to have to review what I told her," Wes admitted. "But what's Sylvain's role? They're VC's, not money managers."

"They could have used information from Alissa in crafting the deal with Algoplex."

"Right. You should find out if the deal was initiated before or after Alissa came on the scene. Her data may have spurred their interest."

"Mike was the one who set up the first date. I wonder if that means—"

"No, because if they had Mike in their pocket, they wouldn't need Alissa. I'm a little surprised Sylvain is even still negotiating with Mike. It might seem like they're being hardasses about the key-man clause, but the fact is most VC's would run screaming when a guy like Rod is removed from the equation. They're trying to act cagey about it, but they still want Algoplex bad. I wonder what their real target is—maybe Rod's patents."

This made some sense, but I was losing my grasp on the whole web of connections. "I also can't figure out Trisha. She seemed like the one in charge at dinner with the Sylvain guys. Mike said Sylvain's main backer on this deal was anonymous. Maybe—"

"She was the one with the capital in the first place," Wes said, finishing the thought I'd been groping for. He laid out a theory about large sums of money, made by Silicon Glamour in some shady way, needing a place to go, a place with a respectable cover. I tried to follow, but my eyes were dropping as if pulled shut by enormous weights.

"You're a bad influence, Wes," I mumbled.

"Now, that's not true, Billy. First of all, I'm not the one getting cold-cocked in the jaw. Second, you'd get no sleep at all tonight if it weren't for me."

I was gone by the time he finished the sentence.

» » » » »

The next day started slowly. Very slowly, and only then because Rita called at noon, jolting me out of cavernous sleep. It took me some time to realize where I was and how a telephone worked.

Actually, first I had to ascertain *who* I was.

Rita said the master tape of the Algoplex film, along with ten VHS copies, was ready. She'd edited out references to Alissa and added an R.I.P. for Rod at the end.

"Thanks, Rita. I'll take them down to Mike. You're a hero."

"Right, so why don't *you* stop trying to be one? Amused as I am by your new Godfather accent, I don't want you to become completely unintelligible."

"I've got to go. It's time for my medication."

When I went into the kitchen, I found out that I'd missed an earlier call from Mike. Apparently he had more bad news about the company. I called him back, but he wasn't in. I was still woozy enough to let Wes talk me into staying on the couch and watching another movie while I waited for Mike's return call.

It came toward the end of the afternoon. He'd just met with one of Rod's original investors, a guy named Carlisle, who wanted to pull out. Mike's voice was strained. "This could be curtains, Bill. It'll put more shares up for grabs and you-know-who will get them. He said Sylvain didn't meddle, it was just that he'd invested in Rod and now Rod's gone."

"We can talk about it more in person," I said. "I've got the master tape of Rod's film, if you want to pick it up."

"Uh, let's see, can you bring it down? I've got a couple of quick stops to make, then some things to take care of at Rod's house before the service tomorrow. Can you meet me there in ninety minutes or so?"

I wasn't crazy about getting in a car, but I agreed. Wes made some scrambled eggs and I thanked him for missing work and being such an excellent nurse.

I swallowed another Vicodin, and, after swinging by Rita's house for the box of videotapes, pointed the Scout down Guerrero to Interstate 280.

Darkness had crept over the city. I turned on my lights and swayed with the curves of the freeway. The autumn time change had just befallen us and the road was a river of lights as people returned home. This time of the year gave me a primal-eclipse kind of feeling, as if the world was coming to end. The Vicodin added to the furry twilight dream. My tongue compulsively explored the gap on the back right side of my lower teeth. I tried to stop, but as soon as I forgot to think about it, my tongue was back in there. Voids are hard to leave alone.

The yellow tape had been removed from Rod's house. His Volvo sat in the driveway. The house was dark for the most part, with a single light on in the entry hall. I didn't see Mike's sports car, so I wondered if Rod's mother was there. I knocked on the door and pressed the bell. It rang forlornly, unanswered. I pressed it again and then commanded the front door to open. It did not click in response. But when I pushed at the door, it swung inward.

"Hello?" I called, setting the box of videotapes on a table inside the door.

Only the hall light was on. I waited. To my right were the dining table and cabinet, hulking in the dimness like sleeping animals. The house was silent. I kept still, listening harder. Then I could hear it, a distant buzz. No, it was a roar: my own coursing blood.

I moved down the hallway, and with a rush the sensation of finding Rod returned to me. I wondered if I should leave myself so out in the open, fingered by the light from the entryway, while the rest of the house was obscured in darkness. Yet I stayed where I was. As my eyes adjusted I made out the leather sofa of the living room, the hearth, the vase, the side table. All were just as they had been that night.

A sense of dread burrowed into my gut. I scanned the living room for a poker or some kind of weapon. The air around me was dense, a fog of darkness, like a thing waiting to pounce. If a weapon was hidden in that fog, I couldn't find it. I felt paralyzed from doing anything but going forward to whatever I would find in the kitchen. I moved as if in a trance, feeling myself a helpless observer, able only to follow the viewfinder down the hall. My steps were short, sliding, silent save for the intermittent whine of a floorboard.

An indirect glow coming through a window gave the kitchen a murky light. It had been cleaned up, the scattered objects put away or taken by the police, the chairs turned upright. Mike's work, I assumed. I touched a light switch but then thought better of it. A faint smear of red still stained the linoleum where I'd found Rod. I considered searching for a knife, but the image of Rod's gashed neck made me leave the drawers alone. Instead, I stopped in front of the refrigerator. A picture of Alissa was there, her features shadowy in the indirect light. But that same smile was still on her face, unchanged, unmoved, promising all yet always just out of reach.

I returned to the hall and looked at the basement door. I could go down there or proceed to the bedroom and den. A dim light came from the bedroom door on the left. I pressed myself against the wall—if I wasn't armed, at least I could make myself harder to strike—and moved down the hall.

The tiny reading light fixed to Rod's headboard was on. I moved slowly into the room and thought about checking the closed closet door. Then I saw that the bedspread was wrinkled. Someone had been lying on it. They'd been on top only, not under the covers. The space seemed faintly warm, though it may only have been the heat from my hand.

I crossed the hall to the den. This room seemed safer, since the struggle the night of Rod's murder had not spilled in here.

The far wall was mostly windows. The same indirect light as in the kitchen filtered through them. There was not a sound in the room, not a stir in the air. I nearly jumped out of my skin when I came upon the motionless figure perched on the love seat.

Her back was straight. A gloved hand was placed on each knee. Her black skirt was pressed and she wore a tailored waist jacket. She stared at the windows, her eyes glassy. She could have been a mannequin. Bare November branches cast a quivering web of shadows across her body. My blood went cold as it occurred to me I'd found another corpse.

Then she blinked. "Who are you?" I said.

I stood a few feet away. She raised her hand slowly to her face, blocking me from view. A shiver traveled the length of her body.

I said, "You better tell me why you're here." I wondered if she had all her marbles, or if she was the kind of oddball attracted by the publicity of Rod's murder. She was dressed as if for a funeral.

Finally the hand dropped. Her face was puffy, her cheeks rough and blemished; her age was hard to read. She turned to the Barcalounger to her right, the chair in which Rod had liked to do his reading. The seat was tipped back, as if he'd just been using it.

The woman's features remained frozen. Only her mouth moved. Barely a sound came out. "I knew him."

"You knew Rod?"

She took in a sharp breath as she looked at me. Even in this dim light, the purple swollenness of my jaw was visible. Her head swiveled again, slowly, to the easy chair. The vacant stare returned.

"He's gone," she whispered.

>> >> >> >> >>

A car door slammed outside. I hoped it was Mike; I'd left the front door open. I offered the woman a hand. "You better come with me," I said.

Her glance snapped over to me and, as if shaking off a spell, animation returned to her face. "I'm sorry. My name is Kim Woodson."

She stood and met my hand with a demure shake. "Bill Damen," I said. "How did you get in the house?"

She looked at my jaw again. "You're hurt. Have you seen a doctor?"

"Yes, thank you—"

Mike's voice came booming down the hall. "Bill! I hope that's you!"

"I'm in the den!" I called back.

We heard every footstep of his approach. I wondered if Kim had listened to my movements in the same frozen position in which I'd found her. Mike did an elaborate double take when he entered. "Who's this?"

Kim stepped forward and introduced herself.

Mike shook her hand and went straight for a table lamp. "Nice to meet you, Kim. I'm Mike Riley."

She and I flinched together as the light burst into the room. Mike plopped himself into the Barcalounger, right at home. Kim returned to her spot on the love seat. I joined her.

Mike let out a big sigh and said, "God, what a day. You a friend of Bill's, Kim?"

"We just met." She gave Mike a smile. "I was a friend of Rod's."

"Oh! I see," Mike said. "I'm very sorry for your loss."

"It must be hard for you, too," she responded. "With the company and all."

"Yes, there's that . . . but I loved him as a friend, Kim. He was a real buddy. How long did you go back with him?"

She waved a hand. "Oh, a ways. When he was with Inter-Dynamics." It had been one of Rod's corporate jobs. "It's been a long time. I shouldn't be this upset. But he was so special."

"He sure was. How well—Were you, uh . . . Well, it's really none of my business."

Kim turned her smile on again. It had a beguiling quality, a way of lighting up her face. Her skin was a golden copper that, on its own, would have been lustrous. But it clashed somehow with her hair, a kind of streaked, shaggy blond that had seen too many colors. The patches of erupted skin over her cheeks and temples added to an impression of her having fallen from grace. So did her throaty growl of a voice and the mixed scents of perfume and cigarette smoke, whiffs of a lost glamour.

Kim seemed to be searching for words. Mike leaned forward. "Honest, I'm sorry, I shouldn't have asked. Can I get you something—a drink?"

A newspaper clipping was clutched in his hand. I said, "What have you got there, Mike?" For some reason I didn't want him raiding Rod's refrigerator.

He held it out and exhaled another big sigh, flapping his lips. "It came in the mail today. No note or anything. I don't know what to say. I really don't."

I got up and took the clipping. It was from a small newspaper in Arizona. A head shot was included in a story about an out-of-town woman killed in a fiery car crash. Her name was Alissa Bevins. The photo confirmed it.

I sank back into the couch, numb. "I guess that's it. Both of them are gone now."

Kim gently pulled the clipping from my fingers. Her gloves were a tight-woven black mesh. She took one look at the story and burst into tears.

Mike rushed to her side, putting an arm across her shoulder. "What is it? Did you know Alissa?"

"No," she sobbed. The back of a glove wiped her nose and she quickly brought the tears under control. "It's just . . . all this death. Was she important to Rod?"

Mike and I looked at each other. "Yes," I said.

Kim drew in a sharp breath. Mike squeezed her shoulder a little more tightly. "They weren't engaged, though. In fact—"

"Did you know Alissa, Kim?" I cut in. She'd answered the question, but I posed it more firmly this time.

She covered her eyes and shook her head. Mike shot me a look that said to lay off. Kim said, "Do you know who killed Rod?"

"We're working on it," Mike said consolingly. "We'll get them."

"We have a good idea," I said. I waited for her to look up at me. I was going to reel off some names and I wanted to observe her reaction. "It's a company called Silicon Glamour Associates. Trisha and Rupert Evans. In collaboration with Sylvain Partners. Possibly in collaboration with Connie Plush and Wendy Bevins. How well do you know these people?"

"I don't," she said, in spite of the visible quivers of recognition. "But I really hope you get them if they did it." Her eyes, still shiny with tears, zeroed in on me. "I *really* want you to. I'll help. Just tell me what I can do."

"That's good of you," Mike said, condescension slipping into his voice. "It's dangerous, though, as you can see from Bill's jaw. I've had some close calls myself. Here, take my card. Do you have a number where we can reach you?"

She recited a number with a 650 area code, which meant it was local. Mike jotted it down. She put Mike's card in a small purse. I noticed, as she stood, that her shoes were scuffed.

Mike's arm hovered near her shoulder. "I'll take you to the door," he said. "Be sure to keep in touch with us."

Kim stopped and shook my hand. She turned to look back at the room. A shudder came over her. "It's so strange to be here. I can feel him. It's like he could walk back in any minute."

Mike squeezed her and took her down the hall. I followed as far as the living room. There was a chill in the house. My skin had goosebumps and I wanted to warm up by lighting the fireplace. I found the switch on the side of the hearth and gave it a twist. It broke off in my hand. A gust blew down the chimney and I shivered. I was starting to think the house was cursed.

17

"We need to talk," I said to Mike.

"I'll say," Mike answered, coming back down the hall from Rod's front door. He flapped his hand. "Boy, I underestimated Rod. He sure knows how to pick 'em."

I'd dropped into the brown leather sofa. A lamp with a green shade cast a lugubrious glow. Unreality was all around me—the report of Alissa's death, the apparition of Kim, the brain-muffling effects of the medication.

"I saw the box with the videotapes," Mike went on, taking a seat. "Thanks for bringing them. I gave one to Kim."

"The master's on the bottom. Make sure you don't give that away."

Mike shook his head. "Whew. What a day."

"Alissa's dead." I was still trying to absorb the news.

"That's bizarre, isn't it? How many more things can go wrong around here?"

"I don't believe it was an accident. They're eliminating everyone who could tell us the truth about Rod and Silicon Glamour."

"But if Alissa was spying for SG—"

"Maybe she wasn't. Erika's intuition was that she really was in love with Rod. If that's true, Alissa may have learned something that made her flee. They caught up with her in Arizona."

"But Bill, these escort people—do they really have that kind of reach?"

"The clipping is probably two or three days old. Plenty of time for those two guys to do the job and come back and give me a purple jaw."

Mike frowned and stared at the cold fireplace. "Maybe we should throw in the towel, Bill. I wouldn't blame you one bit. It's getting too dangerous."

"You're in as much danger as me, Mike. More, if you don't cave in to Sylvain's plan."

Mike chewed on his lower lip. "I don't have many plays left, with Carlisle pulling out. If I had the funds to buy up his shares, I'd do it."

"Borrow money. Do whatever you need to hold them off."

"I'm trying, Bill. But think about this, too: Maybe Sylvain getting controlling interest won't be the worse thing in the world. We keep assuming their intentions are bad, but they might let me run the company as before. At least Algoplex will survive."

"Maybe, maybe not," I said. "It might be Rod's patents they're after. As it stands right now, we've got no chance against these people. The company is the one bit of leverage we have left, the one thing they really want. If you cave in now, then what you said before is true—we might as well give up the fight. Save both our skins."

Mike thrust his chin forward. "I'm not afraid of them."

"You told Kim you had some close calls. What happened?"

He shrugged. "Oh, you know—the general atmosphere. How's your jaw doing? Man, that reminds me of the time I nearly bit through my whole tongue in a rugby match. Hurt like hell to stitch it—"

"My jaw's going to be fine," I interrupted. Like Wes, Mike needed an injury to compare to mine. I didn't know whether it was to compete or to offer sympathy. "Look, Mike, I have no right to ask you to do this. It's not worth your life or mine. But holding off Sylvain is the best hope we have to force them to make a bad move. It'll also give me time to dig at the connection between them and SG. That could save Algoplex in the end."

"Okay. I'll buy us that time," Mike said, his finger jabbing decisively at me. "For Rod, for what he built. But I have to warn you, there will come a point when I have to punt."

"Thanks, Mike." I sat back and closed my eyes for a moment. "Let me get Kim's number from you, too."

His voice turned upbeat. "Yeah, so, what did you think of her?"

I opened my eyes. His hand hadn't moved to the pocket where he'd put the number. "A lot of things. She's not telling us why she's really here. I'd like to know how she got in."

"Yeah . . ." Mike was in charge of the house and didn't like the idea that he might have left the door unlocked, although such a slip was unlike him.

"She looked like a Silicon Glamour type," I added. "My theory is that she worked for SG and was getting an early version of Eternaderm from Plush. You saw the blemishes on her face. Something went wrong and she lost her job."

"Her skin is a little rough, but you can't tell me she's not a babe. I'll liaise with her, Bill. Let me know what questions you want me to ask."

"Mike, I have no interest in her other than what she can tell us about Rod."

"Good. Then leave it to me."

Momentarily stupefied by the fact that he was worried about getting a date when so much more was at stake, I didn't mention the slips she'd made. "I need to watch her face when she answers, Mike. These people are trained to put on a persona."

Mike squared his shoulders. "Whatever you think is best, Bill." He didn't mean a word of it. But he did take Kim's number from his pocket and let me copy it.

>> >> >> >> >>

Wes, ever loyal—or was he just nosy?—had my laptop open in the kitchen when I returned. He'd been making himself useful by searching far and wide on the Internet for Rupert, Trisha, and Silicon Glamour Associates.

"I found nothing, Bill, not a trace. They're either off the grid or they know how to cover their tracks," he said. "I'll run a scan on the Sylvain execs—it's acceptable these days to investigate someone you want to hire. I'll pretend we're looking for a new CFO."

"Don't forget Wendy," I said. "And could you check out this clipping from Arizona, too? I'm tempted to go down there myself, but I've got the memorial service tomorrow."

"Right. I'd like to come to the service with you."

I gave Wes the particulars—the service would be at three—and then excused him from duty. The pain in my mouth had settled into a manageable throb and I'd made friends with the hole in my teeth. I sat in the kitchen for a while after he left, staring out a darkened window. A distinct sense of being in over my head caught up with me. I'd been blindsided by everything

Silicon Glamour had done. I had no way to assess my chances against them because I couldn't tell how big, how fast, or how smart they were. All I knew was that SG and Sylvain worked together to get inside information on target companies like Algoplex. Connie could be their point person at Plush. She used SG associates as test subjects for Eternaderm, and they also moonlighted as models. The treatment kept the associates looking young and fresh. Sylvain, SG, and Plush must have schemed the invasion of Rod's company together. Alissa was given the job of luring Rod in, though it's possible she changed her mind about it in the end. Brendon kept an eye on Rod and had the added motivation of being in love with Alissa. Rod's murder may have been planned from the beginning. Or an unexpected wrinkle had forced Trisha and Rupert into it. The gentlemen who'd ambushed me did the dirtiest of the dirty work.

But this was all presumption. Detective Coharie wouldn't listen to me until I had evidence that forced him to: Rupert had gotten his ear first. I was starting to wonder about Mike, too. Not that I suspected him of collaboration, but it wouldn't surprise me if he was starting to perceive his own interests as separate from Algoplex and Rod. The news about Alissa might have been the most depressing of all. What a terrible way for her to die. Any chance I had of finding out the truth about her and Rod may have gone up in flames with her car.

>> >> >> >> >>

A night of sleep gave me slightly more hope. Wes's research might provide new threads to pull, and there were some wild cards I could turn over myself: Erika, Wendy, Kim. Suddenly, as my eyes sprang open Wednesday morning, it seemed crucial to get to Kim first.

A call to the number I'd gotten from Mike gave me a digitized voice that repeated the number and then beeped. It was a mobile account. I left a message reminding Kim that she'd promised to do anything to help, gave her my cell number, and said I was on my way down the Peninsula.

I stopped in at one of my favorite greasy spoons for breakfast. Silicon Valley didn't have a lot of cultural advantages over San Francisco, but this was one. Most of the everyday diners in the city had been replaced by Starbucks or bagel shops. I was still recuperating and felt the need for a big breakfast: bacon, eggs, and hash browns. Kim called back while I was eating. I said I would come to her place. She said no, she'd meet me. I suggested the coffee shop. She countered with Hoover Tower on the Stanford campus.

The tech boom of the nineties had been good to Stanford. The tower, once visible from everywhere, was hard to find now. I lost my way for a while in the labyrinth of new construction named for figures from the digital age—the Gates Computer Science building, the David Packard Electrical Engineering building, and the huge, still-incomplete James Clark biomedical engineering center.

When finally I found the tower, Kim was nowhere in sight. I waited on the plaza. She arrived wearing a long, shiny black raincoat. It was a gray day, threatening rain later, but still the light seemed harsh on her face. The topography of her cheeks was more rugged than I'd seen last night. A dark wool cap covered her head. The drawn look on her face before she saw me gave her the appearance of a refugee.

She switched on a smile when I approached and repeated that she meant what she said about helping.

"So why Stanford?" I asked. "Did you go here?"

"No." She looked across the plaza, teeming with its bright-eyed crop of students, half of them on wheels, the other half on wireless. "I just like it here. It has a hopeful feeling."

"Shall we sit down?"

"Let's walk," she said. "It's chilly."

I allowed her to quiz me about my connection to Rod as we wandered through the campus. I gave out only innocuous details. It was a way to let her get comfortable with me. She pretended to know nothing of Plush, Sylvain, or Silicon Glamour.

"You haven't asked me about Mike yet," I pointed out.

"Oh, he's being very nice. We had breakfast."

"He moves fast. What did he say?"

"He thinks you're doing a great job."

"Hmm. We're getting nowhere on catching Rod's killers, Alissa is dead, and the company is about to be pillaged. Yeah, we're doing just fine."

Kim didn't reply. She walked with a measured step, as if gauging each word she would say. We'd come to the engineering quad. The character of the students changed. There were more holstered devices here, more buttoned shirts, more people with the kind of preoccupied expression Rod used to wear.

Kim said, "I really do want to know who did it. I want them put away."

"I think I know who did it, I just can't prove it. If I could, I'd probably be dead."

"Who? Tell me. *Tell me.*"

I stopped and looked at her. Her face revealed only contradictions: She was at once guarded and pleading, urgent and remote, beautiful and desolate. "Talk to your friends at Silicon Glamour," I said. "Talk to Rupert and Trisha. Tell me what they say."

She resumed walking. A few silent steps went by. "I don't understand what you mean."

I stopped again. "You can't help by lying to me. Lie to whomever else you want, since that seems to be the norm in this bunch, but not to me. When was the last time you saw Rod?"

She gave me an offended frown, then counted silently. "I don't know, maybe five years ago. Or three."

"He never mentioned you."

Her lips pressed together. Her voice was hoarse and bittersweet. "He wouldn't."

"Were you a couple?"

"It's hard to explain."

People were staring at us. We'd reached a small shaded grotto with a fountain and a few benches. I moved us to one of the benches and pressed ahead. "How did you know Mike was CEO of the company? You'd just met him last night, yet you knew his role at Algoplex."

"I kept track of it."

"What kind of work do you do?"

"I—I don't have a job right now." She looked at her folded hands. The skin was cracked, the nails chipped. Again I noticed the odor of smoke.

"Why did you lie on top of Rod's bed before I found you?"

"It just—" She pressed a palm to her forehead. "It brought back memories."

"You see, this is the problem. You said that last night, too, yet Rod only moved into that house two years ago."

She glanced at me. It was a flash of a look, lasting less than a second, but in that flash was pure, furious anger. Then the tears came. "Please—you're thinking the wrong thing. I can't remember all the details. Maybe it was the same bed. There are so many things in that house. . . ." She hid her eyes.

"You never told me how you got in."

"The door was open," she said in her weary voice.

I looked at the top of her head for a moment, at the brown roots under the blond hair, feeling simultaneously sorry for her tears and annoyed that she wouldn't tell me the truth. "Tell me about your life. Just the past few years. Not everything, but how you made a living, who's important to you. You've got a ring on your wedding finger."

She twisted the ring, then yanked it off. "It's just for protection. I can't talk about these things, Bill. Please just accept that. I can't talk about them. All right?"

I sat, waiting. She remained bent, her elbows on her knees. When she looked up, her face showed resolve. I'd get no further. "At least tell me where the condition on your skin comes from," I said. "Have you used Eternaderm?"

"It's just . . . a disease." Her head bent again. "Like my whole life. Leave me alone, please. I don't want to talk anymore. This was a bad idea."

I wanted to reach over, to comfort her in some way and tell her that I really didn't mean to be so hard on her, especially if she wasn't running a scam on me. What came out was, "Did you hear about Erika?"

A small shake of the head meant either she hadn't heard or didn't know Erika.

"Someone threw a chemical at her," I said. "Disfigured her face. It may be permanent."

The head shake became stronger. "That's terrible."

Again her horror seemed real. But still she didn't look up.

I stood. "I guess I'll see you at the service for Rod this afternoon." I waited a few more seconds for some last offer of information. It didn't come. "Thanks for meeting me here. I don't think you can help, but thanks anyway."

I started to walk away. "Bill!" she called. "Give me a chance. I'll try to find out some things. I'll tell you whatever I can."

I waved to her and left.

>> >> >> >> >>

Once upon a time, I was not so hard-hearted. I'd learned some lessons from the dot-com binge, lessons I'd never been forced to learn in my relatively benign corner of the film world. I'd also learned lessons from having a friend fatally poisoned by a protein engineered into her food. There are good people and there are bad people, but most are in between. The question is which way they will go. Kim struck me as an in-between, but on the edge. She genuinely was upset about Rod, but she wouldn't say why or what her true connection was. Maybe a gentler approach, playing along with her game, would have drawn her out. Usually I'm willing to do that, if only because the game tells me a lot. But my patience for phony identities and simulated motives had run out. Rod had agonized about falling under the spell of Alissa's glamour. I wanted no more glamours cast over me.

I still had time to see Erika before the memorial service. I dialed her cell number from my car. To my surprise, she picked up herself. My number showed on her caller ID, she explained. I asked her about getting into Alissa's apartment. She didn't answer directly, but named a corner and said to be there in half an hour. The tone of her voice told me she'd been hoping I wouldn't call.

She wore jeans and a sweatshirt. A felt hat was pushed low on her head. When she pulled it off in the car, I held back my gasp. Her description of the streaks of white hadn't prepared me for this. It was an act of vandalism, a defacement, as if the vandal wanted to erase her identity. Worse, Erika's body language said that he had succeeded. She slumped in the seat, eyes down. Her hello was listless.

"Erika, I am so sorry. I'm going to do everything I can to fix this."

"That's all right. I have a dermatologist now. I'd just as soon you stay out of it."

"Are you sure you want to go to Alissa's apartment?"

"No. But I'm going to do this one last thing for you. Then I want out."

"I'm sorry I put you at risk."

She shook her head. "Don't apologize. You showed me Trisha's true colors. Having lunch with you was not such a big violation of the rules. I hope you nail them good. But don't call me again until you do."

I waited a few moments before saying, "It would help if you'd come to the police with me and file a report on the attack. Tell them about Brendon, too."

"I didn't see who threw that stuff in my face. And Brendon was just trying to find out where Alissa was."

"Then tell them how SG spies on their clients. We could go to the DA's office."

She shook her head harder and clenched her jaw, biting back tears. "Isn't what already happened to me bad enough?"

I decided not to tell her the news about Alissa. We drove in silence to the Granada. I'd stowed some optical equipment in my Scout this morning: a DV camera, a still camera with a zoom, and a pair of high-powered binoculars. I parked a block down from the apartment building and climbed on top of the jeep with the binoculars. The roof was good and firm; I'd done plenty of shooting from its perch. I scanned the street for a solid ten minutes and saw no sign of the brown Mercedes. We'd have to take our chances if there was someone else. I walked Erika in under a large umbrella, though the rain was not yet coming down.

She had befriended the manager's young daughter last year. Erika had been locked out and the girl had been able to produce a key. Now Erika would knock lightly and call the girl's name. If the manager answered the door, we'd be out of luck.

I waited down the hall and out of sight. Erika's voice came in soft, lilting tones. My hopes rose. A minute later, she arrived with the key. "The manager takes a nap after lunch," she said. "Open the door fast. I'll run the key back down before he wakes up."

We took the stairs two at a time. I unlocked the door. While Erika returned the key, I stepped inside Alissa's apartment. There was a rank, metallic smell. I followed it into the bedroom. Neat red drops were outlined vividly on the tile floor. I bent to touch one. It was fairly dry. The drops led to the bed. I checked under the crumpled covers, but there was nothing there. A drip on the box spring caused me to lift the mattress. Buried beneath it was a paring knife covered with blood, the same color as the blood on the floor. I rushed into the living room, the kitchen, the bathroom. There was no body.

Erika saw the wild look in my eyes when she returned. "What is it?"

I took her into the bedroom and lifted the mattress. "Oh my God!" she said.

"This knife is from Rod's kitchen," I said. "He owned a set of these. Alissa doesn't. The blood wasn't here before, either."

Erika's brow wrinkled. "But how did—"

"The knife was planted. It had to be. Alissa wouldn't put a bloody knife from Rod's kitchen under her own bed."

"Of course not, but—have you been in here before?"

I stopped short. The helpless expression on her splotch-marked face made me tell the truth. "I broke in from the balcony a couple of weeks ago," I admitted. "Rod was worried about Alissa. We wanted to find out if she was still alive."

"That was *you*. . . . Oh my God, I can't believe it!" She rushed to the door.

"Erika, wait."

She wouldn't look at me. She stood in the open door as if fearing an attack.

"Don't go outside alone, Erika."

She shut the door behind her. Some other time I could reflect on the irony of having deceived her the same way I'd accused everyone else of doing to me. For now I needed to complete my search of the apartment and keep an eye on Erika as she left the building.

The clothes that had been strewn around the apartment were now picked up. I found them tossed into the closet and stuffed into bedroom drawers. I checked Alissa's desk for signs of recent activity. A lack of dust on the computer keyboard told me it had been used. I booted the computer, then looked in the bathroom and kitchen. They seemed the same as the last time I was here, except I didn't recall a pot sitting on top of the stove before. And the message board had been cleaned.

I looked at my watch. Five minutes had passed. I called Erika on my cell phone. She didn't pick up. I slipped a piece of paper between the lock and the doorjamb and ran downstairs. A taxi was sitting in front of the gate. Erika must have stopped in her own apartment, because she was shoving a box into the back seat.

"Erika," I gasped through the iron fence, "let me explain."

Her expression was cold. "I wouldn't stick around, Bill. You never know when the manager will show up."

That sent me racing inside again. I did a system search on files that had been modified in the past week. The results showed that files had been opened as recently as yesterday. I opened her email program. But the folders had been cleaned out. Incoming, outgoing, even the folder of deleted messages. Whoever had done the cleaning had been thorough. They'd probably swept the hard drive, too. I'd need sophisticated software to dig up the deleted files.

If Erika's threat about the manager was real, I had no time for more snooping. It wasn't worth the risk. I shut down the computer and got out of there. Once I was safely back in the Scout, I dialed the police and left an anonymous tip to look for a bloody knife in Alissa's apartment.

18

The memorial service for Rod took place at an
Episcopal church in the Valley. I was a bit rumpled for the occasion, having rushed over from Alissa's apartment. I'd brought
a jacket to throw on over my shirt, but Mike and the other business types were in dark suits. Three Sylvain men were there,
along with Connie and Ronald Plush, Ellen Quong, and a large
contingent from Algoplex. I hadn't seen Wes yet. Rod's mother
was up front. Mike rose to deliver a eulogy, one that brought
tears to his own eyes but had one too many sports metaphors
for my taste.

I didn't think anyone from Silicon Glamour would dare
show, but there was Gary, in the back, as we filed out. I pushed
by the exiting mourners to get to him. He crossed the pew to the
left-hand aisle of the church. It felt odd to break into a run in
this refined, slightly aloof atmosphere, but I cut across another
pew and intercepted him. He tried to sidestep me. I turned and
caught sight of Kim's streaked hair. She must have hidden
behind a column during the service. Now she was hurrying to
the porch exit.

"Out of my way," Gary said, reaching a hamlike hand in my
direction.

I stepped back lightly. "Don't try it here."

"Who was that woman?" Gary asked.

"What woman?"

Gary let out a disgusted sigh. He looked uncomfortable in his clothes. His bursting chest squeezed the lapels of his blazer back into his armpits.

"Are you the best SG could send?" I said. "I suppose you're presentable, compared to those other two muggers."

His gaze fixed on my discolored jaw. "You are funny, man," he said, and lumbered back down the aisle.

I went the other way and out the porch exit. Kim was nowhere in sight. I just wanted to make sure Gary didn't find her. I went to the parking lot, then circled back around the front of the church, seeing neither of them. Mike stood at the top of the steps like the master of ceremonies. I lied politely and told him he'd done a good job. He reminded me that I was invited back to Algoplex for a reception.

I thanked him and made a beeline for the Plushes, who were standing below with the Sylvain men. Dr. Plush remembered me as the man with the camera. He asked what new film I was making. I motioned him away from the group. He'd been a hard man to find, and his greeting indicated that Connie hadn't poisoned him too much against me.

"I was thinking that Plush Biologics would be a good subject," I said.

The doctor beamed, his cheeks broad as his tie. "It's a good time to get on board. Eternaderm will be a big, big breakthrough. I'll tell you the whole story. I still remember the moment I came up with the idea. You see, Ellen was doing gene regulation at another company and we got talking about the techniques she used. I'd long believed there had to be better ways to treat skin. Cutting is brutal, topicals have limited effect, and peels are temporary. Speaking to Ellen, it came to me in a flash. Go directly to the genes. They'd unlock what we needed in a devastatingly effective manner. You'll be part of history, Bill. Who funds your films, by the way?"

"Well . . . the company I'm shooting does. Algoplex paid for the film on Rod."

"Oh, hmm, I see. . . ."

"But there are other sources for documentary funding." These days that statement sounded like a wild exaggeration, unless the doc was about sex, drugs, or terrorism. "Of course, I'd have to be more objective then."

He spread his arms. "We've got nothing to hide."

"How well do you know Rupert and Trisha Evans?"

The doctor got no farther than the word "Socially." Though Connie appeared to be attending to the Sylvain men, in fact she'd been monitoring our entire conversation. Now she leaped in.

"Ronald, it's starting to rain. Shall we go?" The sky was a lowering gray, and it was indeed spitting a few drops.

"Hello, Mrs. Plush," I said, extending my hand.

She took it, the picture of pleasantness. "Nice to see you, Bill."

"Likewise. I wanted to tell you something. I've found Alissa."

The smile plunged into a vicious frown. "That's impossible! Alissa is dead."

Her exclamation caused the Sylvain men, a few feet away, to stop their conversation and stare at us. Ronald murmured, "Oh my God."

"Really?" I said to Connie. "How do you know?"

"It was in the newspaper. A terrible thing—car crash in Arizona."

"Which newspaper was that?"

"I don't recall. An Arizona paper."

"You get the *Galatea Gazette*?"

"Someone *sent* it to me, Bill." She couldn't hide the irritation in her voice, just as she had not been able to hide the frown, nor the panic when she declared so definitively that Alissa was dead.

I took a step toward the Sylvain men. "You guys knew Alissa, didn't you?"

They shook their heads quickly and in unison.

"Well, I'm just wondering how seriously your firm is tangled up with Silicon Glamour. They're going to have a lot of legal problems soon."

The most senior of the group turned from me as if I'd never spoken. The others followed suit. Meanwhile, Connie and Ronald Plush had started down the sidewalk. I was about to follow them when I saw Wes motioning me over. He must have come late. I held up my hand to quiet him when I saw another figure behind him: Brendon. He was standing off by himself, next to a rhododendron bush. He made no secret of watching me. Nor did he move when I approached. Wes stood back and kept an eye on us.

I went up and put my nose right in front of Brendon's. His eyes held steady on me. He couldn't have been more than 22, 23 years old. He was good-looking in a UCLA-quarterback kind of way, with wide eyes, overfull lips, and a clear, creamy complexion. His light hair fell over his forehead and his jaw jutted in the manner of a little boy determined to have his own way.

I said, "I didn't know you cared so much about Rod."

"It's not Rod I care about." His glance shifted to the crowd around us. "Follow me."

He cut through an opening in the bushes. We crossed a small lawn and turned a corner to where we could stand unobserved in the shadow of a buttress.

"I need to talk to you about Alissa," he said.

"Why? So you can report back to Rupert?"

"I've quit. I'm not on their side anymore."

"That's what Rupert told you to say, right?"

His lips puckered in a combination of sulk and anger. Maybe he really had left SG. "I heard what Mrs. Plush said. I believe you, not her."

"All I said was I knew where Alissa was. I didn't say she was alive."

"She *is* alive."

He said it with such force it was hard to tell if it was a wish or a fact. I watched his face. "You *do* have the hots for her, don't you?"

He rolled his eyes. He was still part teenage boy. "That's an old thing. I'm telling you, we checked it out. The death is a fake. You should get together with us."

"Who's this 'us'?"

He hesitated, licked his lips, and then said, "Me and Wendy. She went to Arizona and now she's back. She wants to talk to you."

I tried to hide my surprise. Brendon and Wendy? I didn't care what his motives were, I just wanted Wendy in front of me. "When?"

He fingered the hem of his jacket. "Now, if you can."

"Let's go."

›› ›› ›› ›› ››

I followed Brendon in his SUV to Highway 101. We went a few exits before he got off the freeway and turned in at a new apartment complex. The buildings, all cute angles and misplaced windows, had been plopped on the site in no discernible order. We parked and I went with Brendon through an overly elaborate front door into what I assumed was his pad. The furniture was new, sleek, and modern, but there wasn't quite enough of it to fill the living room. Bedding was folded and stacked on one end of a long sofa. The sofa faced a giant television, from which a daytime talk show bleated. No one was watching. Two framed posters decorated the walls, one showing a famous model, one Tahiti. The door to the next room was closed. In the kitchen, dishes were piled high.

Brendon knocked tentatively on the closed door. "Wendy?" he called. A voice came from inside. He turned to me and said, "She'll be out in a minute."

I sat on the sofa. The initials BW were monogrammed into a corner of the bed linen. Brendon paced in front of the TV. His suit was stylish, but a knockoff. The Louis Vuittons appeared real. I asked him for a glass of water. He washed a glass for me and brought it out.

"So what happened between you and SG?" I said.

He waved dismissively. "They're crooks. They want to control your whole life. It's like—who were those people in Russia?—the serfs. I got sick of it."

"What happens when you leave? How do they make sure you stay quiet?"

"I've got confidentiality up the wazoo. Soon as I say a word, their lawyers are on me. Or probably Gary has his way with me first and the lawyers get the leftovers."

"Do you figure that's what happened to Alissa?"

He stopped and, for the first time since we'd arrived, gazed at me. His face showed a mixture of distaste and curiosity, as if I were a fish that had washed up on his sofa. "That's why we brought *you* here."

"We might be able to work together on this. But first I want to hear everything about Rupert and Trisha. They sent you to spy on Erika in the store?"

He turned away from me and looked at the TV as if it had asked the question. He punched it off and said, "Yeah. Yeah, they wanted me to harass her. I don't get it, bro. They acted like they don't know where Alissa is or who killed Rod, when they're behind the whole thing. They were just pushing my buttons, I guess."

"What specifically did they tell you to do?"

"Just, you know, keep an eye on her."

"They didn't tell you to grab her by the hair?"

He hesitated, then said, "Well, yeah. We thought she knew where Alissa was. I was just trying to get Erika to tell us."

"Who threw the chemical in Erika's face?"

"Not me. Must have been Gary or someone like that."

"What about the other two thugs?" I described the guys who'd cold-cocked me.

"That sounds like Larsen and Terry. They were in Vegas last I knew. Trisha sent them down for a whole month. They must have just got back."

That was interesting. "They were down there a week ago?"

"Yeah. Definitely."

"What happened with you and SG?" I asked.

"I couldn't get with the program. I was, like, over it." He stopped and looked at the bedroom door. His ears were more attuned to it than mine. The door opened and Wendy made her entrance.

She flicked glances at us like a queen surveying her subjects. She wore a big-sleeved, billowy blouse, cinched at the waist with an oversized belt. Above a pair of slip-on white pumps were cream-colored silk pants. Her hair was piled high, a few strands loose on her face. Lanternlike earrings swung from her earlobes. A touch or two of Alissa remained: the necklace and the color of her hair. Even so, Wendy was her own glamorous self.

Her lipstick curved into a big, sloppy smile for me. "Bill, it's so nice of you to come."

I took her hand. It was still damp with moisturizer. Conflicting scents battled for primacy in the air around her. She glanced disapprovingly at the occupied space on the sofa. Brendon rushed to the center of the room with an armchair.

"Do you want to sit here?" he said. "Or should I move my blankets?"

She made a show of placing her rear into the chair. "This is fine, dear."

I put mine back in the sofa and said, "I was sorry not to see you at the memorial service, Wendy. But I guess you're not sad to see Rod go."

"Of course I'm sad, Bill. It was a terrible thing that happened to him. And then they tried to make it look like he did it to himself. Poor man. He was a little bit pathetic to begin with—no offense, you understand. Then he became delusional about my daughter. And then he was killed in that horrible way. It's too much."

"I see you know all the details."

She smiled again. "Oh, I keep track of things. I'm sure Rod told you all kinds of silly stories about me. It came out of his delusion. He blamed me for keeping Alissa from him. Of course, I had nothing to do with her feelings. A man like that . . ." She made a gesture of fruitlessness. "He was not a bad man. I thought he and I would be friends one day, once we understood each other."

"He wasn't delusional. Alissa did love him." Even if I wasn't a hundred percent sure of that, I wanted to see the reaction.

Brendon stood abruptly and whipped his tie from his collar. He'd been perched on the sofa arm and had already removed his jacket and laid it neatly on top of the bedding. Wendy halted him with a small motion with her hand. "Dear?"

He stared blankly, then got it. "Oh, right." He folded his tie and said, "The usual?"

"That'll be fine, thank you." She watched him walk to the kitchen with pleasure. "Don't be rude. Aren't you going to offer our guest something?"

"Bill, do you want some wine?" came Brendon's voice.

I said I already had my water, then studied Wendy as she waited for Brendon to return. Her face in the daylight looked pale and puffy, the lips and eyes a little too full, the edges of the face-lift beginning to pucker. I had the impression she was weary, not from overwork but from striving so hard to have the life she thought she should have. Brendon appeared to be providing a much reduced version of it.

She accepted a glass of white wine from him and took a sip, leaving a bruised-claret half moon on the glass, its counterpart a small smear above her lip. Only then did she return to my last comment. "You want to defend your friend, Bill, and that's very nice. I suppose it doesn't matter now how Alissa felt about him." She smiled in a way that was meant to be charming, but her mouth reminded me of a wilted rose. "You and I want the same things: to find Alissa and to get the people who did what they did to Rod."

"What did you find out in Arizona?"

"There's no wrecked car and no body. The editor of the paper claims to know nothing about the story. The reporters, the sheriff, the medical examiner: ignorant as logs. I found a copy of that day's edition and the story wasn't in it."

"So the clipping was faked. Who would gain by having everyone believe Alissa is dead? I suppose Rupert could have pulled it off so that we'd stop looking for her. Which might mean she's dead, anyway."

Brendon jumped up again, as if to attack my words. Wendy pursed her lips, quieting him with a look. She reached into her purse and extracted a pack of cigarettes and a lighter.

"Wendy . . ." Brendon entreated.

"Please," she said in a peremptory tone, "this is no time for rules." She waited with the cigarette between two fingers. Brendon heaved a sigh and fired up the lighter. Wendy took a long drag.

"I don't think she is," she said to me. Her tone was brazen, ready to deal. "I think she's out there and I think you know how to find her."

"Let's say I do—"

"Where is she?" Brendon demanded.

"This is hypothetical, Brendon. Let's say I can find her. What do you have to offer?" I omitted that if I did find Alissa, I'd ask her first if she wanted to talk to Wendy.

"You can't just—"

"Quiet, Brendon." Wendy shifted sideways, throwing her feet over the chair. She let the pumps drop, one at a time, to the floor. "I can't live on maybes. If you find Alissa, we'll talk about that. But let's say I *have* evidence of SG doing the bad stuff we know they do. What can *you* offer me?"

"What do you want?" I asked.

She let her head hang back over the edge of the chair and blew a pillow of smoke at the ceiling. "I want a chance, Bill." She'd turned suddenly wistful. "You know, I was never given a leg up on life. Not even a toe. Everything I've gotten, I had to fight for. When I was nineteen, Alissa's father left. *Nineteen*, Bill: I never had a chance. But that's not when it started, really. No one wanted me from the moment I was born into the world. I was given nothing. You can't imagine. Now, I wanted Alissa never to have to feel the way I did. And I vowed she wouldn't. It's too bad it's taken me so long to keep my promise. But I will. Every time I've been as close as I am now, something has screwed it up. Fate has turned against me. But I've been locked out long enough. It can't happen this time, Bill."

"I'm sorry," I said, "I'm not following you."

"Of course not. How would a college boy like you under-stand?" She leveled a look of injured scorn at me, then let her head hang back again. "You're young and handsome. Not like Brendon, but still you've got plenty to look forward to. By the time this starts happening to you, your life will be set. You'll have your car, your house, your wife. . . . When your skin starts to shrivel, when it sags and loses its shine, it'll just be part of your stupidly contented old age. The world won't see you as a crumpled-up sack."

"You can't be talking about yourself, Wendy. You look very good." And she did, in spite of her airs: It was only in comparison to Alissa that she had the look of the "before" picture.

Wendy came upright again. "I *work* at it. There's a man who's very much in love with me, Bill. A wonderful man, a true gentle-man, generous and respectful. He lives in the hills outside of Reno. It's a beautiful spread. I've been everything he wanted and things he didn't know he wanted. But he's looking at me differ-ently now. Do you know why? Someone said something to him, put an idea in his head that I'm a different age than he thinks. Now he inspects the back of my legs . . . my knuckles . . . my neck. He notices things. He thinks I don't know it, but I do. He was about to pop the question, Bill, and now I see the doubt creeping in. But I'm not going to let life screw me again. I'm going to take this into my own hands."

"All right," I said. "But I still don't see what this has to do with me."

"You have access, Bill. There's a treatment called Eternaderm. I know you know about it." Wendy tapped at the edges of her face where I'd noticed the puckers. "I could get rid of these for-ever! But I'm locked out of it, Bill, unjustly and for no good reason. This is what has to do with you. You need to get it for me. I don't care how you get it: officially, unofficially, whatever. Just get it."

"Have you talked to Connie?"

"Connie is the problem. Connie and Trisha. Trisha's nothing but a showgirl from Las Vegas trying to go respectable. Connie's stuck up. They scheme together—you wouldn't believe what I know about them. And I will tell it to you, if you do your job." Wendy exhaled another cloud of smoke and said, "There's always someone, Bill, always someone out to ruin me. You'll say I'm paranoid, but you haven't lived my life. I frighten them."

"And they frighten me," I said. "But why Eternaderm? There are a lot of treatments available, from what I hear: lasers, peels, retinoids. . . ."

Wendy dismissed them with a wave. "I'm tired of subtracting little bits of time, Bill. It always slides back on you. I want this because it goes below the surface. It fixes the problem at its origin."

"Yeah." I began to see the confluence between Wendy's interests and mine. "What are Connie and Trisha up to together? Trisha's the money behind Sylvain, isn't she?"

Wendy wagged her finger. "Uh-uh. Not until I see some product."

"Who's going to administer it? How do we make sure it's safe? And what makes you so sure I have access to it?"

She finished the last of her wine. "Those are the problems. Now they're yours."

"I need to know more about what you've got, Wendy. I won't go off on some detour to get you your Eternaderm."

"I've already told you about Trisha and Connie. The rest is juicy stuff, Bill. You'll get to avenge your friend. But I need to see progress first." She tossed the butt into her empty glass, suddenly nonchalant. "It's up to you. There's no rush, right? I mean, Rod's not going to get any deader than he is."

I stared out the window. Drops of rain spattered on the glass. I'd have to at least pretend to help in order to get more from her. I didn't say anything right away, though. My silence apparently worried Brendon.

"Aren't we going to tell him about the party?" he blurted.

Wendy gave him a glare, then said, "The Wings of Silicon Charity Ball will be held Friday night. Your friends from Sylvain and Silicon Glamour will be there. You can't afford it yourself, but if you come through for me, we'll get you in."

"All right, Wendy," I said. It was finally sounding worth the trouble. "I'll be back here tomorrow. But I still want you to answer one question before I leave. Why did you show up at the Sylvain dinner pretending to be Alissa?"

A look of horror crossed Brendon's face. Wendy stayed it by holding out the ash-speckled wine glass for him to bus. "I have a very good reason for that, Bill," she said, "and I will explain it to you when the time comes."

Brendon took the glass. I stood up. After getting their phone numbers, I said I'd go to work on the Eternaderm. I privately hoped that would amount to nothing more than a chat with Ellen while I pried more information from Wendy. Meanwhile, I could entertain myself trying to figure out how a spoiled brat like Brendon ended up playing yo-yo on the end of Wendy's string.

19

A light rain pattered on my windshield as I drove to Algoplex. It was after five and a few people still were left at the reception following the service for Rod. Tables with food and drink were set up in a common space at one end of the second floor. The furniture had been moved against a wall to open up the space. The windows looked out over the Frisbee field.

I might have predicted that Wes would stick around to try to enhance his social life. He tore himself away from a conversation to slouch with me in a pair of beanbag chairs along the wall. I described my visit with Wendy and Brendon and asked if he'd seen Ellen Quong.

"No," he answered, "but you should check out this woman I saw lurking around Mike Riley's office. She's not my type at all—kind of a fallen-blond look—but I think she's got a thing for Mike."

It sounded like Kim. "You're sure it's mutual—it's not just him after her?"

"She was the one lurking. Hold on, don't go anywhere yet. I've got more research to tell you about."

"Make it quick."

"Silicon Glamour is virtually invisible on the net. I didn't get a single hit and I was using my best spyware. You don't cloak yourself like that without some know-how. I did learn a little about Sylvain. They've tracked every point along the tech arc and they changed their name at each stage. First they brokered stocks, then did IPO's. They backed a couple of small success stories, then were accessories in one of those nineties IPO Ponzi schemes. Their CEO got probation and disappeared. The rest reconstituted themselves as Sylvain and dipped into a few dot-bombs. Everything turned around two years ago when they rescued a router company. They suddenly got respectable and went on to do set top boxes, net auctions, Plush, and now Algoplex. Their role's hard to pin down, though. They present themselves as a venture firm, but they also do some M&A and some investment banking. One way or another they wind up with a major stake in each company. More so than you'd expect from a small concern like Sylvain. Myself, I'd want to deal with a firm that hasn't spread itself so thin. Yet they make it work. Their results are solid now."

"And no visible tie to Rupert or Trisha Evans?"

"Totally stealth. Unless you've got some new leads for me to follow."

"Brendon gave me the names of those guys who hit me: Larsen and Terry. Terry sounded like the younger one, Larsen the older."

Wes shook his head. "I need full names. An image file would help, too."

"I'll ask them to pose for a snapshot next time. Brendon said they were in Las Vegas when Rod was murdered. So they might have an alibi there, but Wendy mentioned that Trisha was from Vegas. That could help us connect them."

"And it's just a short hop from Vegas to Arizona."

"I guess you didn't check out that clipping. It was a fake. Alissa's still alive, as far as we know."

Wes made a small whistling sound. "That's good news, huh?"

"Let's hope so. Thanks for the research, Wes. It helps."

We pushed ourselves out of the beanbag chairs. Wes returned to his socializing and I crossed to the other end of the building. The door to Mike's office was slightly ajar. Voices came from inside. But the female voice was not Kim's, and it was not happy. I knocked and went in.

Connie Plush stopped in midsentence and gave me a not-you-again glare. She was on the opposite side of the office, pacing, toying with the glasses at the end of her silver necklace. A black cashmere sweater was draped over her shoulders. Mike was leaning back in his chair, bouncing the eraser end of a pencil off his knee. "What's new, Bill?" he said.

"Nothing much." I considered for a moment, then decided to go right at Connie. "Why won't you let Wendy test Eternaderm for you, Connie? She worked for you just like Alissa did. Are you afraid it only works on skin under thirty?"

Mike looked puzzled. "Was Wendy here?"

Connie crossed her arms in a ready posture. "Eternaderm works on all kinds of skin. Whether or not I let that woman use it is my business."

"What's your beef with her?"

"Don't trust anything she says, Bill. How did you find her?"

"She found me. She was full of interesting tidbits. So was her friend Brendon."

"He's the young guy from SG, right?" Mike said. "What's he doing with Wendy?"

"He quit Silicon Glamour. He's got it bad for Alissa."

"He quit?" Connie's exclamation came out before she could stop it. "Oh, Trisha must be steamed. He was her little pet."

"Well, now he's licking Wendy's hand," I said.

"You've got it backwards: Brendon's the one who holds the leash. He's worthless, but Trisha turned to jelly around him." Connie could barely suppress her glee. Talking about Trisha brought out a whole new side of her. She picked up a wine glass from a nearby shelf. The wine seemed to be putting her in an expansive mood.

"What kind of hold did he have over Trisha?" I asked.

"You saw him. She's not a deep woman."

The tightness around her mouth had relaxed and her eyes had a silvery sparkle. I wanted to take advantage of it. "I'd been under the impression you and Trisha were pals," I said. "I guess I was wrong."

"I hope none of us have any illusions about Silicon Glamour," she replied. "Or Sylvain. If—"

"How does the connection work?" I interrupted. "Does Trisha run both of them?"

One corner of Connie's mouth turned up. "That's our best guess. But we've never been able to pin her down."

"You're kidding me," Mike said. "Trisha's in charge?"

Connie's small grin turned into a smirk. "Wake up, Mikey-boy. You're in the women's world now." She must have liked Mike. I hadn't heard her tease like that before. "Listen, guys," she went on, "if you can get Brendon on your side, you can strike at Trisha's heel. Wendy's, too."

"Trisha, yes," I said. "But Wendy's got some hold over Brendon. I figure it's because she's dangling Alissa in front of him. He claims to be over her, but he's lying."

"Dangling a dead woman?" Connie objected.

"Alissa's not dead. The clipping was a fake."

Mike sat up. "That's great news, Bill!"

But Connie's face had tightened again. She took a sip from the glass, put it down, and murmured, "Let's hope you're right. I have my doubts."

I sat down in a chair across from Mike, wondering why Connie preferred Alissa dead. "You said Sylvain couldn't be trusted, Connie. Why?"

Her eyes and Mike's met across the desk. She made a slight shake of the head, but Mike said, "It's okay. I want Bill to hear it from me."

Mike turned to me. "Sylvain has made me an offer," he said. "A pretty nice parachute if I bow out and let them have their way with Algoplex. Hell, what am I saying, it's a silk parachute with gold trimmings and a full bar."

He stopped and watched me. He wanted to draw out my reaction. I kept waiting.

"I won't take it, of course," Mike went on. "It would violate the spirit of Rod's company. I see myself as the guardian of his legacy. But I would be lying if I said it wasn't tempting. The fact is, I think they're going to get control, anyway. I'll end up on the street with nothing. But I'd rather do that than sell out Rod."

Connie was watching Mike carefully.

He returned her gaze and said, "Connie has offered to help me. As I told you, Bill, this company will come to a dead halt without an infusion. Connie thinks Plush can give us a bridge."

"Doesn't Sylvain already effectively control Plush?" I said. "Wouldn't giving her equity amount to giving Sylvain what it wants by other means?"

Connie broke in sharply. "That doesn't deserve an answer, Michael." The steel had returned to her eyes, flashing betrayal and anger. "I've been generous with you today, Bill. Yet you question my motives to my face."

"It's a financial question with a financial answer," I said, backpedaling. "If I'm wrong, just tell me."

She folded her arms. Her glance snapped back to Mike. "The offer stands. You let me know. But don't take advice from people who don't know what they're talking about."

Mike watched her walk to the door. "Thank you, Mrs. Plush." His voice was apologetic.

The door was beginning to close. "Where's Kim?" I said loudly, so that Connie would hear. Mike paused, waiting for the door to click shut. It didn't.

I got up and opened the door. "Connie? Is there something else?"

The look in her eyes surprised me. Her mouth was tense with worry and consternation, the kind of worry you'd see on a mother's face. Our eyes met and a moment of understanding passed between us. I didn't yet comprehend what was understood, but her unexpected vulnerability told me that something about Kim mattered to her deeply.

She turned quickly to leave and I closed the door. Mike let out a big sigh. He slumped in his chair and said, "Bill, you're doing a great job for the most part, but sometimes you go too far."

I wanted to say: Just driving in the dark, Mike, like always. Instead I contrived a smile of collusion. "I knew I smelled another perfume besides Connie's in here. Where are you hiding her?"

Mike returned the smile. "She's the one playing hide-and-seek. When Connie came over, Kim disappeared."

"Connie knows Kim. Do you know how?"

Mike shrugged. "First I've heard of it."

"Be careful, Mike. With both of them."

"Connie's playing straight, Bill. She told me things about Sylvain, about what they'd done with Plush, that would normally be very closely held. She wouldn't have if this was just a trick to get Algoplex into Sylvain's hands."

"What did they do with Plush?"

"The same kind of thing they're trying to do to me."

The pieces began to click into place. I wasn't quite ready to share them with Mike, though. I didn't necessarily buy his noble line about defending Rod's legacy. Experience told me the last thing that bothered a CEO was selling out. Instead I said, "You should be careful with Kim, too. She's a complete unknown."

Mike grinned again, did a half-swivel in his chair, and showed me the front of his hand. "I've got to say, Bill, I'm a little tired of the ol' palm pilot, if you know what I mean. It's been a long time since I met a woman like Kim. I'm feeling that special tingle."

"I don't mind what you do in your own bedroom. Just don't give her information. Remember what happened to Rod."

Mike's grin froze. "I can take care of myself."

"Listen, have you heard anything from the police?"

"Jesus, yes. I was waiting until we were alone to tell you. They think they found the murder weapon. A kitchen knife, smaller than the one Rod had in his hand, covered with blood. And get this: It was in Alissa's apartment."

I whistled. "Whoa. Are they sure it's for real?"

"The lab's running tests right now. This throws us for a loop, doesn't it?"

"Let's wait for the lab results. Even if it's true Alissa is alive, I think she's being set up. You know who's got access to her apartment: Rupert Evans. This'll bring us one step closer to him in the end."

Mike nodded. "That makes sense. I didn't know what to think."

The way his eyes kept flicking to door, as if awaiting an arrival, told me it wasn't the head on top of his shoulders doing the thinking right now. I stood to go. "I better get back to the reception."

"Me, too," he said. "Go on ahead. I got to lock up. I'll see you around."

"You sure will." Sooner than he thought.

>> >> >> >> >>

I had a tough choice. Ellen Quong had been talking with some of the engineers and now she'd come back to get her coat and umbrella. I wanted to talk to her, but I also wanted to keep an eye out for Kim. Wendy had Brendon on her string, but Kim had two people, maybe more, on hers. I wanted to know why.

Wes was alone in his beanbag now. I asked him to go on Kim duty, preferably from a place where he could watch the parking lot. Meanwhile, I caught Ellen as she was leaving.

She was warm as usual. She expressed concern about the purple shade of my jaw. I told her I was all right, just had a little space between my teeth that I'd have to fix someday. Then I asked if we could have another conversation about Eternaderm.

She glanced around the room. No one from Plush remained. "Connie doesn't like me to talk to you. But you know what? That's her problem. I've got to get home to my family, but come over tomorrow. Call me first and I'll let you in by the side door."

I thanked her. The waiters who'd been attending the tables were starting to pack up. Outside, the Frisbee field was obscured in gloom. Darkness had descended over it and the rain was coming down with conviction now.

I kept thinking Mike would have to stop by the reception one last time. After five minutes passed, I decided his rendezvous with Kim was already under way. I hurried down the corridor to find Wes. He was standing by a stairwell window, hands in his pockets, squinting into the soggy dusk.

"Any sign of her?" I asked.

"Nope. Mike left a few minutes ago. And there's your friend Ellen getting into her car."

"Thanks, Wes. You're off duty now."

"Where are you going? I'll come."

"Sorry," I said, "it's kind of delicate."

"You're spying on Mike and Kim, aren't you?"

I didn't answer. We descended the stairs and parted ways in the puddling parking lot. The Scout's small wipers did their best to clear the flat panel of windshield glass. I checked Mike's house first, in Redwood City. No cars were parked in front and the windows were dark. Still, I had a look around back. An umbrella would draw too much attention, so I went without it. By the time I'd jumped his back gate and returned, I was pretty well soaked.

There was one other place to try: Rod's house. It would be weird for them to choose it, I thought, and yet it might be exactly the place Kim wanted. Mike seemed to feel no compunction about lounging there.

His Ferrari was parked in the driveway. A white compact rental car was across the street. I parked the Scout two doors down and ran across the front lawn to the side of the house. A yellow flicker played on the living-room window. But the window was high and I'd have to chin myself up to see inside. That'd be too noisy. I wasn't feeling eager to play the voyeur, either. I went back around to the front and rang the doorbell.

After a second ring and then a third Mike answered. He was startled for a moment: not because I was dripping wet but because it was me. He recovered enough to invite me in. He felt guilty about something: the date, the venue, or maybe something more.

"I hope I'm not interrupting anything," I murmured.

"Well, we can't leave you out in the rain, can we?" he said, hiding his annoyance.

Kim drew in a breath when she saw me. She'd been sitting near the center of the sofa and moved quickly to the end. But I could tell by the position of the drinks on the coffee table that she and Mike had been cozily close. She gave me a cool hello. The fire was roaring in the fireplace.

Mike made an effort at sounding hearty. "Have a drink, Bill. What'll it be?"

I shivered involuntarily and sat on the brick shelf in front of the hearth. The flames warmed me. "I thought the fireplace was broken," I said.

"Kim got it going," Mike called on his way into the kitchen. "Rum and Coke all right? That's what we're having."

"Fine," I called back, then looked at Kim. "Sorry, I didn't mean to break up the party."

She averted her eyes. Her legs were crossed. She swung a foot nervously. Mike returned and stuck a glass into my hand. It was a small one.

"Here's to Rod," I said.

Mike sat on the couch but kept a respectful distance from Kim. They raised their glasses. After taking a gulp, he said, "What brings you here, Bill? I'm sure you have other places to escape the rain."

I fumbled for a moment. What was it exactly? Then I glanced at Kim and knew. "I don't recall if I told you, Mike. I got some big news today, good news. Alissa's still alive. The Arizona story was phony."

Mike let out an impatient grunt. "Are you losing your mind? You said that to me in my office half an hour ago."

But it wasn't Mike I was watching. It was Kim, and I saw the millisecond of panic traverse her face. She recrossed her legs and looked past me into the fire.

"Really?" I said to Mike. "You're right, I must have holes in my brain. Too many facts to keep track of. Too many fake identities."

Kim's other leg was swinging now.

"Yeah. Well, like I said, that's great news," Mike replied. "Maybe you still can find her."

"Yep, probably I can."

Kim stood. "I'm so sorry, Mike, but I've got to go." She looked at her watch. "I've got a yoga class tonight."

"Oh Jeez, that's a shame, Kim," he said, standing with her. "You can miss one class, can't you?"

She gathered her coat and bag from a chair. "No, it's important."

Mike turned to give me a vicious scowl, then followed her down the hall. I didn't watch, but I knew what was happening: the peck on the cheek, maybe more; the promise to call, to see each other again; the door closing.

"You bastard!" Mike barked, returning. "You knew I had a date with her!"

I drank the rest of what was in my glass. "How did she start the fire?"

"I don't know! I don't care! I was in the kitchen."

I rubbed my jaw. "I'm in pain right now, Mike. I better go, too."

"You're a dirty player, Bill Damen. If you're interested in Kim for yourself, why don't you come out and say so?"

I opened the door and peered down the street. The taillights of the compact were disappearing. "I really am sorry, Mike. I'll see you later."

I shut the door, raced to the Scout, and peeled out to catch the taillights.

20

"Odd face job, Alissa," I called out.

The front gate at the Granada apartments was swinging shut behind her. I caught it. She turned casually, as if I must be talking to someone else, then hurried up the walk.

I followed her to the door of the building. "Most people try to improve their looks," I said. "Why'd you go the other way?"

"What do you want from me, Bill?" Her voice was both weary and irritated. She fumbled her key into the lock and opened the door. I put my foot in to keep it from closing.

"Just the truth, Kim. Or Alissa. Or whoever it is on her way to Alissa's apartment."

She stopped at the bottom of the foyer stairs. "Please leave me alone. Otherwise I'll have to scream for the manager."

"That would answer one of my questions. Rupert got you this apartment, and the manager's his friend. It would tell me you're on Rupert's side."

She shook her head but she did not scream. She seemed paralyzed.

"I'm not going to hurt you," I said. "Let's go on up. Apartment 304. Maybe you can also explain how you turned on the fireplace in Rod's house. The manual switch was broken, but it could have been activated by voice. By Alissa's voice. The front door could be opened the same way."

She hesitated, then trudged slowly up the stairs. She gave a small gasp when we reached the third floor and she saw the yellow tape marking the apartment.

"So this is your first time back," I said. "You didn't know about the knife."

"Quiet!" she commanded, putting the key in the door. We ducked under the tape. She closed the door and said, "Don't talk in public like that."

I held her hand from the light switch. "People may be watching the place. Maybe the police, maybe someone else. I didn't see anything in front, but they could be in back."

She took this in stride and glanced around the apartment. "What knife?" she said briskly.

I felt my way through the shadows to the sofa. She wriggled out of her raincoat and tossed it on a chair. "We'll get to the knife," I said, sitting down. "Let's talk about some other things first. What did you use to change your appearance—Eternaderm?"

She sat cautiously at the other end of the sofa. Our eyes adjusted to the dimness and she gave me a curious look. "You're all wet," she said, then burst out laughing and left the room.

I waited there, wondering. She returned with a towel, which she threw at my head. I gave my hair a quick rub, then wrapped the towel around my neck. The room was chilly.

"I wanted to try a new look," she said, flipping her hair. "I thought Rod would like it."

That made no sense, and neither did the new brightness in her manner, but I played along. "So what went wrong?"

"Nothing! It's just a new me."

The girlish tone sounded odd. Then I realized she was using it to disarm me. She still hadn't admitted who she was. "I want to find the people who killed Rod," I said in a slow and careful voice. "I want you to help me do that. Unless you start telling me the truth, I'm going to assume you're on their side. If you're on their side, I'm not going to be very nice to deal with."

The smile slowly disappeared. Her hands clasped in her lap. "You only see this from your point of view," she said. "Your life is hunky-dory. You probably have a family you can fall back on if things go bad. Or friends. A skill. A life."

"That's all true," I admitted, "except for the hunky-dory part. I've got a hole in my teeth and things could get a lot worse before they get better. So let's help each other. Let's start with simple stuff. Like our real names."

She snorted. The gruff sound was a surprise after the girlish act. "Real names. It's easy for you to be Bill Damen. People give some respect to 'Bill Damen.' What kind of respect does Kim with the bad skin get? You know what Mike was after. It was all I had to offer. I needed someone to be on my side. He likes playing the white knight."

"Okay, then, who would *you* like to play—if people gave you respect?"

Her hand flew to her eyes. I didn't know why until she spoke. Then I realized she was crying. "Just a regular person, Bill. Not someone who's desperate, not someone who's indentured for four years to a sleazy agency. I'd take any decent job—administrative assistant, bookkeeper, anything. I just want fair pay without having to sell myself."

"Everyone in the Valley is selling themselves, but . . . I get your point. You want to be able to be yourself in your work, not some created persona."

"I don't know who 'myself' is anymore. I'm no one right now. I'm starting from scratch and I've got nothing left. Not a thing."

She was still holding back the specifics. I took a shot at filling them in myself. "Alissa went away. You didn't want to be recognized when you came back. That's why you changed your appearance. Alissa is finished. You're Kim now."

Her shoulders slumped. "Never use that name again. Alissa. Just forget it, wipe it out. It wasn't my real name, anyway. Rod was in love with her. She's gone, and now he's gone, too." The tears came harder. "It's my fault. What they did to him—I should have let him in on my plan. I should have thought of another way. I was trying to give us a new life."

I moved closer, but she shrank away from me. She didn't want comfort. "Tell me if I've got it right," I said. "You wanted to be with Rod. In order to do that, you had to escape Silicon Glamour and the three years left on your contract. You staged your disappearance. What were you planning to do when you came back?"

Kim wiped her face with her hands. I handed her the towel. She pressed it to her face and shook her head. "I don't know. I mean, I thought Rod and I could just be together. But I hadn't thought it out. What if he hated me the way I look now?"

"What were you going to do, just walk up and ring his doorbell?"

She laughed. "That's pretty much it. 'Hi, Rod, remember me? Not the other me, this me. You can't have Alissa, but you can have Kim. So now let's get married!'" The laugh turned acrid. "What a fool."

"No," I said gently. "It might have worked. He did love you, Al—I mean, Kim. I think he loved you all the way through, not just on the outside. The biggest danger was that Rupert might have found you out. I hear he's got a good eye."

"Yeah, but why would he ever need to see me? Rod and I could have our life together. He didn't need Silicon Glamour anymore."

"That's not quite true." She gave me a startled look, and I explained, "Silicon Glamour is hooked up with Sylvain Partners. In fact, Trisha seems to be calling the shots for both. With Sylvain as Rod's new backer, Trisha would always be lurking."

Kim's eyes were wide. "She scares me, Bill. More than any of them. Rupert is a sweet man. Underneath it all I think he really cared for us. But his big sister . . . she's the one who'd skin me alive if she found me out."

"I imagine she already had the evil eye on you because of Brendon," I said. "Because he wanted you."

She nodded. "I dreaded both of them. I was caught in between: If I didn't act nice to Brendon, he'd bad-mouth me to Trish. But if I was too nice, Trish would punish me. I had to get out of there. I mean, it was for Rod, that's the real reason I left, but . . ."

We looked at each other in the murky light. Finally I felt as though I was hearing the rock-bottom reality. "You needed something better than a simple disguise to pull this off. Someone at Plush came up with ways to change your face. They've been working on melanin, and they used that to modify your skin tone. I suppose they had compounds to make it rougher, too. Who was it—Ellen Quong?"

"The rough skin is a nice touch, huh? Who'd ever deliberately do that to themselves? But please don't ask who it was at Plush. I can't give that away."

"You also had to concoct the fake clipping from Arizona. I suppose you know someone at a newspaper who could do that."

Kim seemed to settle back into herself. "It's actually kind of a relief not having to fake it anymore, Bill. You can't imagine, that first night I met you, how hard it was to pretend I hadn't seen Rod for three years. It killed me, being in his house like that, the house where I'd spent time with him just two or three weeks before."

"I'm sorry, Kim. You went through all this to be with Rod, and then you come back and he's gone."

Her hand went to her face. "Don't get me started again. I cried so much the first day I was back. I can't believe I have this many tears inside me."

She hid behind the towel. A new anger rose up in me at the fact of Rod's death. I thought I was right about how he would have reacted to Kim. He would have been happy with her. They both would have been happy. In that alternate stream of events, Rod would have had to endure the news of Alissa's death. How would he have handled it? How long would Kim have waited before coming back to relieve him of his grief?

Then it came to me who was helping her. It was the person who insisted Alissa had met her demise in Arizona.

"Connie Plush," I said to Kim. "She's your benefactor. She had full access to her company's technology. She could order up the compounds for you. No wonder I pissed her off so much. She was afraid I'd blow your cover."

Kim let the towel fall to her lap but said nothing. For some reason I became aware of my sodden clothes. "Am I ruining your couch?" I asked.

"Who cares? It belongs to SG."

We both laughed. A strange intimacy was growing between us, the intimacy of a shared secret. I said, "Who else knows who you really are, Kim? Does your mother know?"

She held me with a steady gaze. "First of all, Kim is who I really am. She might be a work in progress, but there's no other 'real me,' okay? Second, Connie would kill me if I admitted she helped me. Third, no, my mother knows nothing about this. You might think it's weird not to tell my own mother, but—"

"Not in this case," I said. "Look, I'm not going to blab to anyone. You never admitted Connie helped you, I figured it out myself. I just need to know who else knows."

"You. You, Bill, and now you have a huge advantage over me. I have no idea if I can trust you, and to be honest, I don't really care right now. So do whatever you want."

"I want to get who killed Rod. That's it. Does Mike know about you?"

She snorted again. "Mike the eager beaver. No, he doesn't. He's gentleman enough not to ask too many questions."

I couldn't really blame Kim for her aggressive tone. She was right about the advantage I had. "Be careful with Mike. Sylvain's trying to buy him out. He could switch sides any minute."

"I'm careful with everyone, Bill. Or did you forget what my previous job was?"

I gave what I hoped was a soothing smile. "How did you get involved with SG, anyway?"

"*Rupert*," she said. "He lured me in. Made it sound like a great business opportunity. Working with executives, learning different tech sectors, eventually moving into SG's investment department. I meant what I said, he did care for us, but he also neglected to make clear to me that my real job, at first, would be going out on dates."

"Is their investment department the link with Sylvain?"

"I wish I could tell you. I asked lots of questions about it until Trisha told me to shut up."

Since Kim was in such a blunt mood, I asked, "Did you pass Algoplex information on to Rupert?"

Her eyes flashed. "It was part of the job. We got bonuses. I had to play the game, I had to feed them something. I didn't know I was going to feel about Rod the way I did. There was so much to him, Bill, so much more than people know. I kind of unlocked something in him. I sound like I'm bragging, but I'm not."

"Exactly how much information did you pass on to Rupert?"

"You talk like it was easy for me, Bill. I hated it! But I couldn't let them get suspicious. And I couldn't tell Rod—I was afraid he'd dismiss me on the spot." She twirled a strand of hair around her finger. "Did Rod talk about me? What did he say?"

"He suspected you were spying. In fact, he pretty much knew. He loved you, anyway, Kim. He couldn't help himself."

She massaged her brows. "He had such a hard time believing how I felt about him. He didn't realize how great he was. I knew how to do the glamour thing, my mother made sure of that. Rod thought he was out of my league. I told him I was sick of it, sick of the veils, the come-ons, the string-alongs, the market-place mentality about relationships. I was sick of feeling like a *product*. It worked in the other direction, too: Women looked at their potential mates like investment opportunities. The sad thing is, I didn't know any different until I met Rod. Then I saw what could be with him. I still had my training and my old habits, and I had to use them in public. I admit, I even used them to reel him back in if I thought he was slipping."

"Slipping?"

"Losing interest," she said impatiently. "Don't you under-stand? My big fear was he'd never want me if I dropped all the veils. I'm just *me,* I don't have a good education or upbringing or anything. I didn't know much, but I knew I wanted more from my life. I wanted the kind of thing I had with Rod."

"So turning into Kim was the last veil. The one that would put an end to all the others. I have to say, you've got a certain look down. I mean that as a compliment."

She made a face. "Yeah, who'd *choose* this persona?"

"The change is kind of a jolt," I admitted, thinking of the photograph of Alissa. "But Rod was all about substance. He would have been thrilled when he found out it was you. His wildest dream would have come true."

Kim was suddenly silent. I hadn't meant to pose what they'd both lost so starkly. "I'm sorry—" I began.

"Never mind. You forget that I grew up with the feeling we'd already lost everything. At least I'm still on the planet; I'll have another chance someday. It's Rod you should feel sorry for. I still can't believe he's gone. I keep going back to the house. Maybe it's not right, but I can't stop myself. I keep thinking he'll come walking up the stairs from the basement office. You're right, he programmed things like the door and the fireplace so they'd be activated by my voice. But there were other things, too, silly little messages he left in different rooms. If I went into a room singing, the furniture would talk to me. Funny things, like 'Here comes Alissa, most beautiful woman on earth,' or 'At the sound of the beep, please remove your clothes.' When I was in the house, that first night you found me, I'd been going around picking up those messages. I was in a state."

We sat in silence, thinking of Rod and his delight in gadgets. Rain gusted against the sliding glass door. After a while, I said, "Weren't you worried about someone recognizing your voice?"

"I planned to stay away from people who'd known me. But just to be careful, Connie helped me alter it. I've been practicing to make it deeper. I've also been smoking, and drinking abrasives, to make it rougher."

"And you told Rod nothing about the plan, not even a hint?"

Kim sighed. Her voice quivered. "He's a lousy liar. I knew Rupert would grill him. I thought I was protecting him by making him think Alissa had disappeared."

I nodded. "If it makes you feel any better, I think you were right."

"Who do you think killed Rod?"

"Right now, I'd say it was Trisha and Rupert. They have the most obvious motives. At first I thought it was because they believed Rod had kidnapped you. Now, with Trisha being the real power behind Sylvain, it looks like the motive was to take over Algoplex."

"*Get her*, Bill." Kim's tone was almost vicious. "I'll bet Rupert wasn't involved or didn't know what was really going on. But I want you to get Trisha."

"I will, if she's the one. Tell me more about her and Silicon Glamour. Wendy says she started as a showgirl in Vegas?"

"I heard that once at SG, too. I could believe it. But I don't have much else to tell you—she knew everything about us, and we knew nothing about her. That was how it worked. And you already understand how SG operates. You said something earlier today about Erika—do you know her?"

"Yes." I recounted my date with Erika and the liquid that had been thrown in her face.

"Oh, no," Kim gasped. "Oh, *no*! That was because of me, too, wasn't it?"

"No, it was because of me. She took a risk for me. We just have to hope the damage isn't permanent."

"I feel awful about that."

"Connie should, too. She refused to help Erika."

Kim sighed. "She probably had to, in order not to arouse Trisha's suspicion. Well, when this is all over, I'll call Erika. Is she still in the building?"

"No. Call her on her mobile. Listen, at SG, did you meet a couple of thuggish guys named Larsen and Terry?"

Kim shook her head. "No. I don't think I ever heard those names."

"What about Gary? Tell me about him. And Brendon."

"Gary's just—well, he's Rupert's boyfriend for one thing, but he's like the bodyguard. So he has to act tough. He's actually very sweet. He'd hurt somebody if they were attacking one of us, but I can't picture him killing Rod. And Brendon, all I know about him is he had that crush on me. I don't know why he picked me for his obsession; maybe because I was the one woman who didn't swoon over him. Brendon was so used to getting what he wanted. The more I said no, the harder he tried. He made fun of Rod all the time."

"Do you know he left SG and has teamed up with your mother?"

Kim's hand went to her mouth. "Oh my *God*, you're kidding! That's ridiculous! To do what?"

"To get to you—or Alissa. He thinks Wendy can deliver you. As for Wendy, she seems to think he—and I—can procure Eternaderm. She's desperate for it. Apparently she's got this guy in Reno, and he's—"

"Like *most* men," Kim interjected. "I'm sure Brendon wouldn't give me a second look now. But I hope Reno works out for Mom."

"Sounds like you're keeping a safe distance."

"Rod was right. I need to take a break from her. I mean, she's my mother, and I want to be there for her—eventually. But I want to start my new life first. Whatever that means. A widow who never was married."

"Why won't Connie let her test the treatment?"

"I don't know. Mom and I did some photo shoots with Plush once. It was a little, um, tricky. It seems like Connie should be nice to her, but . . . somehow Mom always screws up. Connie agreed with Rod. She wanted me to get away from Mom."

"That would explain why Wendy hates both of them. She was afraid they were stealing you from her, shutting her out. Trisha, too, I imagine."

"Rupert always said that SG was my family now, not Wendy."

"What else should I know about your mother, Kim?"

"She's not such a bad person," Kim said. "She just wants a break in life, that's all. I mean, a big break, bigger than most schlumps get. That's what she called them, the people we were supposedly better than. She said we were destined for great things. She would take me on these real-estate tours, you know, tours of expensive mansions, and promise that one day we'd live in one. We deserved them, she said, for—I don't know, for just being us. It's kind of pathetic. Rod and Connie were right, her values are in the wrong place. But I can't hate her. I hope Brendon isn't taking advantage of her."

I chuckled. "She'll be fine. He'll do anything for her. I think it's because she creates a very passable likeness of Alissa when she wants to." Kim grimaced, and I said, "Yeah, it's weird all right. Anyway, it'd be a big help if Connie would at least pretend to put her on the Eternaderm list. Wendy and Brendon know things about Trisha that I need to know."

"I'll talk to Connie."

The rain had let up. The sound of car wheels squished in the alley. Kim got to her feet. "I don't want to stay here much longer, Bill. I just came to get a few things. You said something about a knife."

"Yeah, the knife. Well, it seems to be the one that was used on Rod. And it was found under your mattress, covered with blood."

"*What?* That's horrible! You can't think—"

"I think that Trisha or Rupert planted it here. But we'll hear from the police tomorrow about what prints and whose blood are on the knife."

She shivered and looked around. "How did they get in?"

I didn't want to tell her it hadn't been so hard. "This is an SG apartment. I'm sure Rupert had access to a key."

"You're right. Okay, now I really want to get out of here. You've got my number. It's better if you don't know where I'm staying."

I stood up. "I'll walk out with you."

"No, you go on ahead. I just, you know—I want a minute alone. Here, you can take this towel to stay dry."

"I'll be fine. I'll call you in the morning."

"Thanks," Kim said. She wandered into the kitchen, preoccupied with her own thoughts. I slipped the door open, checked the hall, and made my way down the stairs.

I turned up my collar as I went down the walk. A light rain was still falling. Absorbed in thoughts of my own, I never saw the guy lurking outside the gate. As I came through it, he slammed me up against the iron fence.

I reacted instinctively and threw my elbow into his nose. He let out a yelp and swung at my head. I ducked, but he caught the top of it. I hit him in the chest. He staggered backward. We circled each other in the dark.

"Who are you?" I said.

"Who are *you*?" he said.

I faked a couple of punches at him. He flinched, then announced, "I don't want to hurt you. Just leave Kim alone."

I straightened. "You're with Kim?"

"I'm watching out for her. It's dangerous around here. Maybe you didn't know that."

I shook my head. "Okay, calm down." I backed my way toward the Scout, keeping an eye on him. He stayed by the gate.

I had a little too much to think about as I drove back up 101 to San Francisco. Alissa. Rod. Connie. Kim. She'd been so convincing. I'd been ready to believe her story, hook, line, and sinker. Now I remembered how she'd claimed to be at my mercy, knowing all the while a guy was waiting outside to jump me.

21

Thursday morning dawned cold. Long red fingers reached across the icy waters of the bay. I'd woken before light, brewed some coffee, and then walked down to the waterfront. I think best when I walk. Rod once told me that the mathematician al-Khwarizmi, in his calculation of reduction and restoration, called the unknown for which he was solving *shai*, "the thing." For me, the thing was who killed Rod. I tried to devise an algorithm of motives and opportunities, means and inferences, to solve for that unknown.

Motives to kill Rod were plentiful. The clearest belonged to Rupert and Trisha—especially Trisha, if she was the real power behind Sylvain. Rupert's talents leaned more to the daily operation of SG. My theory was that Sylvain provided a secret outlet for SG's profits. Trisha had used Alissa and Sylvain to lure Rod into the alliance with Plush. Eliminating Rod had opened the way for her to get her hands on Algoplex and Rod's brilliant software at a cheap price. Trisha used the SG associates for espionage and Larsen and Terry for muscle.

I'd crossed the 20th Street bridge. Now I turned left down Illinois, toward China Basin. The rain had stopped sometime during the night and the high pressure that usually followed a storm had moved in. The air was chilly enough that I needed to wear a hat and gloves.

Wendy and Brendon also had motives, less calculated but still strong. Both, for their own reasons, felt Rod had stolen Alissa from them—perhaps literally, or perhaps by winning her heart. Wendy also blamed Rod for conspiring to keep Eternaderm from her. The only problem was, she and Brendon didn't strike me as competent enough to carry off a murder. Not only that, killing Rod would deprive them of what they presumed was their lead to Alissa.

I couldn't rule out Mike Riley, either. A new picture of him was coming into focus. The story arc of this picture was that he would throw up his arms on Algoplex, cash out while the cashing was good, waltz off with Kim, and move on to the next target. His heartfelt words about Rod were window dressing. Or, even if he felt them at the time, they wouldn't get in the way of his doing what today's executive needed to do. Nor was it impossible that he and Kim had planned the whole thing from the start. Mike's competitive streak might have given him delight in stealing his boss's girlfriend, even if it was a setup all along.

After the way last night ended, I didn't know what to think of Kim. I'd believed her up until then; her emotions seemed so genuine. But I'd witnessed enough spells cast over the past week to doubt my own perceptions. Mike's allegedly new infatuation with her could be a ruse. The fact that Connie Plush was helping both of them meant she could be in on it, too.

Trucks rumbled down Third Street and rowers cut along the Central Basin inlet. I walked out on the Agua Vista pier, where a few fishermen were making their morning casts. The sky was a pale, endlessly receding blue now, the bay placid. I leaned over the railing and gazed at the water's changing face.

The next operation in solving the equation would be to nail down means and opportunities. Wendy was the one who'd set up Rod for the Cheshire Cat that night. That could mean everything or nothing. I'd seen her at the club, which gave her an alibi, but she might have sent Brendon to Rod's house. He was strong enough to overpower Rod. Brendon had said Larsen and Terry were in Vegas. Gary had claimed that he, Rupert, and Trisha were at a hospital charity dinner. That could be checked out. The whereabouts of the rest were an open question.

Detective Coharie might know the answers. It was unlikely he'd give them to me, though. Being COO of only my camera, I didn't rate on his chart. I'd ask Mike what he'd said and what the lab discovered about the knife. That might help pin Trisha and Rupert. I still wondered how the killer got into Rod's house. Knowing Rod, he'd just opened the door when the bell rang.

I labored back up 20th Street. The sun had risen. My head swam with too many variables. I needed to solve them soon, before Algoplex was lost to Sylvain. If Rod was here and the victim had been otherwise, he'd probably be able to reduce the terms and hand me a clean answer. He had his own form of magic, one of switches and operations, repeated recursively until a revelation was reached. He'd told me once that he believed nothing occurred after death: It was blank, the ultimate null. This, he'd admitted, squinting and blinking, was only a conjecture. But that was what made life interesting: the unknown.

Perhaps my answers could be found in more coffee. It was always worth a try. I went into Scoby's. No sooner had I sat down with a roll and a tall new cup than my cell phone rang. I fumbled it open and made for the door. People did use their phones in Scoby's, but we regulars looked down on them.

"So what happened last night?" Wes demanded.

I told him the Kim story in the order it had occurred. I had him and myself believing everything she'd said, right up to the moment the guy pinned me to the fence. Wes expressed a desire to run a scan on him.

"I need to find out who he is first," I said. "I'll call you back when I know."

I'd been pacing on the sidewalk as I talked, dodging passersby. It was not much better than using your phone in the café. I'd just clicked off with Wes when the thing rang again.

"Are you up?"

It was Kim. I said I was. She launched into an apology for last night. I told her to save it. If she wanted to talk to me, she should be at my flat at three o'clock this afternoon. She promised she would. I didn't add that it was a test to see whether she came alone.

I went back to my table to discover my roll had disappeared from my plate. No one in the café appeared to have it. Then I saw the dog sitting on the stoop, licking his lips. Usually dogs stayed outside, but this one had snuck in. He gave me a mixed look of guilt and hope. Guilty as he was, he hoped I'd provide more. A few crumbs remained on the plate. I set it at his feet, and went home.

>> >> >> >> >>

I showed up at Mike Riley's office at ten o'clock. His shirt was untucked and his hair mussed as if he'd already put in a full day. "You should have called first," he complained as he closed his door behind me. "I'm very busy."

"I wanted to hear what you've learned from the police." I didn't add that I also wanted to watch him face-to-face while he answered.

He sat in his swivel chair and rattled if off to me. "They're convinced now that the knife is the actual murder weapon. Whoever did it must have put the other knife in Rod's hand to try to make it look like suicide. But here's the really weird thing: The blood is not Rod's. It came from a cow."

I sat down, trying to take the news in stride. "Both the blood on the knife and the drips on the floor?"

"All of it." He stopped his swiveling, opened his mouth, and made me wait for the next words. "Detective Coharie traced the anonymous tip to your cell phone. He's asking questions about you."

I tried not to show my consternation. I should've used a pay phone. "Were there prints on the knife?"

"Smeared and fragmentary. Nothing positive."

"Has he said anything to you about suspects? Has he asked people where they were last Wednesday night?"

"He's finally given up the suicide idea, thank God. He thinks it was a crankhead, maybe two, trying to burgle the place. The only other person he wonders about is you. I mention this to you as a favor."

"He needs to zero in on Trisha Evans," I said. "She has two guys working for her, maybe from Vegas, named Larsen and Terry. They're the ones who hit me in the mouth."

"Did you file a report on that?"

"No. But I can. It'll give me a good reason to see Coharie."

"I would proceed with caution if I were you, Bill," Mike said. I noticed his wording: He was talking about me separately from the job. "It already looks bad enough with the call about the knife."

"I gave him the murder weapon. He could at least say thank you."

Mike leaned his elbows on the armrests and again made me wait for his words. "I'm sorry to have to do this, Bill. But I think it's time for Algoplex to part ways with you. Give me an invoice and we'll settle up." His manner was brisk, his eyes averted. He wasn't sorry at all.

"I thought you were going to rename the company." It was all I could think of to say.

Mike turned his head slowly to scowl at me. "It's no longer your concern, Bill. We appreciate your services, but we find they no longer benefit the company. We don't feel you're playing on the same team."

"Do you mean the Algoplex team or the Mike team?"

"That's a low blow, Bill. You're not welcome here anymore."

I stood up. "I'll leave. But I'm watching you, Mike. I'm watching what you do with this Sylvain offer. I'm watching the outcome of the key-man clause, which you put in the contract."

"That was for Rod's protection!" Mike exploded from his chair. He stood, fists clenched, steam building inside like in a stout little teapot. I knew he wasn't responsible for the key-man clause, but I wanted him to come at me. I wanted to find out how strong he was and how combustible: whether he could have killed Rod.

But the steam ebbed. He shook his head and sat back down. "I warned you. And yet you keep pushing."

I opened the door and turned before I left. "You won't get that invoice, Mike. I don't want anything from you."

» » » » »

I've been told that when one door closes in life, another opens. I'd closed the door on Mike, but found Connie's open to me when I arrived at Plush Biologics. Kim must have spoken to her.

I wouldn't have known Connie had a warm side, but she greeted me as if I were her favorite nephew. This was a point in her favor, and also in Kim's.

We danced around the subject of Kim for a few minutes. I asked Connie if she'd heard anything more about Mike and the Sylvain offer. She said no, but she'd let me know if she did. I said I appreciated her help. She said she was glad to oblige. When finally I blurted Kim's name and said her secret was safe, Connie replied with a conspiratorial shush. "Certain things are better not spoken aloud, Bill. We know what we know."

I hadn't focused on it before, but Connie had a small overbite. That and the look in her eyes yesterday when I'd first mentioned Kim made her seem more human. I pushed my luck a little farther and said I didn't realize Plush's melanin research was so far along. Connie didn't seem to mind explaining it to me. Melanocytes were one of the easier skin cells to manipulate. They'd been working on genes expressing tyrosinase and endothelin-1, factors regulating the production of melanin, which determined skin pigmentation. The program had taken a back seat to Eternaderm in part because other companies were farther ahead. An Australian firm had plans to release an implant drug called melanotan that would induce a suntan and guard skin from UV damage. In high doses, the drug turned green frogs jet black.

I told Connie I was impressed with the work. That pleased her. I felt ready to take the next leap and tell her about Wendy. I asked if I could get some help using Eternaderm as bait.

Connie thought about it for a minute and then said, "It can be arranged. Temporarily, you understand. She'll never receive the full course."

"Can you tell me what it was that Wendy did wrong?"

"It's not related to Rod. She did some modeling work for us, as you know, and then tried to take advantage of it. She's the kind of person who's constantly grasping for more. She always wants what someone else has."

Given our new diplomacy, I didn't push Connie for details. "Should I bring her over to the clinic?"

Connie folded her arms. "Wendy will not enter this building. You and Ellen can administer it together. I'll leave the mechanics to her."

"Fine. I'll go talk to Ellen in a minute, if that's all right with you."

"Very good." She hesitated, then played with the glasses on the end of her necklace. "I hope you understand, Bill, about our first few meetings. I was in a protective mode. Odd that it should be evoked now—Ronald and I never had children. The business, the employees, they were our offspring. But now I find myself . . ." She shook her head as her words trailed off.

"I think I understand. Rod brought a protectiveness out in me. Some people just get to you. You're not even sure why."

"Yes." Again our eyes met as they had outside Mike's office. I had a feeling she understood why I wanted to find Rod's killer so badly.

"One more thing before I go," I said. "Are you going to this Wings of Silicon Charity Ball tomorrow night? Wendy says Trisha and Rupert will be there, along with the Sylvain honchos."

Connie raised her eyebrows. "Trisha's getting uppity, isn't she? It's one of the most prestigious events of the year. The money's used to put software in schools. She must be planning to raise her profile. Pretty soon she'll be applying to the polo clubs and denying any connection with Silicon Glamour. Not bad for a woman who started as a Las Vegas escort."

"So it's true what Wendy said. She started in Vegas and moved the business here."

"Actually, she was a little smarter than that. She saw an opportunity for a more legitimate venture in Silicon Valley. SG may do plenty that's underhanded, but the associates always stay just this side of legal. She's a viper, Bill, but I have to give her credit. She did it all on her own. Trisha and Rupert live very, very well, each in their own mansion in Morgan Hill."

"Did you know that SG associates gather inside information from their dates and pass it along to Rupert and Trisha, who then pass it along to Sylvain?" I said.

Connie paused. "Our mutual friend did tell me something about it. I wish we could introduce her to investigative authorities. But that would be too dangerous for her. I'd be glad to help you nail them for that in other ways."

"What about Erika?"

Connie looked away. "I felt very bad about that. It was hard to send her away, Bill, but I had no choice. Trisha was watching. I couldn't do anything that might give away our other friend. I also knew that the damage was temporary; skin cells are a marvel of rebirth, you know, they turn over every month when you're young. In the meantime, I think we better leave Erika out of it."

"All right. Are you pretty sure Trisha's the one running the show at Sylvain?"

"I have no proof, but I'd be shocked if she wasn't. There's nothing illegal about that, of course, unless we can get them on the spying and insider-information charges."

I got up to leave. "Or murder. Thanks for your help, Connie."

Connie put out her hand. "If I see Trisha at the Silicon Ball, I'll have a little chat."

I checked my watch and went across the building to make arrangements with Ellen. I'd have to hurry. It was close to two, and Kim was coming to my flat at three. I wanted to be sure I was there well before her.

>> >> >> >> >>

Kim gave me a jaunty greeting. I could have sworn she was genuinely happy to see me and in a more cheerful mood than she'd been since I met her. She looked that way even before she saw my face. I'd observed her approach from my Scout, down the block, to make sure she was alone, then had surprised her on my doorstep.

We sat at my kitchen table. I cleared it of clutter and brewed her a cup of tea. Since she'd taken up smoking, she said, she'd given up coffee. She picked up her apology about last night where she'd left off. I wanted to know who the guy was.

"Just someone I met. In a bar, okay? Two nights ago. His name's Travis. I told him some people had been bothering me and I might need his help. I was planning for Mike to be there when I went to the apartment, but you messed that up. So I called Travis on my way over. He was just going to sit outside and make sure no one hurt me. When you left—so much had happened—I forgot to call him and tell him you were okay."

"He didn't do a very good job. He should've caught me on the way in. What do you have going with this guy?"

"*Nothing,* Bill. I don't even know his last name. He's just a harmless gentleman who was helping me out. He knows nothing about me."

I shook my head skeptically, and then she lit into me. "*You* don't have people hunting for you, killing your lover, maybe wanting to kill you. So I met Travis in a bar, so what? I take help wherever I can get it. You have no right to judge me."

"Fair enough," I said. It was vaguely possible she was telling the truth. Certainly she was adept at playing the diva in distress; Connie's manner had inched me toward believing the distress was real. "Let's drop it for now. I have some other things to show you."

I went down the hall and found the folder with the pictures of Rod and Alissa that Rupert had given me, along with Alissa's letter to her mother. It was the letter I wanted to ask her about, but Kim picked up one of the pictures first.

It was the telephoto shot of Rod and her kissing. Her eyes went shiny and she said, "Oh my God, I remember this so well. I found out how much passion Rod had in him."

"What made you go for Rod?" I asked. "I'm sure you had other options."

"Plenty of guys *wanted* me, Bill," she replied with disdain, as if it had been too obvious to say. "But they didn't *know* me. Rod, when he focused on me with that intense concentration . . ." She shivered. "Where'd you get this picture, anyway?"

"Your friend Rupert was keeping an eye on you. I'm sure he'd say it was for your own protection."

She wrinkled her nose, then picked up the picture in which Rod was trying to keep her from getting out of the Cabriolet. "This was a little act I put on. I figured SG was watching me by then. I wanted it to look like I was having a fight with Rod so they wouldn't think we eloped or something."

I tossed the copy of the letter she'd written about Rod to Wendy across the table. "What about this?"

Kim actually laughed as she read it. "You must think I'm terrible! Talking about the Girlfriend Experience as if I was faking it with Rod. Mom was so jealous of him, I had to invent an excuse to tell her. I also had to make her not worry if I disappeared. That's why I told her I had to go underground."

"So you allowed your mother to think Rod might hurt you."

"Well . . . yes. I don't know, maybe that was wrong. I didn't want to hurt *her* by saying I needed a break from her. So I let Rod take the blame." She thought about it for a minute, picked up the car photo, and then said, "Oh no, you don't think she told Trisha that Rod kidnapped me, do you? I never thought they'd think that because it—well, it was unthinkable."

It's hard to manufacture panic: The look on Kim's face seemed real. The picture in my own mind was taking shape. I couldn't bring myself to make her feel worse than she did, so I replied, "I'm sure they'd already made their plans, regardless of what Wendy said. I just have to ask you again about one other thing. How much information about Algoplex did you pass along to Rupert?"

Kim wrung her hands. "I honestly don't know. I only did it three or four times—I think that's right—the last one because I absolutely had to, to get Trisha off my back. You can't believe how she pressured me. I was terrified of her at the end: terrified of what she'd do if I kept seeing Rod, and what she'd do if I didn't. I didn't read what was in the files, I just copied them. I hoped the whole thing would go away."

"When was that last time?"

"Four or five weeks ago. It's hard to remember because so much has happened. Do you think his company can be saved?"

I waited, held her eyes, and said, "Do you really want it to be?"

"Of course I do, Bill! It was his life's work. It was just starting to take off. When I think about how he's not here to see it . . . Oh, I can't stand it. It makes me so sad."

She was choking up again. Either she was very good or very innocent.

Neither of us spoke for several minutes. She stared into her tea cup as if an answer would appear somewhere in the grounds. Finally I said, "Have you heard about this Wings of Silicon Charity Ball that's happening tomorrow night?"

Kim's face slowly hardened. It was not for lack of emotion, but to control it. "Rod and I were supposed to go. It was going to be our first big social event—I mean, an event that's not a conference or business dinner—together. It was going to be a sort of coming-out party."

"Your mother says she can get me into it. Trisha, Rupert, and Sylvain will be there. So will Connie."

"You should go. I'll go, too, if you want. Or whatever you need me to do."

"No, it's too risky for you to come. You'll be found out."

"Maybe I will, maybe I won't. Connie says skin color is still a big marker in this society. It makes people put you in a different category. I don't care anymore who finds out who I was, anyway. Let them do whatever they do to me."

"Don't feel bad, Kim," I said. The words came out before I thought about them. My gut was telling me to trust her, as Erika had trusted me. "I made mistakes, too. I never should have left Rod alone that night. If I'd been doing my job . . ."

Her head snapped up. The spirit came back into her voice. "Wait, Bill. Let's not do this. Let's just get them. We have the whole rest of our lives to feel bad."

22

Getting ready for the Wings of Silicon Charity Ball on Friday afternoon was like stepping into a fairy tale. Wendy took the lead role as Cinderella. She kept Brendon busy retrieving pins and fasteners for her outfit, a lace-up corset number with a layered ruffle skirt. We didn't know who'd play the role of the prince just yet, but judging by her anticipatory enthusiasm, Wendy planned to find him. When I asked about Mr. Pop-the-Question in Reno, she declared that absence would make his heart grow fonder. Call her butter because she was on a roll: Wendy had Eternaderm and the future was hers.

Ellen and I had brought the apparatus over that morning. Eternaderm was administered by a grid of superfine pins that delivered the transcription factor subcutaneously. Wendy got so distracted by the pins that she didn't ask whether the formula was the real thing or a placebo. That was a relief: It was a placebo. Ellen refused to dispense actual Eternaderm under these circumstances. The point became moot when Wendy decided her face could not be used as a pincushion the morning of the ball. Treatment would begin tomorrow instead. Brendon asked to receive it as well. Ellen told him that if he got any creamier, he'd turn into Twinkie filling.

At four o'clock Brendon ceased being Wendy's valet and said he and I had to get dressed. He knew the banquet manager at the hotel where the Ball was being held, and had secured waiting jobs for himself and a friend earlier in the week. I was taking the friend's place. For my uniform, I'd brought the black pants Erika had picked out and three of the many white cotton shirts I owned. Brendon declared the pants suitable but all three of the shirts lacking. He lent me one of his own to wear.

We had to be at the hotel in San Jose by five o'clock for setup. We left Wendy to her ruffles and drove down in the Scout. On the way, I mentioned to Brendon that I was impressed with his hotel connections.

He snorted. "Connections. Yeah, we 'help' in the Valley know each other. I see them at these functions, and then later on at the clubs. The ones we can afford."

"Are you sorry you had to leave behind the good life at SG?"

Another snort. "The good life. It was all right, I guess. Trisha liked me. But you get sick of it, you know? Being patted on the head. Behaving." He grinned a private grin. "I did have her drooling for me. Even now, she's letting me keep the pad until I find a new one."

"What about you and Wendy?"

He blew out a long stream of air. "I can't explain, dude. She's got her finger on my control key. Not my style. Once I find Alissa, we're out of there."

"Alissa's special. I can tell from her picture. What did Trisha say about her?"

"Hands off, boy. She didn't care what happened to Alissa, as long as she did her job and I stayed away. Alissa was Rupert's project. That's why he killed Rod."

"How do you suppose that knife got into Alissa's apartment?"

"Rupert, of course. He's trying to set her up."

"And you're sure it was Rupert?"

He looked closely at me. "Aren't you?"

I gave a shrug: I wanted him to try to convince me. I pulled into the hotel's back parking lot and we went into the ballroom. The partitions that usually divided it into multiple spaces had been taken down; tonight it would officially qualify as a "grand ballroom." Bare-branched trees strung with small white lights clustered in strategic spots along the wall. A pair of giant wings, carved from foam and painted gold, hung from the ceiling. A small stage for the musicians was on the right side and the dining room was off to the left. Portable bars and appetizer tables were being erected in the main room.

We found Cathy, the banquet manager. Brendon introduced me as "Dirk," the friend he'd promised to bring. She looked pleased to see Brendon. He got a big kiss and I got a quick hand-shake. We both got black vests and white waiter aprons. Cathy told us to put them on and come into the dining room for the wait staff meeting.

The ball had sold out: Five hundred guests would begin arriving for cocktails at seven o'clock. Dinner would be served at eight-thirty. The theme of the event had to do with education soaring on the wings of technology. The featured drink was champagne and Chambord, which tonight would be called a Purple Eagle. Brendon and I would be two of the twenty wait-rons floating through the room with exclusively these drinks on a tray.

"Repeat the name every time you serve one," Cathy said. "The Purple Eagle. Don't forget to give them the cocktail napkin with the embossed eagle. And smile."

"That's the hard part," Brendon said. Cathy responded with a mock pout, as if he was the most charming thing in the world.

We got to work polishing the dinner flatware and wine glasses. The florists made us hold on until each arrangement was properly fluffed before allowing us to set the table. At six-thirty a giant ice sculpture of a kid with wings sitting at a computer was wheeled through the double doors and positioned in the space between the dining room and ballroom. Purple pin lights were focused on it from the ceiling.

Brendon tugged on my sleeve to look at the sculpture up close. "These guys are wizards with a chainsaw."

"Art that melts," I said. "Cool."

Brendon checked his watch. "We've got a few minutes. Let's go to the kitchen."

I didn't know much about being a waiter, but I knew we weren't supposed to go any farther into the kitchen than was necessary to pick up trays. The prep crew was busy assembling them. Brendon breezed in, greeting the crew with familiar nods. He steered me away from the main hive to a counter where an eighteen-inch-long filet mignon sat on a butcher block. The ends had been trimmed and tossed back into a stainless steel bowl. Parts of the middle had been cut into paper-thin slices. Blood oozed from it.

"Ever had carpaccio?" Brendon asked. He glanced around to make sure no one was watching. "Buddy of mine butchers these babies. The cows live it up before they—" He made a throat-slitting motion. "Totally organic."

He popped a slice into his mouth, then followed it with a toast round from a nearby platter. The next slice he dipped into a mustard sauce. As he tossed a few capers after it, a hand grabbed his elbow.

"Hey, asshole!"

Brendon turned and briefly arm-wrestled with a guy in a bloodstained apron. Then each of them broke into a grin. Brendon introduced me as Dirk or Bill, or whatever.

The prep cook gave me a nod and returned to his carving. "One more apiece," he said, dangling a maroon slice in front of me. "Then get the hell out of the kitchen."

I took it. It was good beef, all right. But what stayed in my mind was the pool in the bottom of the stainless steel bowl. The whole thing was less appetizing when, instead of being presented on an hors d'oeuvres platter, it was piled in a red heap swimming in its own blood. Even less appetizing was what it told me about who killed Rod.

>> >> >> >> >>

I'm a cinematographer, so colors stick in my mind. When they enter or re-enter the frame I remember them, like a dog remembers a scent or a musician remembers a chord. The runoff from the carpaccio was a color I knew well. But I needed to know more before I decided what to do about it.

Cathy's voice rang into the kitchen, calling the troops to order. I went with Brendon to pick up our first tray of Purple Eagles from the bar station. He licked the carpaccio juice from his fingers, self-satisfied and oblivious.

The bartender popped a bottle of champagne and added a dollop of Chambord to each glass, followed by two raspberries. The string ensemble hired for the cocktail hour began to play. The doors opened and the first arrivals trickled in. By some miracle my first tray of long-stemmed glasses did not crash to the floor when I lifted it into position with one hand.

"Let's float," Brendon said. It was the term Cathy had used to mean we'd wander on the floor offering drinks to whoever wanted them. It was a good way to circulate and to see who was there. I was more invisible than a cameraman.

At first, without many people, it was easy. I got the feel of balancing the tray. Then suddenly the doors gushed with guests. The music was drowned out in a rumble of voices rebounding through the ballroom.

I worked my way to the middle of the floor, turned to offer a round of drinks, and came face-to-face with Mike Riley. His broad grin shrank like plastic on hot iron.

"Purple Eagle, sir?" I said. But my own smile disappeared when I saw his date. It was Kim, in a long, slim evening gown. Her hair was done up with flowers and she looked great. She gave me a demure greeting. I motioned her aside.

"Oh no you don't," Mike said, interposing himself. "Not again."

I handed him the tray. He took it by reflex. I slipped past him and took Kim's arm.

"What are you doing here?" I demanded.

"He invited me." Her voice was sweet and smoky. "I want to help you, Bill."

"Rupert's here. Your mother's here. You're going to blow it."

The smile stayed on her face, but the sweetness left. "Don't tell me what to do."

I didn't have time to argue. "It's your choice."

"I'm listening to what Mike and Sylvain talk about. I'm going to tell you everything. It's funny, it's like being back in my job with SG."

Mike was barking my name and prodding me in the small of the back with the tray. I turned to take it from him. He was about to bust a button. Before he got any more words out,

Connie and Ronald Plush moved in. Mike took Kim's arm and squired her away.

"Thank you, waiter," Connie said to me in a dry, mock-haughty tone.

Ronald was confused. "Wait a minute. Aren't you—?"

I shrugged. "Got to pay the bills."

Connie cut in front of Ronald, who didn't seem to mind, and leaned close to my ear to speak. "I did everything I could to keep her away. She insisted. She says she's going to find out what happened to Rod. Help me keep an eye on her."

"I'll do my best. I've got to continue the waiter act a little while longer."

She took the last glass of violet champagne and lifted it in a silent toast. I filled the tray with empty glasses and headed back to the station. The crowd was so thick I had to hoist the tray over my head to get through. Previous jobs had required heavy lifting, but not like this. Somebody squeezed my ass as I went by. I twisted my head over my shoulder. It could have been any one of ten men or women.

When I brought out a new tray, I found Wendy, surrounded by three men, in her corset number and strappy Manolo Blahnik heels. She snatched a glass without so much as a wink at me. I supposed it wouldn't do to pal around with the help. She wore pearl wristlets and her new favorite lipstick, the bruised-claret color. The men appeared fixated on her mouth.

I moved on. Rupert, wearing a three-piece suit, hailed me. "Bill! I see you've found a new profession."

"Yes," I said, offering the tray. "I've got a potion that makes people tell me their secrets. You'd be amazed at how much I've learned since I last saw you."

He took a glass. "Share a little of that with me."

My shoulder was tapped and I had to turn to let some guests grab drinks. I didn't smile and I didn't call them Purple Eagles. One glass was left when I turned back to Rupert. I took it, lowered the tray to my side, and said, "I know who killed Rod."

"Bravo!" He clinked my glass. "Who was it?"

"An employee of yours."

Rupert pretended to be taken aback. He gestured toward an hors d'oeuvres table from which Gary was feeding. "I know where Gary and Trisha and I were that night."

Gary glanced over as if he heard us talking about him. He looked uncomfortable in his tux. He wasn't any more at home in this crowd than I was. Rupert motioned for him to stay put, then said, "In fact, I know where almost all our employees were that night. Which one gave us the slip?"

"I might tell you, but I need some reciprocation. You're going to have to explain why you and Trisha are using Sylvain Partners to carve up Algoplex."

He laughed and threw up a dismissive hand, smooth as ever. "Ah well! I guess I'll have to wait and read about the case in the papers."

A sharp voice made me glance to my right. "Security! Manager!" Trisha shouted.

Brendon stood slouched in front of her, a champagne flute in his hand and a smirk on his face. A new boy, even younger than Brendon, was on Trisha's arm. The new one's ears were shaved close and a shrub of dyed blond hair sat on top of his head. He wore a look of disgust, as if Brendon had just revealed something of a personal nature about Trisha. Brendon's posture almost invited him to attack. But the boy appeared as likely to bolt from Trisha as to defend her honor.

"No one can hear you, Trisha," I said.

She lowered her eyes on me. "Are you in this with him? I'll have you both thrown out."

"Let me tell you something first, then. I've been talking to Rod's lawyer. The key-man clause is invalid."

This was complete fiction, but I wanted to see her response. She jabbed the toe of a lethal suede pump in my direction. "That's *preposterous*, Bill—"

Her mouth snapped shut with a look from Rupert. Brendon— feeling naughty, I guess—said, "No, it's true, Trisha. I heard that, too. The whole thing's off."

"You little punk, you don't even know what we're talking about."

Brendon, for all his insolence, shrank back from her. But he'd hit the right note. I said, "Your company's in trouble, Trisha. Both of them."

Rupert had given a wave to Gary. He shouldered Brendon and me aside, flexing his fingers as if he'd like an excuse to put them around our throats. Brendon smirked at Trisha one last time and said, "Later, babe."

He headed back toward the bar. Trisha gave me a wary scowl and turned the other way. Rupert touched me on the elbow. We weren't done yet.

While Gary kept an eye on Brendon, Rupert murmured casually to me, "It's a shame what Alissa's done to herself."

"I think you mean what you did to her. You used SG associates to spy on your takeover targets. Add that to the murder investigation and things are going to be rough for you."

He rubbed his lips together. "We're not involved in any murder. You know that. It's Alissa's safety you should be worrying about. I know I am."

"That's easy to say when you've got no idea where she is."

He leaned in confidentially. "Oh, I know where she is."

I followed his eyes. They fell on a pink rose in a nest of blond hair about eight yards away. Mike's laugh could be heard even at this distance. Kim happened to look around and met my eyes. She gave a quick wink of a smile. She was perfect: She seemed not to notice Rupert at all. Nonetheless, he made a little bow. He knew.

I stood stunned for a moment. I saw what I had to do now, but there was one more thing I wanted from Rupert. A waiter passing by slapped at my sleeve and pointed at my empty tray. "We could use some help, pal."

"Just a minute," I said, handing him the tray. He glared, grabbed it, and left.

Rupert's voice remained casual. "As I said, it's a shame what's happened to her face. But you know, it's only skin deep. The smile, the dance in her eyes: They're still there. I'd recognize Cindy anywhere."

"Cindy?"

"Cindy Bresloff. Her given name. I felt badly for her—that mother, you know. I wanted to help, to give her a chance to get free of Wendy. Alissa didn't have much in the way of a skill set. When the bottom dropped out of the tech economy, she was desperate. She wasn't cut out for our kind of work, but she insisted we give her a chance."

"You tricked her into it."

"Take a minute to listen to me, Bill. We're on the same side." Rupert spoke indulgently, like an uncle on a stroll in the park. "She had that something special. I'd have done anything for her, but Trisha allows only one kind of contract at entry level. I laid it out for Alissa. She still wanted to do it. So I took it upon myself to make it as easy as possible. Well, Alissa just drips with charm: She could have been a knockout on dates, melting men left and right. But it was hard on her. Her mother is a consummate phony, and Alissa was afraid she'd go down that road herself. I tried to bump her over to the business side. Trisha wouldn't have it. But I also saw that Alissa's business ethics weren't up to the job. They weren't quite—how should I put it?—*micro* enough."

The party roared around us, but I barely heard it. I was ensconced in a small cocoon of knowledge shared only by myself, Rupert, and Connie. My fear was what would happen when we left that cocoon. He could use threats to Kim to shut me up about the takeover of Algoplex. To keep him talking, I said, "She could have gone a long way."

"She could have had the *world* in her hands. Alas it was not to be. Bill, I tell you this from the bottom of my heart. I wanted the best for her. Trisha did require certain contractual obligations to be fulfilled, but I refused to push Alissa. She didn't have to damage her face like that. I would have let her go if she'd spoken openly to me."

"But what about Rod? What if she wanted to leave you for him?"

Rupert sighed. He stared at the bubbles in his glass, considering the idea. "Maybe she did belong with Rod. Stranger couples have happened. I couldn't get a read on his feelings. I knew the lust was strong, but was there more? And then it seemed all too likely he was responsible for her disappearance. Engineers, you see—the socially withdrawn types like him—don't know women. Obsession can make a decent man do bad things."

"You must see a lot of that at Silicon Glamour. Brendon's obsession with Alissa—why didn't you grill him about what happened to her?"

Rupert chuckled. "Trisha had her methods. The boy's a dreamboat, but I knew to keep him at arm's length. I do wish my sister applied her famous discipline to her own indulgences. Nevertheless, Brendon's frantic demeanor betrayed him. He didn't know where Alissa was."

"What about the attack on Erika?"

The avuncular tone disappeared. "I can't talk about that," he snapped. "She'll be all right. Now look, I've spoken frankly with you. I want you to do the same with me."

"I have been."

"No. I want to know who killed Rod. And why Alissa—Kim— is with Mike."

"She's afraid. Especially of you. She has reason to be."

"She has reason to fear whoever killed Rod. *Who was it?*"

"I'll tell you," I said. "First tell me how you're going to stop Sylvain from eating up Rod's company."

"Bill," Rupert began. He folded his arms in displeasure, then looked at the food table. Brendon was there, chatting with a guest. "Never mind. I'll ask your new best friend about it."

I watched Brendon pop a little fish-shaped pastry into his mouth as if he didn't have a care in the world. "Wait," I said to Rupert. "I'll talk to him first."

Rupert gave me one of his unctuous smiles. "You do that."

23

"Brendon," I said, "come with me."

"What's up? You find out something from Rupert?"

I just nodded and took him into the kitchen. The walk-in refrigerator was the only place I could think of where we could talk alone. A sous chef gave me a dirty look as I opened the door. I walked around the boxes of produce, flats of eggs, and bins of iced fish to the other side of the refrigerator's middle rack.

Brendon had some idea of what I was going to say. My theory was that he wanted to be caught: Otherwise why had he made the throat-slitting motion when he talked about the beef? Standing before him in the frigid, misting air, the sweat contracting into tiny beads on his skin, I saw how unformed his face was, how little he knew himself. The smirk, the cool, the James Dean insolence, were masks he'd learned. He had little idea what lay beneath that pretty surface. He hadn't lived enough for character to take root beyond the dreamboat gaze and the childish demand to have every desire fulfilled. He knew he could make people fall in lust with him, and this allowed him to get what he wanted. But he had no idea what it was he did want. Until Alissa, that is. And she, along with her mother, were the two women in the world who could resist him.

Now, suddenly, he'd lived too much. He was sinking and in need of a lifeline, even if it bound him by the hands. He waited, eyes receptive, lips slightly parted, emitting small breaths of champagne-scented steam. He'd downed enough drinks to allow his mixture of apprehension and exhilaration to show.

"It was nice of you to share the carpaccio with me," I said. "The blood in the bottom of that bowl looked a lot like the blood on the knife in Alissa's bedroom. I imagine your butcher friend has plenty of it to spare."

He hardly blinked. Obviously he knew about the knife. "Rupert did that."

"You gave him the blood? And the knife?"

"No! I gave the blood to Wendy."

"Let's back up," I said. "The main thing I want to know is if you killed Rod on your own or if someone asked you to do it."

"That's wrong!" He shook his head furiously. "I wrestled him to the ground. I had him in my grip. *Wendy* used the knife."

"Wendy?"

The head shake turned into a nod. "I hated the fucker. But she hated him more. I didn't want to kill him, I didn't *need* to. Alissa would have chosen me."

Pride was in his words, but his eyes showed revulsion. I pictured him on the kitchen floor, subduing Rod; Wendy grabbing the knife from the drawer; Brendon shrieking in horror when the blood spurted from Rod's neck. When they realized what they'd done, Wendy stowed the murder weapon and fit the larger knife in Rod's still-warm hand. There had been plenty of blood available to coat the new knife.

"All right," I said. "Let's say Wendy is the killer. You need to fill in the rest for me. What were you doing in Rod's house?"

"He had Alissa. Wendy and I both wanted her back. You know my reason. Why Wendy wanted her—I guess because she was her daughter, but also because Trisha offered a big reward, plus access to Eternaderm. Trisha's the one who said Rod was hiding Alissa. Wendy talked me into joining up with her. She reminded me of Alissa. I was a sucker. I admit it."

"How did killing Rod get you closer to Alissa?"

"It didn't!" Brendon burst out. "It was self-defense. He kept coming at us."

"Why didn't he have any clothes on?"

"He was getting ready to go to the Cheshire Cat. He answered the door in his boxers. Shaving cream on his face. We wanted to force him to tell us where Alissa was. We were sure he'd kidnapped her; Trisha told us so. Him pretending to meet her at the club was to fake us out."

"Wendy set that up, not Rod," I said.

"Yeah, but he called her bluff. I mean, that's what we thought at the time." Brendon hesitated, then went on. "The club was also a way to get *you* out of the picture. She figured you'd be concealing yourself at the Cheshire Cat when we went over to Rod's. You hid well—she never saw you—but the fact was, the plan worked. We got Rod alone."

"So you went to talk to Rod. To force him to give up Alissa. How did you end up sticking a knife into his neck?"

"Wendy," he repeated impatiently. "Rod tried to chase us out. I had to make him listen. He had to tell us where Alissa was. He got away from me and ran into the bathroom. Wendy threatened him with a nail file. She scratched him on the arm a few times. Rod wrapped a towel around his arm to protect himself. He hit her, too. That made her mad. We kind of bashed around the house until we ended up in the kitchen. He threw a toaster at me. Wendy hit him with this pot of coffee. It burned him. I got him down. I was finally going to make him talk to us. He looked at Wendy with this hatred and started talking about how she was a vicious, poisonous mother. Wendy screamed back at him. Then she put the knife—"

Brendon broke off and looked away. I kept my eyes on him. "The only problem," I said, "is that I saw Wendy at the Cheshire Cat at ten forty-five."

"She wanted you to see her. She went right after it happened."

It was plausible. But it was also plausible Brendon had convinced himself Wendy bore responsibility for his actions. I kept going. "What about the note? 'Sorry.'"

"Wendy wrote it to make people think it was a suicide. She used her left hand."

"Then a few days later, you got the beef blood from your butcher friend. You still had the knife, and now you immersed it in the blood."

He stamped his foot. "Bill, you're not listening! *I* got the blood. *Wendy* did the rest."

"She put the knife in her own daughter's bed?"

Brendon slammed a fist into a box of lettuce. "*That's* what I don't get. She said she was going to plant it on Rupert. That was our whole plan. You thought Rupert did it, and we were going to set him up for you. I freaked when I found out the knife was at Alissa's. Wendy said Rupert must have moved it there. He had a key."

"Do you believe her?"

The fist slowly unclenched. "I don't know. She's stopped talking about Alissa since you said you'd come through on the Eternaderm."

"Wendy could have dressed herself up like Alissa to get into the apartment."

Brendon stared at a box of radishes. His real gaze was a thousand miles away.

Our teeth were chattering now. My sweat had dried, giving me a clammy feeling. "Let's go," I said. "We'll take Wendy down together."

"She's the one who did it," he repeated.

The refrigerator door opened. "What the hell is going on in here?" Cathy bellowed.

Brendon went around the middle rack, arms extended. "Sorry, Cathy," he said, grasping her by the elbows. Then he threw her out of his way and ran through the door.

I raced past Cathy and came out of the refrigerator in time to see Brendon grab a carving knife from a cutting board. He swung it wildly to chase people out of the way, then barreled through the swinging doors and back into the ballroom.

I grabbed a large serving tray to use as a shield and plunged after him. Waiters and party hosts were herding the guests toward the ice sculpture and the dining room. I bulled my way in the other direction, fighting the tide. Screams came from somewhere ahead of me. Someone knocked me into a food table, and a four-tiered serving platter of pink mush went flying. I saw Connie's and Ronald Plush's heads moving to the left, in the direction of a set of double doors that opened onto a smoking balcony.

Another scream came from the balcony. This one sounded like Kim. I bulled harder and suddenly was through the crowd. I ran with the Plushes toward the balcony doors. A bartender came racing in the other direction. He tried to grab me. "Don't go out there! Get security!"

I shook free of him and pushed by the Plushes to get to the large, semicircular balcony. The floor above provided a roof, but the front was open to the street, guarded only by a stone balustrade. The area was furnished with upholstered couches and armchairs for the comfort of cigarette and cigar smokers.

A small bar to the right of the door served single malts. Mike Riley had a bottle in his hand. He crouched in a defensive position in a niche in the back left corner of the balcony. The niche contained a sofa, coffee table, and some large potted palms on a platform raised like a small stage. Pressed together into the sofa were Wendy and Trisha. Their body language said they wanted to hold on to each other for protection, but some force of repulsion kept them apart. Trying to get to them, waving his knife, was Brendon. Mike blocked his way. Rupert and Gary stood near the stage, a few feet behind Kim, who stood near the edge of the platform at an equal distance from Brendon and Mike. Trisha's new boyfriend cowered near the bar.

"Stop it, Brendon!" Kim screamed.

"I don't want to hurt you, but I will," Brendon said to Mike. "Get out of my way."

I joined Rupert and Gary. The Plushes followed breathlessly behind me. "Good God!" Dr. Plush cried. Connie shushed him.

I came forward cautiously to stand next to Kim. I raised the tray in front of her in case any knives came flying our way. "Stop, Bill," Brendon ordered.

"Brendon," I said, edging closer to the platform, "this is not what I meant about getting Wendy."

Brendon pointed the knife at me. "This is *my* business!"

Gary's eyes darted from Mike to Brendon, waiting for an opening. "Nobody's arguing with you, man," Gary said in his low rumble. "Just let Trisha come down here."

"No way! She's as bad as Wendy! She said Rod had Alissa! You're all a bunch of liars!"

"Brendon, darling—" Wendy began.

"Shut up!" he screamed. "You set up your own daughter for murder!"

Mike judged Brendon sufficiently distracted to make his move. He took a quick step and brought the bottle down toward Brendon's head. But Brendon was faster. He sidestepped the blow and stuck the knife into Mike's left shoulder. Mike let out a sickening shriek. I dropped the tray and dove for Brendon's leg. He kicked me away and wrenched the knife from Mike's shoulder in the same motion. Gary wasn't fast enough, either, to prevent Brendon from hopping over the coffee table and landing on the couch.

Wendy and Trisha split like pea pods. Trisha swung an open hand at Brendon, catching him in the eye. The blow allowed her to slip away. Brendon grabbed Wendy by the hair.

Trisha nearly ran me over on her way off the stage. Gary stepped up to receive her. She pushed him back, saying she was fine. Mike, clutching his shoulder, writhing in pain, rolled off the edge of the platform.

Two hotel security men burst onto the scene. "Help him!" Connie said, pointing to Mike.

"Stay back!" Brendon ordered.

He had Wendy firmly in his grip now. The knife was at her throat. Her eyes were wild with fear. I rose very slowly and carefully into a sitting position on the platform. Brendon and Wendy must have been in a similar frenzy when Rod's murder occurred.

"Let me go, darling," she whimpered.

"Quiet, *darling*," he said sarcastically, "or I'll do to you what you did to Rod."

"No!" Kim screamed. "Brendon, listen! It's me, Alissa!"

A hush came over the scene. Kim's jaw quavered.

"You're not my daughter," Wendy objected.

"Yeah, you're Kim," Mike gasped from the floor. "Alissa's—"

"Shut up, you dork!" Brendon bellowed. He gazed at Kim for a moment, then said, softly, "It's really you." He giggled. "I was afraid you were dead!"

Kim stepped onto the platform. "Alissa *is* dead."

"Honey, is that really you? Help your mother," Wendy pleaded.

"Why did you do it, Mom?" Kim said. Her voice was cool and even, as if she were speaking to a stranger. "Why did you kill Rod and put the knife in my bed?"

"I didn't—" Wendy began. Brendon pressed the knife to her skin and she altered course. "We thought he'd kidnapped you, honey."

"Why'd you try to frame Alissa?" Brendon demanded savagely.

Wendy's answer was broken and incoherent. "I just—we thought she was gone—and it'd never stick—we could say Rupert—"

Sirens squalled on the street below. "Let her go," I said to Brendon." She's admitted what she did."

His teeth clamped down in anger. He clenched Wendy's hair tighter.

"Brendon," Kim said quietly, "let her go. Do it for me."

Slowly Brendon's hand opened. Shaking, he placed the knife on the cushion beside him. Wendy flew from his grip. "Oh, Cindy, darling!" she gasped.

Kim folded her arms and angled her body away from her mother. "You killed Rod. He was right about you."

"No!" Wendy wailed, then laughed tearfully. "I just said that because Brendon was making me. Don't you understand? Brendon did it. I was at the Cheshire Cat when he—"

"No, Wendy," I interrupted. I'd crept forward to sit on the coffee table, staying close to the knife just in case. "You were at

Rod's. Rod had a small red streak on his arm the night I found him. At first I thought it was blood, but the color was slightly different. It was the color of your lipstick."

"Don't listen to him, Cindy," Wendy said. "Somebody help me—somebody tell her. Rupert, Trisha: I was helping you find Alissa, remember? You said Rod had her!"

"We wanted her back," Trisha said coolly from her spot below between Rupert and Gary. "We accepted help from anyone."

"No, you promised—the reward—" Wendy's tone turned malevolent when she saw she was getting nowhere. "Tell them, Trisha, or I'll tell everyone how Silicon Glamour really works."

"No one believes anything you say, Wendy," Trisha replied.

"There are plenty of others who know," I said. "It'll come out."

Brendon had been slumped on the sofa, head back. Now he straightened and said to Trisha in a weary voice, "Don't forget I know a few details, babe."

"Murderers," Trisha spat. But I was watching Rupert and the way he chewed his lip during the exchange. My conversation with him gave me an idea he was ready to revise the way SG did business.

"You'll be hearing from our lawyers, Trisha," Mike croaked. The security men had succeeded in dragging him away from the action. A small crowd had gathered in the ballroom, rubbernecking through the balcony doors. More security had arrived to keep them out.

"Connie!" Wendy appealed. "Help me!"

Connie smiled. "I'm sure you'll talk some nice lawyer into defending you."

"I'll tell them!" Wendy warned. "I'll tell them about the fake photos!"

"That little prank? Eternaderm is so far beyond that, it'll dwarf any accusation you make. But if you want to add black-mail to your list of offenses, go ahead."

"Alissa and I faked before-and-after pictures for their pro-motional brochure," Wendy announced to anyone who cared.

No one much did. Kim had taken a step away from her. Wendy stumbled in her direction again, grasping at her daughter. "Don't leave me alone."

Kim took yet another step back, coming down from the plat-form. Her expression had turned to one of wounded and betrayed contempt.

Wendy saw it clearly. Before Kim could speak, Wendy struck first. "You hypocrite!" she cried, standing above Kim on the platform, snapping her arm out at her daughter. "After all I did for you. The sacrifice. You'd have just run off with him and left me in the dust. You should have taken care of your own mother first. But no, you had to grab for it all—the life I was supposed to have."

"And you had to take it away from me."

"What about *me*? You thought you could shed me like an old skin, didn't you? Well, I've got news, girlie. You don't belong in that world. You're no better than me."

The cops had arrived by now. They parted the crowd, but when they got to the stage, they could see the drama had been spent. Kim turned away and began to sob quietly. Rupert led her back in the direction of the bar. I stayed near Brendon and the knife.

Wendy looked wildly for an exit, then rushed to the balustrade. Gary grabbed her as she tried to climb it. An officer cuffed her. Brendon pushed himself to his feet and went quietly.

Paramedics tended to Mike. A police sergeant got up on the platform and asked everyone to remain in the area. Statements would be taken.

I picked my way through the crowd to join Rupert and Kim. She managed a smile for me. "Are you all right?" I said.

"I'll make it," she said, resting her head on my shoulder.

Connie approached and took Kim gently by the elbow. "Come with me. I'll help you talk to the police, then take you home."

Trisha had her eye on them. She aimed a red fingernail at Kim and said, "You're under contract, young lady!"

"Leave her be!" Rupert commanded.

For once, Trisha seemed to listen. She spun and went to have her say with the sergeant.

Rupert extended a hand to me. "Congratulations," he said. "I had a feeling about Brendon, but you followed through."

I gave his hand a quick, reluctant shake. "We have unsettled business, Rupert. The Algoplex takeover. The way you use your associates to spy."

He waved it off. "It will be settled, Bill. Trisha is the one you want for that sort of thing. I myself would be happy to go back to running Silicon Glamour just as it was—before her ambitions got out of hand."

"So that means you'll cooperate," I said. "Especially when it comes to Algoplex."

He chuckled and looked down at my chest. I wondered what was funny. He reached over and removed a bit of pink mush from my vest.

"Salmon pâté," he said, sniffing his finger. "A man of taste."

24

Most of the consequences had shaken out a few weeks later. Brendon was offered, and accepted, a manslaughter plea in exchange for testifying. The sample of the red streak the police lab had taken from Rod's arm matched Wendy's lipstick. Traces of his blood were found in her car. Using a good set of Wendy's fingerprints for comparison, the lab was able to match them with the fragmentary ones on the knife. She insisted on going to trial, anyway. The prosecutor was confident it would end in a second-degree murder conviction.

Wendy doggedly blamed Brendon and denied putting the knife in Alissa's bed. In truth, it was hard to figure why she should have framed her own daughter. One of the first people to call after the arrests and invite me to lunch was Connie Plush. She'd heard from Kim about my lunch with Erika, and offered to take me back to the Rotunda Room. I couldn't think of a reason to say no. I'd been in touch with Erika and had made the same offer to her, but she wanted to wait until the white streaks were purged from her skin. They were gradually disappearing, as Rupert and Connie had promised they would.

I asked Connie if she could explain Wendy's motives. What made her such a princess in the first place?

Connie tried to restrain a smirk, then said, "If the crown fits . . . No, seriously, that's how she thinks. Wendy is a cauldron of emotions. So are we all, but hers stay at full boil. She resented Alissa for so many things. Alissa was making her own way, starting at entry level. Wendy had never had the patience to do that. She was jealous of Alissa for taking a different path and for succeeding at it. She also despised Rod for the life he would provide Alissa."

"I think what drove Wendy over the edge was the way he shut her out," I said.

"I agree. With Alissa distancing herself, Wendy wanted desperately to draw her close. She planted the knife to make Alissa need her mother again. Wendy hoped it would draw Alissa out of hiding, and had good reason to believe a murder charge wouldn't stick to Alissa. In the meantime she'd be Alissa's best friend when her daughter was most in need."

"That's twisted enough to make sense."

"Wendy lives in a perpetual desperation of her own making," Connie said. "She suffers from the 'I Should Have That' disease. It's endemic. Restless people spending criminally excessive amounts of money on toys and luxuries to fill a hole in themselves and create envy in others. Wendy shouldn't live in a place like Silicon Valley. She should be somewhere quiet."

"She is now, if you count prison as quiet."

"Just watch, she'll have more cigarettes than any inmate on her cell block."

"She was dying to get Eternaderm," I said. "You kind of make your money on people like Wendy, don't you?"

Connie looked stern for a minute. "Don't forget who's paying for lunch, Bill." She smiled. "No, you're right. But we'll use a chunk of that money to develop treatments for rare diseases that most drug companies ignore. I've promised that to Ellen. And I live in a reasonable manner. Ronald doesn't care for luxury, either; all he wants is the spotlight. I told you from the beginning, Bill, I know who I am. People like Wendy have no personal core. Aging is a part of nature, it's a part of life. We age and then we die. We can do it gracefully or with a lot of whining and complaining."

I nodded. "Trisha bears some responsibility for Rod's murder, too," I said. "She egged Wendy on by putting the idea that Rod was all to blame in her head. Not to mention the fact that she ran that whole racket of selling romance and intimacy for business purposes."

"She was a genius at using male desires against themselves, I have to admit," Connie replied. "You're right, she won't get the blame she deserves for Rod's death. But she got in over her head when it came to Sylvain and real business. Now that we know what we know about Sylvain and SG, Mike will be able to save Algoplex. I'm also confident I'll be able to pry Sylvain's tentacles off of my company. And as an added bonus, Trisha won't dare show her face at the next big social event."

>> >> >> >> >>

I visited Mike Riley in his office the next day. His convalescence was going well. He enjoyed describing his stab wound to me and detailing the gory aftermath. It beat all his rugby injuries put together. I declined an invitation to view the wound.

Mike marveled at how thoroughly he'd been taken in by Kim's magic act. He hadn't had a clue she was Alissa transformed. "But that's why we love 'em, right, Bill? They're always keeping us off balance."

"Right. Have you got Sylvain where you want them now?"

"You bet I do. We've got enough on them and SG's spy techniques to force Sylvain to restructure the deal. In the long run, Connie and I will push Sylvain out altogether and line up new backers. It won't be hard once Eternaderm makes its big splash."

Mike also told me, in a sensible tone this time, to send him an invoice. I did.

Rupert Evans called me a couple of weeks later. He reported that Trisha saw the clouds of investigation gathering and was about to order a pre-emptive disbanding of Sylvain and Silicon Glamour. This would give Plush and Algoplex even more leverage in dictating the terms of the exit. Trisha's energies were now directed toward scheming how to keep hold of her fortune, the one Sylvain had been created to enlarge. That would be a full-time job, Rupert said. As for himself, he was content to supervise the shutdown of Silicon Glamour and eventually resume the business—without the spying—under a new name. He was also going to sell his house to put some distance between himself and his sister.

I saw Kim a couple of times in the month before she left. She was moving to Oregon to start over. She'd have to come back for Wendy's trial, but she was eager to get out of the Valley. Just before her departure, we met again at Stanford. After we'd walked and talked for a while, she said good-bye with a kiss as warm and real as any I'd ever received. At last I caught a glimpse, if only fleeting, of the smile I'd seen in the photograph. She turned and I watched her leave, her long black raincoat swinging from side to side, on her way to a place where no one knew her and she could re-create herself from the ground up.

As I walked slowly back to the Scout, I stopped to watch some students play Ultimate Frisbee on a green field. The dirt under the grass was soft from winter rains; the longer I stood still, the more the mud sucked at my feet. I thought back to Rod on that warm day, his pacing and his nervous hands. Alissa had been an apparition then, a ghostly figure who had never materialized. She remained an apparition and, I now knew, had always been. Just as the persona of "Erika" had been, just as Brendon's James Dean flair had been. Just as their clients used SG associates to make themselves look like studs.

I also understood now that the apparitions were not mere illusion, but magic. I'd been forced to reconsider my own binary code, the opposition between surface and depth. I'd always assumed depth was superior, the real thing. But what if it amounted to only one layer of skin after another? The idea was disorienting: I'd been taught it was a law of life that pretending didn't make it so. And yet I'd chosen a profession, filmmaking, that was all about faking it. Even in documentaries made to look "gritty," the camera angle, composition, lighting, editing, and sound told you how to feel about the people on the screen.

In recent weeks I'd seen how people could cast a spell over others and, more important, over themselves. Alissa pretended to be enamored of Rod and then found that she was. Sylvain pretended to be a venture firm and found itself with controlling interest in several companies. Rod's code simulated how molecules interacted with real skin, and that's how they did. It seemed that if you pretended thoroughly enough, it might not matter whether your illusion was false: If it was powerful enough, it became reality.

I had talked about some of this to Kim. She'd replied that it was baloney. She'd reached a point where knowing the difference between glamour and actual beauty was essential. Wendy had pretended that life was obliged to give her what she wanted, and look where it got her. Alissa was buried, Kim told me, and Cindy was a husk of the past. She was Kim now, starting from scratch. Yes, the identity was an adopted one, but after all she was pretty much an orphan now. She would hone the skills she possessed in Oregon and learn new ones. Take classes. Find a job. Build a life from the few materials she had at hand. Meet someone, if she was lucky, for whom she cared as much as she had Rod. Get married, buy a house, have children. But it would start with a single brick, as real and solid as she could make it.